D0864226

Also by Jennifer L. Schiff

A Shell of a Problem

Something Fishy

In the Market for Murder

Bye Bye Birdy

Shell Shocked

Trouble in Paradise

A Sanibel Island Mystery

Jennifer Lonoff Schiff

Shovel
& Pail
Press

TROUBLE IN PARADISE: A SANIBEL ISLAND MYSTERY
by Jennifer Lonoff Schiff

Book Six in the Sanibel Island Mystery series

http://www.SanibelIslandMysteries.com

Cover design by Kristin Bryant

Formatting by Polgarus Studio

ISBN: 978-0-578-67893-1

Library of Congress Control Number: 2020909029

The path to paradise begins in hell.
—Dante Alighieri

Florida is a strange place: hot, beautiful, ugly. I love it here, and how nothing makes sense but still, somehow, there is a rhythm.
—Roxane Gay

PROLOGUE

As Guin sat on the closed lid of the toilet in her unfinished bathroom, in her unfinished house, staring at the body in the tub, she wondered if things could possibly get worse. It had already been a hellish four months, and she was starting to think the house was cursed, or maybe she was.

First, there had been a problem with the closing. The owner apparently had some unpaid bills, resulting in a lien on the house, which had caused the closing to be delayed.

Then she had had problems finding someone to renovate the place. All of the contractors she had reached out to were either too busy or too expensive. Only one, Funt & the Son Construction, had a) replied to her email, and b) submitted an estimate that matched her budget. That should have been a tip-off. But she was desperate to get the renovation going as she had to be out of her condo by mid-November.

Sure enough, problems began cropping up as soon as she paid Funt & the Son the deposit.

First, they (really the "son," Frank Funt, Jr.) had stalled on applying for a permit, making all sorts of excuses. Then, after the City of Sanibel building department finally issued a permit, after going back and forth with Funt for weeks, Funt hemmed and hawed about starting work. Then, when work finally did start, Funt refused to give Guin a schedule. Making matters worse, when Guin would ask Funt questions, perfectly reasonable questions, he would treat her as though she were a simpleton or yell at her.

Finally, fed up with the lack of progress and having been yelled at again by Funt, she had hired a lawyer to have a little chat with Mr. Funt, letting him know he would not receive another dime until substantial progress had been made. That had done the trick, and Funt had had crews working at the house since. Though there was still a lot of work to be done. And Guin was nervous about the quality of the work. (Half of the guys she had seen at the house seemed clueless while the other half thought nothing of getting plaster or paint all over the floors.)

But instead of complaining, she would tell Frank what a great job he and his guys were doing, hoping that praise would spur him on. She also did her best to stay out of his way.

Guin again looked at the body in the bathtub and sighed. This was to have been her dream house, her little piece of paradise. But so far, it had been a nightmare.

It had been nearly two years since Guin had moved to Sanibel from New England, after being laid off from her job and then finding out her husband had been having an affair with their hairdresser. She had been sent to Sanibel on a freelance assignment for a magazine and had instantly fallen in love with the place. A few months later, she had returned to Sanibel, with her cats and whatever possessions she hadn't sold, and had gotten a job working for the local paper, the *Sanibel-Captiva Sun-Times*.

She had made new friends and found new love. And a few dead bodies. (But that's another story.[1])

---

[1] See *A Shell of a Problem, Something Fishy, In the Market for Murder, Bye Bye Birdy*, and *Shell Shocked*.

Guin glanced again at the tub, then got up off the toilet and left the bathroom, walking back into the main room. What was taking the police so long?

The police. Instantly, she thought of Detective William O'Loughlin, Sanibel's chief (and only) detective, a former cop from South Boston who had moved to Florida a few years before Guin had. The two had a fiery relationship. Though maybe *fiery* was not the right word. More like smoldering.

The two of them had unmistakable chemistry. Whenever they were together, you could almost see the sparks flying. One of those sparks had burst into a full-on fire that spring when they had gone to the East Coast to see a Spring Training game and had wound up watching the sun set over Hutchinson Island afterward. The detective had kissed Guin on the beach, a kiss that ignited something in Guin that she hadn't felt for a long time.

And then nothing. The detective had stopped returning her calls and texts shortly after they had returned to Sanibel. Guin had at first been confused, then angry. What had she done for the detective to have ghosted her? She had thought about going to the police department to confront him, but she knew that would be foolish. And besides, she had other things to worry about.

Her best friend Shelly's son, Justin, had been dumped by his girlfriend, a pretty blonde co-ed whom Shelly had disliked, just before finals, and he had not handled the breakup well, swallowing a handful of painkillers in hopes of killing himself.

Fortunately, he had texted a friend just before he took the pills, and the friend had called 911. But it had been a close call, and Shelly and her husband Steve had insisted that Justin return with them to Sanibel once he had been released from the hospital.

Shelly had been a wreck for weeks, and Guin had done

her best to be supportive, trying not to burden Shelly with her own relationship woes.

Guin glanced at the phone. Part of her wanted to tell Shelly about finding her contractor in her bathtub. But she knew she should probably wait. The police should be there any minute.

She would also need to tell Ginny, her boss at the paper. Ginny would no doubt want to cover the story, though the thought of that made Guin shudder. Would Ginny allow Guin to cover a murder—well, assuming it was a murder; Funt could have had a heart attack—that had happened at her house? Probably not. No doubt Ginny would assign the story to Craig Jeffers, the paper's crime and fishing reporter.

Like Guin, Craig had had a rough few months. He had been diagnosed with prostate cancer and had been undergoing treatment. The prognosis was good, but the radiation had taken a lot out of him, and Guin wondered if it was a good idea to involve him in a potential murder case. Well, it was out of her hands.

Guin's beloved cat, Flora, had also been diagnosed with cancer that spring. However, she hadn't fared as well as Craig and had to be put to sleep. Guin had cried for days and her other cat, Fauna, had seemed sad as well.

Yes, it had been a bad few months.

As Guin stared out the window, lost in thought, she heard sirens.

"Pull yourself together, Guin," she admonished herself.

She took a deep breath, then went to the front door to greet the police.

CHAPTER 1

Guin watched as two police cars arrived at the house. One was driven by Detective O'Loughlin and the other by Officer Pettit, who Guin knew, who was accompanied by another uniformed officer, who Guin didn't know.

"Detective," Guin said, as he got out of his car. "Thank you for coming."

"Ms. Jones," replied the detective.

They stood looking at each other for several seconds, neither one speaking until one of the officers cleared his throat.

"Won't you come in?" Guin said, addressing the officers.

She led them inside and pointed toward the guest bathroom.

"The body is in there."

The detective and the two officers made their way to the bathroom, stopping just outside.

"The EMTs should be here any minute," the detective informed Guin, as he pulled on a pair of disposable gloves. "Did you touch anything?"

"Well, the door, obviously," said Guin. "And the body. Pretty sure he's dead, by the way."

"Anything else?" asked the detective.

"I sat on the toilet," said Guin. "The lid was closed," she quickly added.

"And what were you doing in the house?" asked the detective.

Guin had written to him that summer that she had bought a house and had sent him the link to the listing. But he hadn't written her back.

"Checking on my contractor."

The detective continued to look at her.

"He was renovating the place."

"Did you have an appointment?" asked the detective.

"As I own the place, and he was supposed to be here working on it, I didn't think I needed one," said Guin a bit more snippily than she had intended. "I just figured I'd stop by as I had been out walking on the beach."

"What time did you arrive at the house?"

"Around nine? I wasn't wearing a watch."

The detective was writing in the little notebook he always carried. Guin craned her neck to see but was unable to.

"And did you notice anything odd when you arrived?" asked the detective.

"Odd?" said Guin.

"Anything unusual or out of place," he clarified.

"No, not at first. I saw Frank's pickup in the driveway. Frank's the contractor. He owns Funt & the Son Construction."

The detective raised an eyebrow.

"I know, it's a stupid name," said Guin. "It's a pun. You know, on 'fun in the sun.'"

The detective shook his head.

"Anyway, they came recommended."

"Who recommended them?"

"Actually," said Guin, "I found them online, on one of those home renovation sites."

The detective looked skeptical.

"I checked them out and spoke with references," Guin

added, feeling defensive. "They've done a bunch of work on the island."

"Never heard of them," said one of the officers.

"Anyway," said Guin. "I hired them, and they were supposed to be done with all the renovations by the end of October. But as you can see, they're a bit behind schedule."

That was putting it mildly.

The detective glanced around. There was the sound of a siren in the distance, though it was getting closer.

"Must be the EMTs," said the detective. "Pettit, take some pictures. Just be careful not to touch anything. Mulvaney, go search the place and let me know if you find anything. Pettit will join you when he's done here."

Guin and the detective watched as Officer Pettit began taking photos inside the bathroom. When he was done, he looked up at the detective, who nodded. Then he left the bathroom.

The detective turned back to Guin.

"So, you said you didn't see anything odd at first."

"Right," said Guin, somewhat distracted. She had been watching Officer Pettit and staring at the body. "Like I said, I saw Frank's pickup parked out front. Figured he must have been working on site. So I went in and called his name, but there was no answer."

"Was the door locked?" asked the detective.

"No," said Guin. "But I figured that was because Frank was inside, probably waiting for his guys to show."

The detective was writing in his notebook again.

"Then what?" he asked, looking up at her.

"I called out, 'Frank? You here?' But there was no answer. So I went to have a look around. The place, as you saw, is a bit of a mess, though he'd made a bunch of progress the last couple of weeks."

"Did you see anyone?"

"No. I checked all the rooms, but there was no sign of anyone."

"So you went into the guest bathroom and…"

"There Frank was, in the bathtub. At first I thought he was asleep. But then—"

Before she could say more, there was a loud knock on the front door, and a man and a woman entered.

The detective greeted them, then led them to the guest bathroom.

The woman, clearly the senior of the two, examined the body, then stood up.

"He's dead."

(Guin could have told them that, but she kept her mouth shut.)

The EMT continued to examine the body.

"Any idea what he died from?" asked Guin.

"Won't know until they do an autopsy," said the male EMT. "Okay for us to take him?" he asked the detective.

"Give me a minute," the detective replied.

The EMTs stepped outside the bathroom and the detective entered. He squatted down on the bathroom floor and examined the body, making notes in his little book. Guin hovered over him.

"You see anything?" Guin asked. "I didn't notice any blood. Do you think it could've been a heart attack?"

The detective ignored her, continuing with his investigation. When he was done, he stood up.

"Okay, you can take him," he said to the two EMTs.

They had gone out and returned with a stretcher and gently placed Frank's body on it, covering it with a sheet.

Guin watched as they wheeled the body out to the ambulance.

"Where were you earlier this morning?" the detective asked Guin.

"On the beach, like I told you."

"Can anyone vouch for that?"

"You don't seriously think *I* killed him?" said Guin, staring at him.

"What about last night?"

Suddenly, Guin remembered.

"I saw Bonnie Barnes!" Guin blurted out. "She's the treasurer of the Shell Club and works over at the Shell Museum. We said hello to each other. You can ask her."

"You saw Ms. Barnes last night?" said the detective, confused.

"No, this morning," said Guin. "I was at home, alone, last night. Well, except for Fauna."

The detective was scribbling in his notebook again. He couldn't possibly think she had killed the man, could he?

"You find anything?" asked the detective. He was looking past Guin.

"No, sir," replied Officer Pettit. "The place is a construction zone. Hard to tell if anything was moved or removed."

"It didn't look like anything was missing when I checked," said Guin.

"And you say you didn't see anyone?" the detective asked Guin.

Guin shook her head.

He looked over at Officer Pettit.

"Give us a minute? I'll meet you outside."

Officer Pettit nodded and he and Officer Mulvaney went outside.

"I'll need an official statement from you," said the detective, looking at Guin.

"Of course," she replied.

Just then her stomach let out a loud growl. Guin felt her cheeks turning pink.

"You have breakfast?" asked the detective.

"No," Guin replied.

Her stomach let out another loud growl.

"You should eat something," he said.

"I was planning on eating something after I got back to the condo."

"Come with me," said the detective, placing a hand on her arm.

Guin froze.

"Are you arresting me?"

"No, I'm taking you to get something to eat. You look like you're about to pass out."

Guin stared at him.

"Come on," he said, gently leading her to the front door. "We'll stop at the Over Easy for a quick bite, then we'll go to the police department."

"The police department?" said Guin, still confused.

"For your official statement."

"But what about Officer Pettit and the other officer?"

"They already had breakfast," said the detective.

Was that a grin on the detective's face?

They reached his sedan and the detective opened the passenger-side door.

Guin looked over at her purple Mini Cooper, which was parked in the driveway, just behind the contractor's pickup truck.

"You can pick up your car later," said the detective. He turned to the two officers. "I'll see you back at the PD," he called.

Guin still hadn't got into the car.

"Get in," the detective commanded.

Guin opened her mouth to object, but she really was rather hungry.

CHAPTER 2

"One more time," said the detective.

Guin made a face.

"Humor me."

They were sitting in the back of the Over Easy Cafe, where hopefully no one would pay them much mind. Guin had ordered the French toast and egg platter with two slices of extra crispy bacon. The detective had ordered the Ho Hum: two eggs with sausage and a side of toast.

"Fine," said Guin. "As I told you, I got up early and decided to go over to West Gulf Drive, to Beach Access #4. I parked my car and walked down to the beach. It was a lovely morning, and—"

"You can skip that part," said the detective. "Tell me what happened afterward. Why did you decide to go to the house?"

"Well, like I said earlier, I was in the neighborhood, and I figured I might as well check on the place, see if Funt had done any more work."

"That would be Frank Funt, Jr.," said the detective.

"Yes, Frank Funt, Jr.," said Guin. "I've never actually met the father."

"Go on," said the detective.

"I saw Frank's pickup in the driveway and parked behind it. I got out and went over to the front door. It was unlocked.

I went inside and called his name, but no one answered. Then I thought I heard something, so I went to check it out. But there was no one there. I went through the house and there he was, in the guest bathroom."

"He being Frank Funt, Jr.," said the detective.

Guin nodded.

"And he was in the tub," said the detective.

"Yes," said Guin.

"Any idea what he was doing there, in the tub?"

"I don't think he was taking a bath," said Guin, somewhat sarcastically.

The detective gave her a look.

"So no idea why he was there?"

Guin sighed.

"I had complained about the bathtub being too small the last time I was over there. They had just put it in, and I swore it was smaller than the one that had been there before. And sure enough, the new one was fifty-eight by twenty-eight, instead of sixty by thirty."

The detective was giving her another look, the one that said "Really?"

"I measured it," said Guin, in answer to his silent question. "Anyway, I had told Frank he needed to put in a bigger tub, and he argued with me. Said the tub was fine as is. And I said, 'You're what, six feet? Why don't you get in there and tell me it's not too small.' But I didn't think he'd take me literally."

"So you think he was checking out the bathtub?"

Guin shrugged.

"I don't know."

She bit off a piece of her bacon.

"When do you think you'll get the autopsy results?" she asked him.

"A couple of days."

"Will you send me a copy?"

The detective gave her a look.

"What about Funt's guys?" he asked her. "What time did they usually get there?"

"Around eight-thirty?"

Guin wasn't sure, though she knew most workers tried to get on the island early.

"Yet you didn't see anyone there when you arrived."

"Nope, not a soul," said Guin.

They finished their food and the detective signaled for a check.

The waitress cleared away their plates, then returned a minute later with their check, which the detective immediately grabbed.

"I got this," he said, as Guin was reaching for her wallet.

He left some cash on the table and stood up.

"Are you done with me?" asked Guin when they got outside.

"I need you to fill out a formal statement," the detective replied.

Guin followed him to his car and got in. A few minutes later, they arrived at the Sanibel police department, which was housed in a nondescript, gray wood complex that housed most of Sanibel's municipal offices. The police department was located on the second floor, and you could see palm trees out the windows—a far cry from the police departments Guin had been in back in New York and Connecticut.

They climbed the stairs and the detective held the door for her.

"Thanks," she mumbled.

The detective said hello to the woman seated at the reception desk, who buzzed him and Guin back. The detective's office was decorated with Boston sports paraphernalia: Red Sox pennants, a signed baseball glove, a signed baseball, a photo of Fenway Park, a Boston Bruin's jersey, and a signed photo of Bill Belichick, the head coach of the New England Patriots.

"Is that new?" asked Guin, looking at the signed Bill Belichick photo.

"Yeah, Joey sent it to me for my birthday."

Joey was the detective's adult son, who still lived in Massachusetts.

"When was your birthday?" asked Guin, who felt awkward for not knowing.

"A couple of weeks ago."

"Well, happy belated birthday."

"Thanks. You want to take a seat?" he said, gesturing at one of the chairs opposite his file-strewn desk.

Guin took a seat.

"So, what do you know about Frank Funt, Jr.?" asked the detective, taking out his notebook.

"Not a whole lot," said Guin. "As I told you, I found Funt and the Son Construction online. They had mostly good reviews, so I reached out and asked for references. The references all checked out, and their bid was the only one I could really afford, so I hired them."

"Mostly good?" asked the detective.

"Excuse me?" said Guin.

"You said they had mostly good reviews," said the detective.

"There were a few negative reviews, too. But you have to kind of expect that, especially with contractors."

"Did anyone else submit a bid?"

"Yes, Beautiful Homes and Right-On Renovation. My real estate agent, Polly Fahnestock, had recommended Beautiful Homes, and several people in the Sanibel Island Facebook group told me to call Right-On."

"So why did you go with Funt?"

"I wanted to go with Beautiful Homes, but their bid was way over my budget, and they wouldn't be able to start until late summer."

"What about the other company?"

"Right-On? The guy I met with was kind of a jerk, and it took a while to get them to give me a quote. And then he told me it would be cost plus, whatever that meant."

"Why didn't you contact more companies?"

"I did," said Guin. "I must have left voicemails or emails for half a dozen contractors, but no one called or messaged me back, except for those three. And I was eager to get the renovation going. The condo was on the market, and I knew I would need to move out by the end of the year, if not sooner."

"So you hired Funt."

"I did. Though, frankly, no pun intended, I started having second thoughts right away. There was something about him that didn't sit right with me. He was one of those big talkers, bragging how he was the best. And he gave me this line about how some contractors will submit a low bid and then do the old bait and switch, charging you a lot more. Little did I know he was talking about himself."

"Anything else?"

"Frank would get annoyed with me whenever I asked him something, treated me like I was an idiot or a pest."

Guin looked at the detective. Was he smiling?

"I tried to ignore his bad attitude, but work wasn't going well, and then the condo got sold, and I told him I needed him to step it up."

The detective was busy writing. When he was done, he looked up.

"And how did he react?"

"Not well," said Guin. "He started to give me one of his

lectures, and I kind of lost it, threatened to sue him."

"And then what?"

"And then he got real nasty."

"Did he threaten you?" asked the detective.

Guin's mind flashed back to that day. It had been awful. Funt had loomed over her and called her "little girl" and said he wasn't scared of her but that she should be scared of him, and in that moment she had been.

She looked at the detective and nodded.

"I called my lawyer right after that."

"Who's your lawyer?" asked the detective.

She gave the detective the lawyer's name.

"And did you sue Funt?"

"No, it didn't come to that. The lawyer sent Funt a letter, letting him know he wouldn't receive any more money until substantial progress had been made—and that he was not to threaten his client, me, ever again, or we'd contact the police."

"And?" said the detective.

"And it worked. Funt had a crew working at the house a few days later."

"And when was the last time you saw Funt, alive, that is?"

Guin cast her mind back.

"Last week. I think it was Wednesday. He had just put in the tub."

"The one you found him in."

"Yes," said Guin.

The detective made some more notes in his little book. Guin leaned over to see what he was writing, but he was too far away.

"So, are you going to arrest me?"

The detective looked up at her.

"Should I?"

"No," said Guin. "We don't even know if he was murdered. It could have been a heart attack."

Though she didn't really believe that. She had noticed some marks on Frank, which had made her suspicious.

They stared at each other for several seconds. There were so many things Guin wanted to ask the detective, but now was not the time or the place.

"So, am I free to go?"

"For now," said the detective. "Just don't leave the island without notifying me."

"Seriously?" said Guin. "What if I need to go to Publix?"

"Go to Bailey's."

"What if Ginny wants me to cover a story off-island?"

"Text me first."

"Why don't you just put one of those ankle monitors on me?" she asked him.

The detective's lips twitched. Guin was pretty sure he was suppressing a grin.

"Don't give me any ideas."

Guin made a face.

"Well, just so you know, I'll be heading over to the office after I leave here. No doubt Ginny has already gotten word of Funt's untimely demise and will want details."

Ginny always seemed to know what was going on on the island, sometimes even before the police did.

"Thanks for letting me know," said the detective. "I trust you can find your way out?"

Guin nodded and started to leave, then stopped.

"My car. It's still at the house."

The detective ran a hand over his face. He had clearly forgotten, too.

Guin folded her arms over her chest and looked down at him, as if to say, "See, I told you we should have taken two cars." But she let her body language speak for itself.

"I'll get someone to drive you over there," he said.

He picked up his phone.

"Hey, Sue, we got anyone who could give Ms. Jones a lift over to West Gulf Drive?"

Guin waited.

"Great," said the detective, a few seconds later. "Thanks, Sue."

"Officer Rodriguez was just about to head that way. She can give you a lift."

"Thanks," said Guin.

She waited for the detective to say something, but he had already busied himself with something on his desk.

"Well, bye," she said.

He raised a hand without looking up at her.

Guin sighed, then made her way back down the hall.

CHAPTER 3

Guin waved goodbye to Officer Rodriguez, then got in her car. She glanced over at the house before she turned the key in the ignition. Would she ever be able to move in? Would she even want to? She sighed and put the car in gear.

"I hear the police were over at your house this morning," said Ginny. "You wanna tell me what's up?"

Guin removed a pile of papers and magazines from one of the chairs in Ginny's office and sat down.

"I found my contractor in the bathtub."

"Was he taking a bath?"

"No, he was dead."

"You know, Guinivere, before you arrived, Sanibel was a peaceful little town. Now it seems like every other month, there's a murder."

"You're not really blaming me, are you?"

"Just saying," said Ginny. "So, did you kill him?"

"No!" said Guin. "How could you even think that?"

"Well, you weren't exactly happy with him," said Ginny.

"I wanted the house taken care of," said Guin. "Not him. Besides, the man was a good head taller than me and had to have outweighed me by at least eighty pounds."

"I've seen women smaller than you take out men twice their size," said Ginny.

Guin stared at her.

"I cannot believe we are having this conversation. You don't seriously think I killed Frank Funt, do you?"

Ginny looked at her.

"No, I don't. But I wouldn't be a good journalist if I didn't ask."

She had a point.

"So what did Detective O'Loughlin have to say?"

"Not much," said Guin. "You know how tight-lipped he is."

"So what do you think happened?"

"I don't know. I mean, he could have been checking out the tub and had a heart attack, but I'm not buying it."

"Was he naked?"

"Excuse me?" said Guin.

"You said you found him in the tub."

"No, he was not naked."

Guin shuddered at the thought.

"Shame," said Ginny.

Guin stared at her.

"Is it possible he drowned?"

"No," said Guin. "There was no water in the tub."

"He could have slipped and hit his head."

"I don't think so," said Guin. "I didn't see any blood."

"Hmm…" said Ginny, leaning back in her chair and tenting her hands.

"The paramedics took the body," said Guin. "The detective should have the autopsy report in a few days."

They sat in silence for several seconds.

"You tell Craig?" asked Ginny.

"About the body? No, not yet."

"Give him a jingle."

"I don't want to bother him."

"You rather I tell him?"

"No, it's just…"

"Please," said Ginny. "The man would probably jump at the chance to do some investigative reporting. Give him a call."

"What about his cancer?"

"What about it?" said Ginny. "He's in remission, isn't he?"

Guin nodded.

"Look, Guin, the man's probably bored out of his mind. He needs to get back out there. Besides, I can't have you covering something that took place in your house. Journalistic ethics and all that."

"What about Betty?" said Guin, thinking of Craig's wife.

"She'll probably be thrilled to get him out of the house or at least out of her hair," said Ginny.

Ginny had a point.

"Okay, I'll give Craig a call," Guin said. She paused. "So what do *you* know about Frank Funt?"

"Junior or Senior?" said Ginny.

"Both," said Guin.

"Well, Frank, Sr., worked on our home right after we bought it. Did a good job, too. The company wasn't called Funt and the Son back then. Can't remember the name, but Frank was the kind of guy who'd stay late and work weekends to make sure the job was done right. Don't know much about the son. Just heard some things."

"What kinds of things?" asked Guin.

"Some problems with drugs."

"And you didn't think to warn me about him?"

"It was a while ago, and I had no idea the son was running the business. Besides, I assumed you had checked him out with the building department."

"The building department?" said Guin.

"To see if anyone had filed any complaints."

Why hadn't Guin thought of that?

"So I can just go to the building department and say, 'Hey, do you happen to know if anyone filed a complaint against Funt and the Son Construction or Frank Funt, Jr.?'"

"Pretty much," said Ginny. "It's public record."

"Huh," said Guin. It would have been nice to have known that before she had selected a contractor. "Well, I guess I should get going," she said, getting up. "I should have the piece on Congress Jewelers' expansion to you by end of day tomorrow and the 'Fall in love with Sanibel' article to you by the end of the week."

"Sounds good," said Ginny. "And while you're at it, talk to Glen and let me know which places you two want to cover for the Day Trips series. You've got first dibs."

At their last staff meeting, someone had suggested the paper start a Day Trips column. Ginny thought it was a great idea, and the staff took a vote and picked eight places: Cayo Costa State Park, Cabbage Key, Useppa, Boca Grande, Matlacha, Naples, Marco Island, and the Ten Thousand Islands.

"Will do," said Guin. "I just hope I'm not arrested for murder."

Ginny ruffled some papers, looking for something. Guin wasn't sure if she was supposed to wait or if it was okay to go.

"Go on," said Ginny, looking up and making a shooing motion with her hands. "I've got work to do."

Guin headed to the door. She stopped and looked back, but Ginny was already on the phone.

CHAPTER 4

"So, which three places do you want to cover?" Guin asked Glen.

Glen, who was maybe a few years older than Guin, was a freelance photographer who had a regular gig with the paper. The two had worked together a number of times now and got along well.

"Hmm..." said Glen. "How about we discuss it over dinner?"

"When?" said Guin.

"You doing anything tonight?"

Guin stared out the glass sliders in her living room, which overlooked a golf course. She didn't have any plans, but she felt a bit funny going out to dinner with Glen. A working lunch was one thing, but dinner? (It also didn't help that Glen reminded Guin of her ex, Art, who was also tall, blond, and good looking.)

"Hello? You still there?"

"Sorry," said Guin. "Must have spaced out. What was the question?"

"I asked if you wanted to discuss the Day Trips column over dinner tonight. I was thinking we could meet up at Dante's, over at the Sanibel Inn."

"I know where Dante's is," said Guin.

"Good, so shall we say six-thirty?"

"You're going to drive all the way to Sanibel? Isn't that kind of far?"

"It's fine. It's not in season, so traffic should be fine. Besides, it's not that far."

"If you say so," said Guin.

"I do," said Glen. "So it's a date. See you at Dante's at six-thirty."

"It's not a date," said Guin.

Glen chuckled.

"See you later."

He ended the call, and Guin felt embarrassed. When had she become so sensitive? Oh yeah, after the detective had dumped her. She looked out the window again. As she was standing there, her phone began vibrating. She looked down and saw a familiar number.

"Craig?"

"What's this I hear about you finding another dead body?"

"Did Ginny call you?" asked Guin.

"Never mind who called me, are you okay?"

"I'm fine," said Guin. "How are *you*?"

"Good enough," he replied. "Now tell me what's going on."

And Guin did.

When she was done, Craig whistled.

"That's quite a story."

"So, what's your take?"

"Too early to say. You say the detective told you the autopsy report should be available in a couple of days?"

Guin nodded.

"That's what he said."

"Well, if he doesn't share it with you, let me know."

"I will," said Guin.

Craig had contacts everywhere: in City Hall, the police

department, the fire department, the medical examiner's office… He either went fishing or played poker with anyone who was anyone on Sanibel and Captiva, and he had contacts in Fort Myers, too. As an award-winning crime reporter (formerly with the *Chicago Tribune*), he knew how to develop sources and was very good at getting information out of people, often without them knowing it.

"Anything else I can help you with?" he asked.

"If you could chat with some of your buddies, see what they know about Frank, Jr., that would be great. I heard he may have been into drugs, either using or selling them. He also probably had a bunch of unhappy customers, subs too. Whatever you can dig up."

"Not a problem," said Craig. "I'll get working on it right away."

"Thanks," said Guin.

She heard Betty saying something to Craig in the background, but she couldn't make out what.

"That was Betty," said Craig. "She wants to know if you're free for dinner tonight."

"I would love to join you," said Guin. "But I have plans."

"Oh?" said Craig. "Got a date?"

"No, I'm meeting up with Glen, my photographer."

"That the tall, good-looking blond fellow?"

"I didn't notice if he was good-looking," she said, feeling her face grow warm.

"He married?"

"Divorced."

She knew where this conversation was going and wanted to stop Craig before he went any further.

"It's purely business, Craig. We're just meeting at Dante's, for pizza."

"Back in my day, a man met a woman for dinner, even if it was pizza, it was a date."

"Well, it's a whole new world," Guin said. "And it's not a date."

"Well, I hope you enjoy your non-date. I'll do some poking around and get back to you."

"Thanks," said Guin. "And please thank Betty for the dinner invite."

"Will do. Another time."

They said goodbye and ended the call.

"So, Fauna, what do you think I should wear?"

The black cat, who had been napping on Guin's bed, glanced up.

"You think these capris and this tee are okay?"

Fauna yawned.

"Yes, I know it's kind of boring, but…"

Guin looked again at the pair of white capris and the black t-shirt she had pulled out. Why was she being so indecisive? It wasn't as though this was a date. Still, she didn't want to look like a slob. Not that she ever did, but….

She sighed and put on the capris and grabbed a lacy blue top. Then she went into the bathroom. She stared at herself in the mirror, then pulled her hair back into a ponytail and applied some mascara and lip gloss.

"It's not a date," she told her reflection.

She wasn't positive, but it seemed as though her reflection didn't believe her.

"Well, gotta go," she told it.

She gazed at her reflection one last time and removed the ponytail holder. Then she headed into the kitchen to grab her bag and her keys.

She arrived at the restaurant a few minutes late and found Glen seated at the bar, chatting with the bartender. Guin walked over and tapped him on the shoulder.

"Hey!" he said, smiling at her.

"Hey yourself," she replied, smiling back. "You been here long?"

She noticed his beer was half empty.

"Not too long," he replied. You want to grab a table?"

He signaled to the hostess, who led them to a booth.

"So," said Guin, after they had sat down. "You think about the list? Any place you've been dying to photograph?"

Before he could reply, their waitress came over and asked Guin if she wanted something to drink and if Glen wanted a refill.

"I'm good," said Glen.

Guin looked over at Glen's glass.

"What do you have on tap?" she asked the server.

The young woman reeled off a half-dozen beers. Guin picked one of the local brews and the server said she'd be right back.

"So?" she said, looking over at Glen.

"I was thinking we could start with Boca Grande."

"Fine by me," said Guin. "I've never been."

"You haven't? Well, we'll have to remedy that. When do you want to go?"

Good question, thought Guin. She still had to finish her list of things to do on Sanibel in the fall, and there was the matter of finding out who killed her contractor. Though she knew Ginny wanted them to get going on the Day Trips series ASAP.

"You okay?" asked Glen.

"Sorry," said Guin. "Just going through my mental calendar. How about Friday?"

"Let me check my calendar," said Glen, pulling out his phone. "Friday's good! Let me just see what time the boat leaves."

Guin watched as he typed.

"The boat to Boca Grande leaves from Captiva at ten and boarding begins at nine-thirty."

"What time does it head back?"

"It returns to Captiva at four, but we'll need to be at the dock by three-thirty. That doesn't give us much time."

"I guess we could drive there," said Guin. "As I recall, Gasparilla Island is around two hours from here."

"Or we could stay over."

"Though the point of the article is that these are day trips," said Guin.

"True," said Glen. "But it will take us more than a handful of hours to cover the island. And won't most people want to take the boat from Captiva?"

He had a point.

Guin opened her mouth to say something, then shut it as their waitress appeared with her beer.

"Here you go!" she said, placing it in front of Guin. "You two know what you want?"

Glen looked over at Guin.

"Give us a minute," he said to the young woman.

"Sure thing," she said.

They stared at the menus.

"You want to share an appetizer and a pizza?" asked Guin.

"Sure," said Glen. "Whatcha thinking?"

Guin looked back down at the menu.

"How about we share the fried crab balls and get a large pizza with mushrooms and onions?"

"Sounds good to me."

Guin signaled to their server.

"You ready to order?" she asked them.

"One order of fried crab balls and one large pizza with mushrooms and onions."

"Very good," said the server.

She smiled, then headed to the kitchen.

"Getting back to Boca Grande," said Guin.

"Tell you what," said Glen. "Let's plan on taking the boat and spending the day. But take an overnight bag, just in case."

"Just in case of what?"

"Just in case we need to spend more time there," said Glen, smiling at her again.

Guin's stomach did a little flip. It was probably hunger.

"Hopefully, that won't be necessary," said Guin, sounding a bit like a schoolmarm.

"But as the Boy Scouts say, it pays to be prepared."

"Were you a Boy Scout?"

"Briefly."

Guin took a sip of her beer.

"How's your dad doing?" she asked him, hoping to change the subject.

Glen's father was in declining health, which was why Glen had moved back to Fort Myers from New York City. His mother had been taking care of him at home, but they had recently moved to an assisted living community.

"Not great," said Glen. "But at least they're in assisted care now."

They sat quietly for a couple of minutes, drinking their beers.

"How's your mom?" Glen asked. "Didn't you say she was having knee replacement surgery?"

"Wow, good memory," said Guin. "The surgery went fine. She's been in physical therapy."

There was another silence, and Guin wondered if she should tell Glen about her contractor.

Fortunately, she was spared having to say anything as their crab balls arrived.

"Enjoy!" said their server, placing them in the center of the table.

"Those look good," Guin said, spearing one with her fork and dipping it in the sauce.

Glen did the same, popping the crab ball into his mouth.

"Mmm…" he said, his mouth full of crab. "Hot."

Guin smiled. She found it hard to picture Glen in a suit, working on Wall Street. He seemed far too laid back.

They made small talk for several minutes. Then, when they were done, a busboy took away their plates.

"That was good," said Glen.

Guin nodded.

"So, um, are you seeing anybody?" Glen asked, not looking directly at Guin.

"Excuse me?" said Guin, taken off guard.

"Sorry, I didn't mean to get too personal."

"No, it's fine," Guin replied. "It's just…"

The truth was, she didn't know how to respond. Technically, she wasn't seeing anyone. She had broken up with her erstwhile beau, Dr. Harrison "Ris" Hartwick, Ph.D., known to his many female fans as "Dr. Heartthrob," months ago. And any hopes she had of herself and the detective getting together had faded away over the summer.

She saw Glen looking at her.

"The answer is no," she finally replied. "What about you? You seeing anyone?"

"Not right now," Glen replied. "There was someone, but…"

"But?" said Guin.

"It didn't work out."

"Sorry," said Guin.

"Don't be," said Glen. "It wasn't meant to be."

They stared at the large TV over the bar, which was airing

ESPN. A few minutes later, their pizza arrived.

Glen served Guin a slice, then placed one on his plate.

After two slices, Guin was done. But there were still a few slices left.

"You want a box for that?" asked their server, seeing they were done.

"Please," said Guin.

The young woman returned a minute later with a cardboard box.

"Thanks," said Guin.

"Would you like some coffee or dessert?"

"I'll have an espresso," said Glen.

"Can you do a decaf cappuccino?" asked Guin.

"No problem," said the young woman. "Any dessert?"

They shook their heads.

The waitress returned with their coffee a few minutes later. Guin took a sip.

"Oh, I nearly forgot! We still need to pick two more places."

"Hmm…" said Glen, sipping his espresso. "How about Naples and the Ten Thousand Islands? Or would you prefer Cayo Costa? I know how you like to go searching for shells."

"Yeah, but I don't want you to be bored out of your mind. Let's do Naples and the Ten Thousand Islands."

Glen smiled.

"Sounds good."

"Great," said Guin. "I'll let Ginny know."

They finished their coffee, then got the check.

"Thanks for having dinner with me," said Glen, when they got outside.

"Thanks for inviting me," said Guin.

They stood there in the moonlight for several seconds.

"Well, good night," said Guin.

"Good night," said Glen. "You sure you don't want the extra pizza?"

Guin had insisted Glen take the box home with him.

"I'm good," said Guin. "Enjoy."

"Oh, I will. Nothing like a slice of cold pizza for breakfast."

Guin made a face.

"Hey, don't knock it till you've tried it."

They waved goodbye, then headed to their cars.

"See you Friday!" Glen called.

Guin gave him a thumbs-up, then got in the Mini.

CHAPTER 5

Guin spent the next day in front of her computer. She finished editing the Congress Jewelers story and sent it off to Ginny. Then she turned her attention to her "Fall in love with Sanibel" piece.

Guin had reached out to the Bailey-Matthews National Shell Museum, the J.N. "Ding" Darling National Wildlife Refuge, the Sanibel Historical Village and Museum, the Clinic for the Rehabilitation of Wildlife (known as CROW), the Sanibel-Captiva Conservation Foundation (SCCF), and BIG ARTS to see what they had going on in October. Now she felt a bit overwhelmed, she had received so much information. Well, she would just include everything and then edit the piece down later.

She was busy typing when her stomach started to growl.

"Shh!" she told it. But it continued to rumble. "Fine," she said, looking at the clock on her monitor and realizing it was after one.

She took out her phone, which she had placed in her desk drawer, and checked her messages. She had been hoping to receive word from the detective about Frank Funt, Jr., but there was nothing. Of course, it had only been a day, but she was anxious to hear the preliminary findings of the autopsy report. Had Frank died from natural causes or had someone killed him?

She put her phone in her back pocket and headed to the kitchen, where she made herself a peanut butter and jelly sandwich on whole-grain bread. She stood at the counter as she ate, staring out past the lanai. It looked like a nice day. Maybe she should go for a walk. It always helped her to think better.

She finished her sandwich and looked at her phone again. Still nothing from the detective. She thought about calling over to the police department, then put her phone down. A minute later, she picked it up again.

"Just a quick call," she said aloud.

She entered the number for the police department, which she had on speed dial.

"Detective O'Loughlin, please," she told the operator.

"He's in a meeting," said the operator. "Would you like his voicemail?"

"Sure," said Guin. "Thanks."

The operator put her through. At the tone, she left a brief message.

"Hey, it's Guin, Ms. Jones. I was wondering if you heard anything from the medical examiner. Give me a call. Thanks."

She ended the call and sent him a text. Then she went back to work. A couple of hours later, she had finished the first draft of her "Fall in love with Sanibel" article. She knew it was too long, but she would edit it the next day.

She took out her phone and checked her messages. Still nothing from the detective. She sighed and went into the kitchen to get a glass of water. As she was drinking, she could feel her phone vibrating in her back pocket. She put down the glass and took it out, answering it without checking to see who was calling.

"Hello?" she said, a bit too eagerly.

"You're alive." It was her mother. "I was beginning to wonder."

Guin groaned inwardly but plastered a smile on her face. "Hi, Mom. How nice to hear from you."

"Hmm," said her mother.

"I've been meaning to call," Guin continued. "I've just been really busy. Is everything okay? How's your knee?"

"My knee is fine, thank you," said her mother, a bit icily. "Lance even attended a couple of physical therapy sessions with me. And you know how busy he is."

Guin rolled her eyes. Lance, full name Lancelot, was her older brother and their mother's favorite. He owned a successful boutique advertising agency in New York, but he always made time to get together or chat with their mother—and check on Guin. Which reminded Guin, she owed him a call.

"I'm sorry I couldn't have helped, Mom. But I couldn't get away."

Her mother made a noise that Guin knew meant she didn't believe her.

"Really, Guinivere, I don't know what you could have possibly been doing down there. Isn't it hurricane season? Sanibel must be positively dead."

"People live and visit here during hurricane season," Guin replied. "And I couldn't leave with the house not done."

"Ah yes, that house of yours. Lancelot said you were having some issues with your contractor and that you had to hire an attorney."

"I did, but we worked things out."

Guin did not want to tell her mother that said contractor was now dead.

"I hope you were firm with him, Guinivere," said her mother. "I know you have a habit of letting people walk all over you. But you'll never get anywhere in life if you let people take advantage of or bully you."

Guin wanted to laugh. Her mother was a fine one to talk.

"Well, you don't have to worry about him walking all over me, Mother, because he's dead."

Guin immediately covered her mouth. She had not meant to say that.

"Dead?" said her mother. "Did he fall off a roof?"

"No," said Guin.

She prayed her mother wouldn't press her for details.

"So what does this mean for your house? Did he have a partner who could finish things up?"

"His father was his partner, but he's retired."

"Surely, there must be someone who can help. What about the project manager?"

"He was the project manager."

"Really, Guinivere, you need to vet these people more carefully. What about your money?"

What about her money? Guin had been so preoccupied with Funt, she hadn't thought about that. Until now. Then she remembered.

"There's always his girlfriend, Phoebe. She's the office manager. I guess I could talk to her."

Guin suddenly felt guilty. She had forgotten all about Phoebe. True, she had only met Phoebe a couple of times, and had gotten the distinct impression that the woman didn't like her, but she knew she should send a condolence note or call.

"Is this Phoebe going to fix your house?" asked her mother.

"I don't know," Guin replied. "Probably not."

There was another pause.

"Let me ask Alfred," said her mother. "I'm sure he must know someone. Naples must be full of contractors."

Alfred was the son of Guin's step-aunt's good friend, Harriet. He was in his forties and divorced, like Guin, and lived in Naples. Guin had never met Alfred, but it wasn't for her mother's lack of trying.

"By the way," her mother continued. "I heard Alfred broke up with his girlfriend. And now that you're single again…"

"Thanks, Mom. But I'm good," said Guin, not wanting to go down that path.

Her mother made a tsking sound.

"It is not normal for a woman your age to be alone, Guinivere. You need a man."

Guin rolled her eyes. She was always amazed by how old-fashioned her mother could be, at least when it came to relationships.

"Mom, there are lots of perfectly happy single women in their forties."

"They may tell themselves they are happy," said her mother. "But…"

"Can we please change the subject?" Guin pleaded. "Lance said you and Philip were going on a cruise somewhere in Europe."

(Philip was Guin's stepfather, who was British.)

"Yes, we're going to the Mediterranean. There was a last-minute cancelation and we had our travel agent book it. It's one of those small, very exclusive ships."

"A Mediterranean cruise sounds nice," said Guin.

"We shall see," said her mother.

Guin stared up at the ceiling, trying to think of a way to end the conversation.

"Well, I hope you and Philip have a wonderful time."

"We're going to spend a few days in Bath afterward, with the family," said her mother. "You could always join us."

"Thanks," said Guin, "but I don't think I'll be able to get away."

"Your Aunt Lavinia is always asking after you,"

continued her mother. "I bet she knows some nice eligible British men. You will, of course, be attending Lavinia's eightieth next year."

It was a statement, not a question.

"Of course," said Guin, who had completely forgotten about it. She looked up at the clock. "Hey, Mom, I need to go."

"Oh?" said her mother.

"Yes, I have a lot of work to do."

"Very well," said her mother. "I'll let you know what Alfred says."

"You do that," said Guin, knowing it was pointless arguing with her mother.

"And call me next week."

"I promise," said Guin. "Love you."

"I love you, too," said her mother.

Guin ended the call and leaned against the counter, suddenly feeling exhausted.

She took a sip of her water, then went back to her desk, to see what she could dig up on Frank Funt, Jr. No sooner had she sat down than Fauna climbed into her lap and promptly closed her eyes. Guin smiled at the sleepy feline.

"I wish I could take a nap," she said.

She raised her eyes to her monitor.

"Now, let's see what the internet has to say about you, Mr. Frank Funt, Jr.," she said as she typed.

Although she had done a search on Funt & the Son Construction before she had hired them, she hadn't delved into Frank, Jr., personally. Her mistake.

She watched as the screen filled with search results. One in particular, about a drug bust in Fort Myers, caught her eye. She clicked on it and began to read.

CHAPTER 6

The article was from three-and-a-half years ago. Frank, Jr., had been arrested selling drugs to an undercover cop, who was posing as a college student, at a bar in Fort Myers Beach. The article wasn't very long and didn't say much. Guin returned to the search results, to see if she could find more information about the bust. But all the articles pretty much repeated the same basic information.

She sent the link from the Fort Myers paper to Craig, asking him if he could see if one of his buddies knew anything about the bust or if Funt had been busted before or since. Then she reached for her phone. Still nothing from the detective. She was about to put her phone back on her desk when it began to vibrate. Finally.

"Detective," she said. "How nice to hear from you."

"I need you to come down to the police department."

"I'd be happy to," Guin replied. "When?"

"Now."

Guin suddenly had a bad feeling.

"Did something happen?"

"We got the preliminary autopsy report," replied the detective.

"And?" said Guin.

"Just get over here," he said.

That didn't sound good.

"So, what was the cause of death?" Guin asked.

"Are you coming, or do I need to send a car?"

The detective was clearly not in a good mood.

"Are you going to arrest me?"

There was no reply.

"Just give me a few minutes," said Guin. "I'll be there as soon as I can."

"I'll be waiting," said the detective. "Sue'll buzz you back when you get here."

Guin looked up at her monitor. There would be no more searching for now. She went to the kitchen and filled Fauna's bowl with dry food, in case she didn't make it back that evening. Then she grabbed her bag and her keys and left.

"I'm here," said Guin, standing in the doorway to the detective's office.

"Have a seat," said the detective, gesturing to one of the chairs opposite his desk.

Guin stepped into his office but remained standing.

"Please, have a seat," the detective commanded.

Guin reluctantly sat.

"So, what was the cause of death?"

"Drug overdose. Though they're waiting for some additional tests to come back."

"So if he OD'd, I'm off the hook."

"Like I said, that was the preliminary finding."

"Oh," said Guin, sensing that the detective wasn't done.

"They found various marks on the victim, including some scratches on his face," he continued.

"Scratches?" said Guin.

The detective nodded.

"What has that got to do with me?" said Guin, not following.

"We believe they were left by a woman."

"And you know that how?" asked Guin.

"There were traces of nail polish."

"Well, detective," said Guin, holding up her hands. "As you can see, I'm not wearing nail polish."

"You could've removed it."

She looked at him.

"I could have, but I didn't. Besides, I rarely wear nail polish."

They stared at each for several seconds.

"You know," she finally said, "there are plenty of men who wear nail polish: catchers, drag queens, rock stars…"

The detective continued to regard Guin.

"What about Funt's girlfriend?" asked Guin. "Did you haul her down here and check out her hands?"

"Are you done now?" asked the detective.

Guin gave a quick nod.

"They also found a track mark on his arm."

"So he wasn't just a pusher, he used the stuff, too," said Guin.

The detective looked at her.

"I read that Funt had been busted for trying to sell drugs to an undercover cop a few years back and that he was arrested. Did he do any jail time?"

"No," said the detective.

"Any idea why?"

"His lawyer got him off."

"So you said the preliminary finding was that Funt had OD'd. I'm assuming the autopsy report listed the source of the overdose."

The detective nodded.

"They found oxycodone and fentanyl in his system."

"Opioids," said Guin. "Do you know if he had a prescription?"

"We're looking into it."

"So why did you call me down here? I doubt it was just to see if I wore nail polish."

"You ever see Funt taking pills or injecting himself?"

"No," said Guin.

"What about you?"

"What about me?" said Guin.

"You ever take painkillers?"

Guin racked her brain. There had been the time when she had her wisdom teeth removed, but that was years ago.

She shook her head.

"We need to search your condo."

"Wait, what?" said Guin, startled. "Why?"

The detective arched an eyebrow.

"Fine," said Guin. "I've got nothing to hide. Search away. Just tell your people to watch out for Fauna—and not to let her out."

"I'll let them know." He picked up his phone and punched in some numbers. "Go ahead," he said to whoever was on the other end. "Just watch out for the cat."

He listened for several seconds, then hung up.

Guin was staring at him.

"They're there now?"

The detective didn't respond.

Guin mentally went through her medicine cabinet. She knew she had a bottle of ibuprofen and another of naproxen sodium, but she was pretty sure those were the only pain relievers she had. Though now that she thought about it, she was pretty sure she had a bottle of blue nail polish. Hopefully, that wasn't the color of the polish they found on Funt.

"So am I supposed to stay here while your guys ransack my home?" said Guin, a bit peevishly.

"I'm sure Officer Rodriguez will be very careful," replied the detective.

Guin folded her arms across her chest.

"Well, while you're holding me here, maybe you could answer a few of *my* questions?"

The detective looked at her.

"What was the time of death?"

"Sometime between eight and midnight," replied the detective.

Guin tried to remember what she had been doing between eight and midnight the night before she had found Funt. She had probably been in bed.

She saw the detective watching her.

"Because I know you're going to ask, I was at home, alone, Sunday evening." Then she remembered. "Wait, I spoke with my brother, Lance. It was a little before nine. We must have been on the phone for at least half an hour. You can check my cell phone records. Then I got ready for bed."

She realized that wasn't a rock-solid alibi, but it was the truth.

The detective continued to regard her.

"Come on, detective! You don't seriously think I drove to the house, tackled Funt, and then pumped him full of painkillers while having a conversation with my brother, do you? The man was nearly twice my size! Also, where would I have gotten painkillers? I don't even have a doctor here." (Something Guin had been meaning to remedy but hadn't gotten around to.)

"So what was he doing at your house?" calmly asked the detective.

"I have no idea," said Guin, unable to hold back her exasperation.

The detective opened his mouth to say something, but he was interrupted by his phone ringing. He picked it up and listened, nodding his head.

"Okay," he said. "Thanks."

He hung up and Guin waited for him to speak.

"Well?" she said.

"You're free to go."

"That's it?" said Guin. "You don't have any more questions for me?"

"Not at this time," replied the detective.

The detective's phone rang again.

"O'Loughlin."

He listened for several seconds, then asked the caller to hold and covered the mouthpiece.

"I need to take this. I trust you can see yourself out."

His eyes moved to the door.

Guin knew she was being dismissed. She got up and made her way to the door, the detective watching her. She stopped when she got there and turned to face the detective.

"No matter what you think," she told him, "I didn't do it. But I'm going to find out who did."

Guin stomped down the stairs and let out a scream when she got to her car. How could the detective possibly think she had anything to do with Frank, Jr.'s death? She understood that the detective was just doing his job, but still. She paused and wondered what, if anything, the cops who had searched her condo had found. Clearly, if they had found anything incriminating, the detective would have held her, right? Then again, you never knew with the detective.

She got in the Mini and turned the key, only to sit there and stare out the window for several seconds. She turned the car off and dug in her bag for her phone. There was a message from Craig, asking her to call him. She hit redial and called him back.

"Hey, what's up?" she asked him.

"I have some information about Frank Funt, Jr.," he replied.

"Go on," said Guin.

"I'd rather not discuss it over the phone."

"I'm at the Sanibel police department."

"You're at the police department? Is everything okay?"

"I don't know," said Guin. "The detective brought me in for questioning. Seems Mr. Funt died of a drug overdose, and they wanted to search my condo for drugs."

"They find anything?"

"Not that I'm aware of."

"You want to come over here?"

"Sure. Why not? Is Betty there?"

"No, she's playing bridge."

"Okay, I'll see you in a few."

"So, what couldn't you tell me over the phone?" asked Guin, after Craig had led her into the living room.

"Sorry, I didn't mean to sound so dramatic," he said, taking a seat near her. "I asked around, and it seems your contractor had a record."

"A record, as in a criminal record?" asked Guin.

"Yes, though most of the stuff occurred when he was in his teens."

"What kind of stuff are we talking about?"

"The usual: drugs, shoplifting, disorderly conduct."

"What about since he was legally an adult? In that article I sent you, Funt was trying to sell drugs to an undercover cop. And that was only a few years ago."

"Ah yes," said Craig. "According to my sources, Funt was known on the street as a middleman."

"So he *was* selling drugs."

"Though he was never formally charged."

"And who was he selling drugs to, other than undercover cops posing as college students?"

"Probably his other clients."

"His other clients as in his remodeling clients?"

Craig nodded.

"You have any names?"

"No."

"You know if Funt had a drug problem?"

"I don't," said Craig. "You ever see him take anything?"

"The detective asked me that, too. And I told him no. I haven't hung out with a lot of junkies, but if he had been high, I think I would have noticed. Is it possible one of his customers killed him, made it look like he OD'd?"

"It's possible," said Craig. "From what I hear, Frank, Jr., rubbed a lot of people the wrong way."

Including me, Guin thought.

"So, your sources say anything else?"

"No, that was it for now."

Guin looked at Craig.

"And how are you?"

"How should I be?" he replied.

"They got the cancer, right? You're in remission."

"Yeah, supposedly. But you know cancer."

Guin nodded. She knew that once cancer got its claws in you, it didn't fully let go.

"Don't look so sad," said Craig. "I've had a good life. No complaints."

"Don't talk like that!" said Guin, feeling emotional. "You and Betty have many good years ahead of you."

Craig patted Guin on the leg.

"How 'bout we change the subject? Tell me, what else are you working on?"

Guin told him about her Sanibel article.

Craig yawned.

"I didn't mean to bore you," said Guin, though she was smiling.

"Sorry. I've just been tired a lot more lately."

"I understand," said Guin. "I should get going anyway. When's Betty going to be home?"

Craig looked at his watch.

"Any minute. You sure you don't want to stay for dinner? I know Betty would love to see you."

"Thanks, but I've got work to do."

"You still need to eat," said Craig.

Guin was tempted, but she was eager to get home and do some more research.

She gave Craig a quick kiss on the cheek.

"Take care of yourself—and let me know what else you find out about Funt."

"Will do," said Craig.

He walked her to the door and waved as she got into the Mini.

CHAPTER 7

As soon as Guin got home, she opened her browser and looked up "opioid overdose." Immediately, she got thousands of hits. She clicked on one of the first links and scrolled to where it discussed signs that a person had suffered an opioid overdose.

"The person's face is pale and/or feels clammy to the touch."

Check.

"Their body goes limp."

Check again.

"Their fingernails or lips have a purple or bluish color."

Guin tried to remember what Frank had looked like. He had been slumped over, so she hadn't gotten a good look at his face or his hands.

"They start vomiting or making gurgling noises."

Again, Guin had no idea if that had occurred.

"Their breathing or heartbeat slows or stops."

Well, he was dead, so it was safe to assume his heart had stopped.

She sat back in her chair. Why hadn't she taken a closer look at Frank when she had had the chance? But she knew the answer. She had been too in shock and hadn't wanted to touch the body. Still. She turned over her phone and searched her photos. She had taken a handful before the police had arrived, including one of Frank in the tub. She zoomed in, but due to how he was positioned, it was tough to see much.

She turned back to her monitor and typed "Funt & the Son Construction reviews" into her search engine. She had checked their reviews before she had hired them, but she hadn't carefully read all of them. And there were more now. She had begun to read when her phone started vibrating. She looked down at the caller ID. It was Shelly.

"Hey," said Guin. "Everything okay?"

Guin was always nervous when Shelly called these days.

"How's Justin doing?"

"Good!" said Shelly. "He's been working over at Bailey's. I think it's really been helping."

"Great!" said Guin.

"Though I wish he'd think about going back to school."

"I'm sure he'll go back as soon as he feels up to it."

"He's been talking about finishing his degree online. Says he has too many memories back there. But when I think of all the money we spent..." She sighed. "Oh well. The important thing is that he's healing, right?"

"Absolutely," said Guin.

"So, you wanna grab a drink or something to eat? Steve and Justin are having one of their father-and-son dinners, and I don't feel like being home alone."

Guin looked at the clock on her monitor. It was nearly six.

"Sure. Where were you thinking?"

"How about the Sandbar?"

"That's fine," said Guin. "What time?"

"How soon can you meet me?"

"How's six-forty-five?"

"Sounds good," said Shelly. "I'll see you then."

"Do you think we need a reservation?"

"It's September, but I'll call over there."

"Okay," said Guin. "See you soon."

They ended the call and Guin went back to reading reviews of Funt & the Son for the next twenty minutes. The reviews had been mostly good, until around the time Guin had hired them. Of course.

She looked at the clock on her monitor. Time to get ready. She closed her browser and got up.

Guin looked around the restaurant. The bar was busy, but there were plenty of free tables. She didn't see Shelly, but she saw several other people she knew, including Craig's friend, Jimbo.

"Hey, Jimbo!" Guin said, going up to him. "What brings you here? Don't you usually hang out at Doc Ford's?"

Jimbo smiled up at her.

"Thought I'd switch things up. What are you doing here?"

Guin was about to say, "meeting a friend," when, as if on cue, Shelly came rushing through the door.

"Sorry, I'm late!" she said, making her way over to Guin.

"No worries," said Guin. "I just got here myself. Shelly, I believe you know Jimbo."

"Of course," said Shelly. "Catch any fish lately?"

He smiled.

"Not lately, no. Though things should start picking up soon."

He placed some money on the bar and got up.

"Did we chase you away?" asked Guin.

"Nah," said Jimbo. "I've a date."

"A date?" said Guin. "Good for you!"

Guin knew that Jimbo had lost his college-age daughter in an automobile accident a few years back and that his wife had left him shortly thereafter.

"It's no big deal," said Jimbo, looking slightly embarrassed.

"Well, I hope you have a great time," said Guin.

"Thanks," said Jimbo. "Now you two don't get into any trouble."

He gave them a stern look and wagged his finger, but Guin knew he was only teasing.

"We'll try," said Guin, smiling at him.

Jimbo left, and Guin looked down at his now-empty seat.

"Shall we?" she said to Shelly. "Or would you prefer we get a table?"

"I'm good with the bar," said Shelly, taking the empty seat next to Jimbo's former stool.

"Can I get you ladies something to drink?" asked the bartender.

Shelly ordered a Cosmo and Guin ordered a margarita, no salt.

"And could we get a couple of menus?" Guin asked him.

The bartender nodded and handed them two menus.

"So how's Lizzy doing?" Guin asked. "Everything okay with her?"

Lizzy was Shelly's daughter, who worked at Disney World.

"Oh yeah. She loves it there."

They made small talk for several minutes, with Guin asking Shelly about her jewelry business and Steve.

"What about you?" said Shelly. "Anything new? How's the house coming along?"

Guin was spared having to answer right away by the bartender delivering their drinks.

"Thanks," said Guin.

They clinked glasses and Guin took a sip of her margarita. Damn, that tasted good.

"You two ready to order?" he asked them a minute later.

"Give us another minute," said Shelly.

They scanned their menus, then signaled to the bartender.

"So, you were about to tell me the latest about your house," said Shelly, after they had ordered.

"Well," Guin began. She took another sip of her margarita. "I don't have to worry about Frank anymore."

"Did he finish?" asked Shelly.

"Not exactly. He's dead."

"Dead?"

"Dead," said Guin.

"What happened? You didn't finally let him have it, did you?"

"No," said Guin. "It was a drug overdose."

"A drug overdose?" said Shelly. "Did you know he had a problem?"

"No," said Guin.

"So what was it?"

"Painkillers."

Shelly whistled, which attracted several looks. Then she lowered her voice.

"So he was an opioid addict?"

"Maybe," said Guin. "Though something about the whole thing doesn't feel right. I mean, the guy was moody, but he seemed relatively normal, at least for a contractor."

"Lots of opioid addicts seem normal," said Shelly. "Though I've heard that moodiness is a sign of opioid addiction."

"If being moody was a sign of opioid addiction, then nearly everyone I know is an opioid addict."

"Good point," said Shelly.

They sipped their drinks, then Shelly spoke again.

"You speak with Detective O'Loughlin?"

"Yeah."

"And?"

"On the plus side, he hasn't arrested me."

"Why would he do that?"

"Well, Funt was found in my house, and the whole thing is a bit odd."

"You think he was murdered, that someone just made it look like he had OD'd?" said Shelly, wide-eyed.

Before Guin could reply, the bartender came over with their food.

"Can I get you ladies anything else?" he asked them.

"I'm good," said Guin.

"Me, too," said Shelly.

They looked down at their food and began to eat, though Guin was no longer hungry.

"So what's going to happen with your house?" asked Shelly, when they were halfway through their meal.

"I don't know," said Guin. "I guess I need to find a new contractor. The problem is, I have to be out of the condo by the middle of November, and even if I found someone tomorrow, I doubt the house will be habitable by then."

"You know you can always crash at our place," said Shelly.

"I know," said Guin. "But with Justin home…"

"There's always the guest room. Come on, Guin, you're like family."

"Thanks, but…"

"Just know that you have a place to stay if you need one."

Guin smiled at her friend.

They ate some more, then asked for a couple of to-go boxes.

"Would you ladies like some coffee or dessert?" asked the bartender.

"No, thanks," said Guin.

"I'm good," said Shelly. "Just the check."

They split the bill, leaving money on the bar, and got up.

"I need to go to the bathroom," said Guin.

"You want me to wait?" said Shelly.

"No, I'm good. You go."

"Okay," said Shelly. She gave Guin a quick kiss on the cheek. "So, maybe shelling later this week?"

"I'd like that," said Guin. "Text me. Or else I'll text you."

"Sounds good," said Shelly.

She waved goodbye and made her way out of the restaurant while Guin headed to the bathroom. Guin emerged a few minutes later and was heading to the door when she saw Detective O'Loughlin enter with a woman on his arm. She froze.

"Detective," she said, plastering a smile on her face.

She glanced at the woman, who had unnaturally dark brown hair and was wearing a sour expression. She looked to be around the same age as the detective. So definitely not his mother. Did he have a sister? Guin didn't recall him mentioning one.

"Ms. Jones," said the detective, a bit stiffly.

She waited for the detective to introduce her to the woman, but he didn't.

"Well, um, nice seeing you, detective," said Guin, after several awkward seconds had elapsed. "Enjoy your dinner."

She then quickly made her way to the exit. When she got outside, she stopped and put a hand to her chest. Her heart was racing, and she felt sick. Who was that woman the detective was with? Guin turned and looked back at the restaurant. She thought for a second about going in and confronting him, but that was the margarita talking. Instead, she made her way to her car and got in.

"Don't let your imagination run wild," she admonished herself. "It could have been a cousin or a colleague."

But she didn't really believe that.

She took a few deep breaths, slowly releasing them.

"Go home and get a good night's sleep," she said, aloud. Then she turned the key in the ignition and put the Mini into gear.

CHAPTER 8

Guin slept badly that night. She dreamed (though really it was a nightmare) that she was at her new house. She had gone into her bedroom to get ready for bed and had found the detective in her bed with another woman. Horrified, she had run out of the room, down the hall to the guest bathroom, the sound of laughter following her. She had thought to splash some cold water on her face. But when she opened the door to the bathroom, there was the ghost of Frank Funt, Jr., pointing at her. She screamed and instantly woke up.

Guin could feel her heart racing, and her chest felt clammy. For a second she thought she was having a heart attack, but she realized it was probably just a panic attack. She forced herself to take several deep breaths, slowly breathing in, then slowly breathing out, and her heart rate began to slow.

She looked at her clock. It was five a.m. She thought about trying to go back to sleep, but she knew it would be pointless. Instead, she went to the bathroom and splashed some cold water on her face (thankfully, there were no ghosts), then made her way to the kitchen.

She gave Fauna some food, then made herself some coffee, extra strong. It was dark outside, though many diehard shellers were no doubt already on the beach. Should

Guin join them? She stared off into the distance, sipping her coffee. When she was done, she rinsed out her mug, then headed back to her bedroom/office.

She started her computer and opened her email. Glen had been sending her suggestions of places they should check out on Boca Grande and had suggested they rent bicycles. Guin typed "Boca Grande" into her search engine and began to read.

Boca Grande was a small but affluent residential community located on Gasparilla Island, northwest of Sanibel. You could get there by boat (Captiva Cruises had a ship that left from Captiva daily) or drive (via Port Charlotte).

There was a world-renowned tarpon tournament held off the island each May, and Boca Grande was home to the Gasparilla Inn & Club, built in 1913 and listed in the National Register of Historic Places. There were also lighthouses and beaches, a state park, and shops and restaurants to explore. Guin wondered if a day would really be enough.

She bookmarked several pages and typed some notes, then she pulled up her article on things to do on Sanibel in the fall, which she needed to edit. She hated to cut anything, but she knew the piece was too long for the print edition. Maybe Ginny would consider running two versions, a longer version for the online edition and a shorter one for print.

She sent Ginny an email, asking her what she thought of her idea, then saved a separate version for the print edition, which she would prune, hopeful that Ginny would agree with her two-version idea.

While she was waiting for a reply, she went back to the kitchen to eat a little something. There was still no reply from Ginny by the time she got back to her desk, though it was still early. Guin stared out the window and decided to go for a walk around the neighborhood. Walks always helped her think more clearly.

She made her way down to the bayou, admiring the elegant Mediterranean-style houses, the different palm trees, and the pretty red, pink, and yellow hibiscus bushes on her route. It was a beautiful morning, and there were several other walkers out. Guin smiled and said hello to them, stopping to pet a couple of dogs. As she stood looking out at the water, watching the boats make their way to Pine Island Sound, she thought for the hundredth (thousandth? millionth?) time how lucky she was to live on Sanibel.

When she arrived back at the condo, she had a much clearer sense of how she would edit her Sanibel article. She grabbed a glass of water, then headed to her desk. An hour later, she was done, and she turned her attention back to Boca Grande and Gasparilla Island.

Guin made a list of all the places she felt she and Glen should check out, then made a face. There were so many. How could they possibly see them all in a day? Actually, less than that, as the boat from Captiva didn't get to the island until around eleven, and they would need to be back at the dock at three-thirty. Maybe Glen was right about staying over. Though she doubted Ginny would pay for a hotel room, even if they could find rooms someplace at such short notice.

She did a quick search on Airbnb, then checked the Inn. But there was limited availability, and what was available was ridiculously expensive.

She grabbed her phone and sent Glen a text.

"Am rethinking our Boca Grande strategy and thinking we should stay overnight. But everything is super expensive. Thoughts?"

A few minutes later, she received a reply.

"As it happens," Glen wrote, "I have a buddy with a place in BG, and he said we could crash there."

"That was fast!" said Guin. "What's his place like? Is there room for me?"

A minute later, Glen sent her a photo. It was of a large yellow house, right on the beach. Guin whistled. She was about to write him back when her phone rang. It was Glen.

"The place has, like, four bedrooms. Maybe five. I think there's room."

"Who is this guy?" Guin asked.

"Thor? He's a former pro wrestler."

"Thor?" said Guin. "Is that his real name or his wrestling name?"

"It's his wrestling name, but no one calls him by his real name."

"Which is?" asked Guin.

"Mortimer," said Glen. "But don't tell him I told you, and don't ever call him that. He hates it."

Guin smiled.

"So how do you know Thor?"

"We went to college together. He had been planning on going to law school, but he decided to try his hand at professional wrestling instead."

"Wow," said Guin. "That's quite the career change. How did his parents feel about that?"

"They weren't thrilled, but when Thor started winning matches and making gobs of money, they changed their tune."

"So I take it he's good?"

"Oh yeah," said Glen. "I'm surprised you never heard of him. He was a big deal in the nineties and early two-thousands."

"I'm not exactly a big pro wrestling fan. Did Thor even know anything about wrestling? Though I've heard most matches are staged. You just have to put on a good show."

"Thor wrestled in high school and college. He knew what he was doing. And he was a good businessman. He socked away his earnings and bought himself a place on Boca Grande and invested in a number of startups."

"So he never went to law school?"

"No," said Glen. "But you never know. Maybe one day. He talks about going back sometimes. Says it would probably cost him less to go than what he pays his attorneys."

Glen chuckled.

"Will I get to meet this Thor?" said Guin. "He sounds fascinating."

"He'll be away over the weekend, but you may get a brief glimpse of him on Friday, before he heads out. Speaking of Friday, why don't I pick you up at your place?"

"You sure?"

"No point parking and paying for two cars. Besides, didn't you say you're on the way?"

True, thought Guin.

"Okay, fine," she said.

She gave Glen her address, and he said he'd pick her up at nine-fifteen.

"And I'll make us a dinner reservation for Friday night since we're staying over," he added.

Guin was about to say that wasn't necessary when Glen interrupted her.

"Hey, I've got another call coming in. See you Friday."

He ended the call and Guin stared at her phone.

"Guess I'm staying overnight in Boca Grande," she said. "I better let the detective know."

She debated whether to call him or just send him a text. The latter option won.

She stared at her phone for several seconds, wondering if the detective would object. But her phone remained silent. She then placed it in her desk drawer and turned back to her computer. But she was unable to concentrate.

Thinking about the detective made her think about Frank Funt, Jr. She looked at the clock on her monitor and got up.

"Change of plans," she announced to Fauna, who was dozing on the bed. "I'm heading to the Sanibel building department."

Guin climbed the stairs that led to the Sanibel building department and opened the door. There were two desks, one on each side of the room. Guin went over to the one of the left, which had a sign that said Building Department.

"May I help you?" asked the woman seated behind the desk.

"I hope so," said Guin. "I'm trying to find out if anyone has ever filed a complaint against Funt and the Son Construction or Frank Funt, Senior or Junior."

"Hold on," said the woman. "Let me go ask Heidi."

She got up and went to the back room. A few minutes later, she returned.

"Heidi should be with you in just a few minutes."

"Thank you," said Guin.

There was someone in line behind her, so Guin stepped to the side. A few minutes later a pleasant-looking woman around Guin's height, with short hair and glasses, appeared.

"You the one asking about Funt and the Son Construction?"

"That's me," said Guin, smiling at the woman.

"Here you go," said Heidi, handing her a folder. "You can look through it over there."

She pointed to a nearby table with a couple of chairs.

"Thanks," said Guin.

"Just let me know when you're done. Copies cost a buck apiece."

Guin took the folder over to the table and sat down. She took a deep breath, slowly releasing it, then opened the folder. Inside were two contractor complaint forms. One was submitted by a Mr. and Mrs. Miller, Sanibel homeowners, the other was submitted by a Larry Leakey, a local plumber who had done work for Funt & the Son. Guin smiled at the name.

Guin took out her notebook and jotted down their names and contact information. Then she began to read.

When she had finished, she sat back in the chair and shook her head. Why hadn't she checked with the building department *before* she had hired Funt? Well, to be fair to herself, she hadn't known that you could check to see if someone had filed a complaint against a contractor. But as a journalist and homeowner, she should have.

She sighed and looked back down at the folder.

Could one of these people have killed Funt? Both complainants had reason to be angry with him. The situation described by the homeowners, who lived not far from her condo, was nearly identical to her own. Funt had gutted their house, then disappeared with their money. Then they had hired an attorney and got Funt to return, but he did such a bad job, they fired him—and had to pay someone else to finish the job. As for the plumber, he complained that Funt owed him money for two jobs.

Guin picked up the folder and took it to the front desk.

"Thank you," she said, handing it to the woman seated there. She paused. "So, I know you guys aren't supposed to recommend contractors, but I'm in a real bind." She paused again. "I bought this house, which I was having remodeled. You guys issued a permit," Guin quickly added. "But my contractor screwed me over, and now the place is a mess, and I desperately need to find someone to finish up, or else I'm going to be homeless."

Guin knew she was rambling, but she couldn't stop herself. She could also feel tears forming.

"Sorry, I…"

The woman behind the desk, who had the face of one of those kindly grandmother types you see in commercials, glanced around, then leaned over towards Guin.

"Call Clint Mayberry," she said. "Tell him Irma referred you."

"Clint Mayberry?" said Guin. "Is he a contractor?"

"Used to be. Now he's more of a handyman. But there's nothing Clint can't fix or do."

"Do you have his number?"

"Hold on a sec," said Irma.

She bent down and retrieved a large handbag. She rummaged around and pulled out her wallet.

"Here," she said, handing Guin a dog-eared card that looked like it had been shoved in her wallet years ago.

"Clint Mayberry," read Guin. "No job too big or too small. So does he live here on the island?"

"He does," said Irma. "Though he has family up north he goes visit. But if he's around, I'm sure he'll help you out."

"Thanks," said Guin.

She pocketed the card and left, feeling slightly better.

CHAPTER 9

The rest of the day had been uneventful. Guin had sent emails to the Millers and Leakey the plumber, and she had left a voicemail for Clint Mayberry. She had also sent a condolence note to Frank's girlfriend, Phoebe.

The next morning, she got up a little before six-thirty and decided to go for a walk on the beach. When she got back, she checked her messages. But there was no reply from the Millers or Mr. Leakey or Clint Mayberry. She was tempted to reach out to them again but decided to hold off.

There was also no word from the detective. She had let him know of her plans to be on Gasparilla that Friday and Saturday, but he hadn't responded. She had also asked him when she could get back into her house. Again, no reply.

Finally, it was Friday. Guin woke up feeling excited. She had never been to Boca Grande and was looking forward to it—and to meeting the infamous Thor, who she had looked up online.

It was a beautiful morning, perfect for a cruise through Pine Island Sound. Guin got dressed, then brewed coffee and ate a protein bar. There would be no time for a walk, but she'd do plenty of walking later.

She checked her phone, but there was still nothing from the detective. Guin thought briefly about sending him another text, then shook her head. She had done her duty.

If he had a problem with her leaving the island, it was his responsibility to inform her.

She packed her overnight bag, throwing in a dress last minute, in case they were going someplace fancy for dinner. (Glen hadn't revealed where they would be dining, saying it was a surprise.) Though Boca Grande didn't seem like a fancy dress kind of place. Still, you never knew. And she made sure to pack her notebook, a couple of pens, and her microcassette recorder along with some tapes, in case she wanted to interview anyone.

She went through her bag one last time, making sure she had everything. Though it wasn't like she was going camping in the woods. There were plenty of stores in Boca Grande in case she had forgotten something. And it was only one night.

She carried her bag into the hallway and left it by the front door, then went to give Fauna some food and water. The cat had followed her into the kitchen and was rubbing herself against Guin's legs as Guin poured food into her bowl. Guin watched as Fauna inhaled her food, telling her to slow down.

As she stood there, she felt her phone vibrating in her back pocket. It was Glen, letting her know he was downstairs.

"Gotta go!" she told Fauna. "Try not to throw up while I'm gone!"

She stood looking at the cat for a few more seconds, then headed to the door.

"Nice wheels," said Guin, admiring Glen's car, a silver BMW convertible. "Apparently freelance photographers make more than I thought."

"It's a holdover from my Wall Street days," Glen replied,

a tad defensively. "One of the few things the ex let me keep."

He looked fondly at the car, patting the hood.

Guin smiled. Men and their cars. Then again, her purple Mini was like a member of the family.

They got in and drove west to Captiva, parking at the marina.

"I'll go get the tickets," Glen said.

A couple of minutes later, he returned from the ship's store, tickets in hand.

"This way," he said, gesturing towards the pier.

Guin followed him down to the boat, and they found two seats near the front.

"Clearly, you've done this before," said Guin.

"Oh yeah," said Glen. "Captiva Cruises and I go way back. I even took some publicity photos for them."

Guin was about to say something when she was interrupted by a voice over the loudspeaker.

"Everyone, please take your seats!" announced the first mate.

He went over safety protocol, then they were off.

The boat stopped at Cayo Costa State Park first, dropping off over a dozen beachgoers, then headed to Boca Grande. Along the way, the first mate reeled off information about the area, including its history and wildlife.

Guin took notes as Glen stood on the side of the boat and took photos. A short time later, they arrived at the Boca Grande Marina. Glen took Guin's bag and escorted her off the boat.

"Did you rent us bicycles?" Guin asked, looking around.

"Actually…" said Glen.

"Glen!"

Guin turned to see a giant of a man, with long, flowing blond hair, coming toward them. No doubt the famous Thor. He looked a bit older and not as buff as in the photos she had seen of him online, but he was still a mountain of a man, and his nickname fit.

The two men greeted each other warmly.

"Thor, may I present Ms. Guinivere Jones."

"Guin, this is my good friend, Thor Eames."

"A pleasure," said Guin.

"The pleasure's all mine," said Thor, grinning down at her.

Guin felt very small.

"I thought I'd give you a proper welcome and a lift back to my place," said Thor, leading them to the parking lot. "You can drop your things, then take off from there. I have a couple of bikes you can use."

"Thank you," said Guin.

Thor led them to a Porsche SUV and opened the rear passenger-side door for Guin.

"Thank you," she said again.

"Your first time to Boca Grande?" Thor asked Guin as they made their way out of the marina.

"It is," said Guin.

"You're going to love it. I'd give you the guided tour myself, but I'm headed off-island. Need to attend to some business on the mainland. But Glen here is an excellent tour guide. And I made you a reservation at the Gasparilla Inn for dinner."

"Thank you," Guin said for the third time.

A few minutes later, Thor turned into a driveway that was nearly hidden by some of the tallest hedges Guin had ever seen.

"Here we are!" he said, as he stopped the car in front of a yellow house that resembled a Mediterranean villa, at least to Guin's mind. "Welcome to Valhalla!"

Guin got out and looked around. The grounds were gorgeous. It was like stepping into a well-manicured jungle, with hibiscus and other tropical plants everywhere. And the house…

"Come, let's go inside," said Thor. "I'll give you the nickel tour before I go."

Guin glanced over at Glen, who just smiled and indicated for Guin to follow Thor.

Guin tried not to stare or let her mouth hang open as Thor showed them around. But the house was like one of those places you saw in an upscale shelter magazine, and Guin was in awe. And the view! You could see the water out of nearly every window, or else the lush garden.

"And this is your bedroom," said Thor, opening a door.

Guin took a step inside and stopped. It was beautiful. There was a large wooden canopy bed and a matching dresser—and a big bay window complete with a cushioned window seat, perfect for admiring the view.

"I think she likes it," Glen said to Thor.

"Thank you," Guin said, turning to their host.

Apparently, *thank you* were the only two words she was capable of uttering.

"And Glen, you can have the bedroom across the hall."

"If you want to switch," said Guin, glancing into Glen's room, which had a view of the garden, "just let me know."

"I'm good," said Glen. "It's where I usually stay when I visit. I pretend I'm camping in the jungle."

He and Thor exchanged a smile.

"A jungle with a fully stocked bar," said Thor.

Glen laughed.

"Saves me from having to bring my flask."

Guin smiled at the two men.

"Come," said Thor, turning to her. "I need to get going, but I want to finish the tour."

He led them through the rest of the house, including his bedroom on the second floor. It was massive, taking up the whole second level. The bathroom alone was the size of the apartment Guin had rented in New York when she graduated college.

"You can use the Jacuzzi later if you want to," said Thor, winking at them.

Guin blushed.

They headed back downstairs to the main living area.

"Well, kids, I must head out. Help yourselves to whatever's here. Just try not to trash the place."

"Will do," said Glen. "And thanks for letting us crash."

Thor waved him off.

"Just promise me you and Ms. Jones will come back when I'm in residence."

Glen cast a glance at Guin, who was nodding.

"I think we might be able to arrange that."

"Oh, and feel free to use the Fiat, if you'd rather not bike," said Thor. "Just leave me with some gas." He turned to Guin. "No gas stations on the island, just a pump at the marina."

They then said their goodbyes and Thor left.

Guin stared out at the water.

"I could stand here all day."

"I know the feeling," said Glen. "But we have work to do."

"We do," said Guin. "I made a list of all the places we should visit. I was thinking we could bike down to the lighthouse and then work our way around the island."

"Sounds like a plan," said Glen. "Though, you sure you want to bike it?"

Guin thought about it.

"Well, we should check out the bike trail, but as it's already past noon…"

Guin's stomach let out a loud rumble.

"Sounds like someone could use some lunch," said Glen, smiling at her.

Guin's stomach let out another gurgle.

"Let's take the car and go to the Pink Elephant," Glen suggested. "Then we can walk around town afterward."

"And hit the bike trail tomorrow morning," said Guin.

Glen nodded and offered Guin his arm.

"Shall we?" he said.

"We shall," Guin replied.

To call it "work" just seemed wrong, thought Guin. She was having too good a time. Lunch at the Pink Elephant had been delicious. And they had gotten ice cream afterward.

She had been making notes and taking photos on her phone, but it still felt like she was on holiday. And being with Glen felt easy, like they had known each other forever.

Around five o'clock they headed back to the house.

"What time is our dinner reservation?" asked Guin.

"Seven o'clock," Glen replied. "Plenty of time for a shower and planning tomorrow's activities."

"Shall we meet in the living room at six-thirty?"

"Sounds like a plan," said Glen. "I may duck out to take some more photos, but I'll make sure I'm back by six-thirty. And the restaurant is just a few minutes away."

"Okay," said Guin. "See you in a bit."

Guin stood in the shower, her eyes closed, luxuriating in the pressure and steam. Her shower at the condo was good, but this… this was heaven.

She begrudgingly emerged ten minutes later, feeling relaxed and sleepy. She put on the terry cloth bathrobe she had found hanging on the back of the bathroom door and sat on the window seat.

It was still light out, though the sky had that magical pastel glow it got just before the sun dipped below the horizon.

Guin got out her notebook and pen and reviewed what she had written. Then she took out her laptop and started typing. They would need to cover a lot of ground tomorrow, but she was up for it. Especially with Glen as her guide.

A little after six, she put on her dress and applied some makeup. Then she headed to the living room.

"Drink?" said Glen. He was standing behind the bar.

"What do you recommend, bartender?"

"Hmm…" he said, scrutinizing her. "I'm thinking blood orange margarita."

Guin gave him a funny look. Margaritas were her go-to drink, but she didn't remember telling him that.

"What?" said Glen.

"How did you know I liked margaritas?"

"I just remember you ordering one that time we had drinks."

"Ah," said Guin.

She watched as Glen made the margarita.

"Here you go," he said, handing it to her. "One blood orange margarita, no salt."

"Mmm…" said Guin, after taking a sip. "That's good."

"My friends used to call me the psychic bartender."

"Oh?" said Guin, taking another sip of her margarita. "How come?"

"I think it was because I could sense what drink a person would enjoy."

"A very useful skill," said Guin, continuing to sip her margarita.

"Indeed," said Glen. "Got me a lot of invitations to parties. And into some trouble."

He smiled at her and held up his glass.

"To the day-tripper series and getting to know each other better."

"To the day-tripper series," said Guin.

They clinked glasses.

"We should get going," said Glen a few minutes later. "You ready?"

"Let me just grab my bag," Guin replied.

Dinner at the Gasparilla Inn had been lovely. The food was good and the service even better. She and Glen had made small talk, then wound up swapping divorce stories over a bottle of wine.

Glen's story of why his marriage broke up was reminiscent of what had happened with her and Art, except the other way around. Well, sort of. Like Art, Glen had been a workaholic, often leaving early for work and coming home late and barely having time for his wife. However, in Glen's case, it was his wife who had cheated on him, with her tennis instructor. Then she had filed for divorce, claiming abandonment, and had received a generous divorce settlement. Amazingly, to Guin at least, Glen didn't seem bitter, or too bitter. He claimed he had known the marriage was over before the affair, and if he had had the guts, he would have left her before she left him.

Guin was impressed and wished she had had the guts to leave Art before he began boffing their hairdresser.

She had told Glen about it, and he had been sympathetic. And they had laughed about how hard it was to find a good hairstylist.

"So what happened with you and the woman you were dating?" she asked him.

Glen sighed.

"We just wanted different things."

"Different how?" asked Guin.

"She wanted to get married…"

"And you didn't," said Guin, finishing the sentence.

Glen nodded.

"I'm not sure I want to get married again, at least not right now."

Guin could relate.

"What about you? I know you broke up with that professor. Can't say I blame you. He sounded like bad news."

"You can't believe everything you read in the paper," said Guin, realizing the irony. "He was actually a good guy. I met one of the women who had accused him. She confessed that she had made up the story afterward, by the way. But the damage had been done."

"You ever regret breaking up with him?" asked Glen.

"No," said Guin. "Besides, he's in Australia."

"Australia?"

"Long story. Anyway, I'm fine being single."

"Me, too," said Glen, polishing off the last of his wine.

Their server came over and asked them if they wanted dessert or coffee.

"We have the best key lime pie on the island," she informed them.

"Guin?"

"Do you have decaf cappuccino?" Guin asked the young woman.

"We do," she replied. "And you, sir?"

"I'll have a double espresso, and a slice of your key lime pie, two forks."

"Coming right up!" said the server.

She returned with their coffee and the pie a few minutes later.

"You have to try this," said Glen, breaking off a piece of the pie with his fork and holding it up to Guin's mouth.

"If you insist," said Guin.

She opened her mouth and Glen popped the piece of pie into it.

"Oh my God," she said, savoring the tart-sweet flavor and luscious texture.

She picked up the extra fork and took another bite.

"You mind?"

Glen smiled.

"Be my guest. That's why I asked for two forks. Their key lime is pretty irresistible."

That wasn't the only thing Guin was finding hard to resist. But she didn't say anything.

CHAPTER 10

Guin stared out the window as Glen drove them back to the house, although it was dark, and she couldn't really see anything. She had a lot on her mind.

"You want a nightcap?" he asked her after they had gone inside.

"Thanks, but I think I should turn in," she said, suddenly feeling awkward around Glen.

"Okay, I'll see you in the morning then. What time do you want to head out?"

"Seven-thirty? Eight? I want to bike down to the museum first thing and check out the lighthouse."

"Let's say eight," said Glen. "I need my beauty rest."

Guin smiled.

"Eight it is." She paused. "Say, did Thor leave us any food?"

"Don't tell me you're hungry."

Guin smiled.

"I couldn't eat another bite. Just wondering if there was stuff for breakfast."

"Ah," said Glen. "Well, knowing Thor, the kitchen is well stocked. Shall we go take a look?"

He led her into the kitchen, which, like the rest of the house, looked like something you'd see on one of those HGTV shows, with sleek stainless steel appliances and granite countertops.

Glen opened the refrigerator. It was filled with Champagne, wine, beer, hard seltzer, sparkling water, and orange juice; every condiment imaginable; and containers of chopped vegetables and fruit.

"Looks like he was preparing for a cocktail party," said Guin. "What's in the pantry?"

Glen opened the doors to the pantry, and they glanced inside. There were boxes of pasta, crackers, canned goods, various flavors of protein powder, and some cereal.

"Hmm…" said Guin.

She went back over to the fridge and opened it.

"Aha!" she said, moving some things around.

"Find something?" asked Glen.

"Eggs and some yogurt." She opened the freezer. "And bread."

"We could always go out for breakfast."

"I'm fine eating here. That is if that's okay with you."

"Fine by me," said Glen.

Guin yawned.

"I'm going to head off to bed."

"Sweet dreams."

"You're not coming?" said Guin.

"Is that an invitation?"

Guin blushed.

"I just meant… Well, you know what I meant," she said.

"I do," said Glen, smiling. "Good night, Guin. I'll see you in the morning."

Guin stood there a few more seconds, then turned and headed down the hall.

Guin had no idea what time it was when she woke up. There was sunlight streaming into her room, and she panicked, thinking she had overslept. She had turned off her phone before going to sleep, not bothering to set an alarm as she never slept past seven. Though, surely, Glen would have pounded on her door if she had overslept. Then again, Glen had had more to drink than she had and had stayed up later.

She grabbed her phone and waited as it booted.

She sighed with relief when the display showed it to be only seven-thirty. Still, she needed to get dressed and eat something quickly if they were to head out at eight.

She went into the bathroom, then got dressed and checked her messages. Nothing from the detective. She didn't know if that was good or bad.

She made her way to the kitchen and saw a nearly full pot of coffee on the counter, though no sign of Glen. She took the mug Glen had no doubt left out for her and filled it. She took a sip, closing her eyes as the warm liquid made its way down her throat. She took another sip, then took her mug into the living room, staring out at the water in the distance.

"Hey there."

Some coffee went splashing over the side of the mug as Guin nearly jumped, startled to see Glen.

"Sorry," he said.

His camera was slung over his shoulder and his pants were rolled up.

"I went out for a walk on the beach. Sunrise is my favorite time of day. That is, when I'm not asleep."

He gave her a big smile.

"Mine, too," said Guin. "Thanks for the coffee."

"No problem. Hope it's not too strong."

"It's perfect," she said. "You eat?"

"I'm not much of a breakfast person."

"Well, I'm going to make something. Care to join me?"

He followed her into the kitchen.

Guin took out eggs and bread and a stick of butter.

"I can make enough for two."

"Fine, go ahead."

"You okay if I scramble the eggs?"

"Anyway is fine," he replied.

A short time later, they were seated at the counter, eating their scrambled eggs and toast.

"Not bad," said Glen, who had finished every last bite, despite not being a breakfast person.

"Thank you," said Guin. "I see you hated your food."

She smiled at him, and he smiled back.

Guin went to wash their plates, but Glen took them from her.

"Allow me," he said.

Guin watched as Glen cleaned the dishes and had a flashback to when she and Art used to do the dishes together in happier times.

"Penny for your thoughts?"

"Sorry, just spacing out," said Guin. She looked at the clock on the wall. "We should get out of here."

They biked to the Boca Grande Lighthouse Museum, then to the Gasparilla Island Lighthouse, then back to Thor's. Guin was exhausted yet happy. She couldn't remember the last time she had spent a morning biking. And the weather was picture-perfect, with the coastal breezes cooling the air.

She was also hungry.

Instead of biking into town, they decided to take Thor's red Fiat 500, which seemed a ridiculous vehicle for such a big man. They had lunch at the Eagle Grille, then continued their exploration of the island, Guin taking notes and snapping photos with her phone while Glen captured images with his camera.

"We should get back to the house and get our stuff, so we don't miss the boat," said Glen, a little after two-thirty.

"But how are we going to get back to the marina without Thor here to drive us?" asked Guin. "Is there some kind of car service?"

"Thor said we could leave the Fiat there. He'll have someone pick it up."

They returned to the house and gathered their things.

"What about the house?" said Guin. "Shouldn't we lock up?

"I texted Thor that we were leaving and taking the Fiat. He's going to have his guy pick up the car at the marina and then lock up."

"Nice to have a guy," said Guin.

She looked back at the house.

"Goodbye, house," she said wistfully. "It's been nice."

"You'll be back," said Glen, smiling at her. "Now get in. We should just be able to make it."

Guin was quiet on the boat ride back to Captiva. She had put Frank Funt, Jr., and the detective out of her brain (mostly) the last 24 hours, but now, as they made their way back to Sanibel, they were all she could think about. Well, them and her unfinished house.

"You okay?" said Glen. "You're awfully quiet."

"I was just thinking," said Guin. "And enjoying the view."

"Ah," said Glen, looking out at the water.

They sat there, looking out onto Pine Island Sound, neither saying anything, for the rest of the journey.

"I found my contractor in my bathtub," Guin blurted out as they approached Captiva.

Glen turned to look at her.

"Excuse me?"

"He was dead. The medical examiner said it was a drug

overdose. But I have a feeling he was murdered."

Glen didn't know how to respond.

"And now I'm a suspect, and I have this unfinished house with no one to finish it, and I have to move out of my condo by mid-November."

Glen rubbed the back of his head.

"I think I know someone who can help you, at least with the house."

"You do? Who?"

"Me."

"You?" said Guin, staring at him. "What do you know about remodeling?"

"My dad loved to build and fix stuff. Taught me everything he knew. When I was in college and grad school and needed some money, I'd pick up work as a carpenter or painter or handyman. I was pretty good, too, if I do say so myself. I can probably dig up some references if you need me to."

Guin smiled.

"That won't be necessary." She paused and shook her head. "Photographer, bartender, and handyman, too. Is there anything you can't do?"

"I don't like to cook, though I make a mean PB and J."

Guin laughed.

"But if you need someone to paint your apartment…"

"You're hired!" said Guin. "Though maybe you should see the place first. It needs more than a little paint."

"You can show it to me later if you like."

"What about work? Don't you need to develop some photos?"

"I've got plenty of time. The perk of working for oneself. I get to choose my own hours. Well, most of the time."

"Okay," said Guin. "But I don't want to take you away from any gigs. And I insist on paying you."

"Which is good as I insist on being paid," said Glen, smiling at her.

Guin smiled back at him.

"It's a deal," she said, extending a hand.

Glen shook it.

"You want to show me the house after we get off the boat?"

"Sure," said Guin.

She just hoped there wouldn't be any policemen there— or more dead bodies.

"So this is where you found the contractor?" said Glen, staring into the now-empty bathtub.

Guin nodded her head.

"And the medical examiner said it was a drug overdose?"

"That's what I heard."

"Hmm…" said Glen.

Guin wondered what Glen was thinking. She had shown him around the place, pointing out what still needed to be done. It seemed like a lot to her, but Glen said it wasn't so bad.

"You okay giving me a key? It'll go a lot quicker if I can just come and go."

Guin hesitated.

"Or you can let me in if you don't trust me," he said.

"It's not that," said Guin. "I'm fine giving you a key. It's just…I feel guilty. It's a lot of work. And I hate to think of you spending all your free time here."

"I can handle it. And I wasn't planning on doing everything myself."

"You weren't?" said Guin.

"I've still got friends here who are in the business. I'm sure I can get them to help out. That is if that's okay with you."

"Hey, the more, the merrier," said Guin. "Especially if it

gets me in here by mid-November."

"What happens mid-November?"

"The condo was sold. That's when the closing is."

"Ah," said Glen. "Well, it'll be tight. And we may not have everything done, but you should be able to move in."

"Great," said Guin. "And thank you."

"Don't thank me yet. So when can I pick up the key?"

"Frank, he's the contractor, or was, had the extra one." Guin frowned. "I'll make you a duplicate of mine. You want to meet me back here tomorrow?"

"Sure," said Glen. "What time?"

"You tell me."

"Does three work?"

"Three it is," said Guin.

She turned to go, then realized Glen had driven her.

"Would you mind giving me a lift back to the condo?"

Glen smiled.

"Hop in."

They listened to a jazz station on the way back to Guin's, neither talking. When they got to Guin's place, she let herself out and said goodbye.

She had just walked in the door when her phone started buzzing. She pulled it out and saw the number for the Sanibel police department. She thought about not answering but knew that would be foolish.

"Hello?" she said.

"I need you to come here," said the detective.

"When?" asked Guin.

"Now."

"I just walked in the door. Can you give me half an hour?"

"Half an hour," said the detective. "Or else I'm sending a car to get you."

Guin was about to say something snarky, but the detective had already ended the call.

CHAPTER 11

Guin had just walked into the detective's office when she was attacked.

"She's the guilty one, detective! Arrest her!" shrieked Phoebe, pointing at Guin.

Guin hastily took a step back.

"Go on, detective, ask her!" Phoebe shouted. "Ask her if she was in love with Frank and then killed him."

"Excuse me?" said Guin, staring at the madwoman in front of her.

"Oh sure, deny it," said Phoebe. "But I know!"

"Know what?" said Guin, truly baffled. "I assure you, detective, there was *nothing* going on between me and Frank Funt." (Except a mutual animosity, Guin thought.)

Phoebe made a face.

"Please. I saw the way you two looked at each other," she said to Guin.

Guin was trying not to stare, but the woman was insane.

"Of course, you wouldn't be the first woman attracted to Frank," Phoebe continued. "All you pampered princesses are the same. You see a good-looking guy who knows his way around a toolbox, and you go for it."

Guin had to cover her mouth to keep from laughing out loud. Was this woman serious? She looked over at the detective. Was this the reason he had wanted to see her, so that Phoebe Costanza could hurl baseless accusations at her?

Phoebe continued to fume.

"Phoebe," Guin finally said. "I promise you, there was absolutely nothing going on between me and Frank."

Phoebe squinted at her.

"Then why was he always talking about you?"

"I don't know," said Guin. "Though he was working on my house."

She looked over at the detective, silently begging him to help her and stop this nonsense. But he continued to remain seated behind his desk, not saying a word.

"You killed him!" Phoebe shrieked. "Just admit it!"

"According to the medical examiner, he died of a drug overdose," said Guin, calmly.

Phoebe made another face.

"Frank didn't do drugs. The medical examiner must be wrong."

Guin turned again to the detective.

"Detective, I give you my word, there was absolutely nothing going on between me and Frank Funt, Jr.," she repeated. "And I had nothing to do with his death."

"Then what was he doing at your house Sunday night?" shrieked Phoebe. "You lured him over there, and then when he told you he didn't want you, you killed him!"

"No!" cried Guin, exasperated.

"Then explain why was his body found at your place!" demanded Phoebe.

"I can't," said Guin. "I have no idea what he was doing there."

She felt exhausted and badly wanted a drink.

"You telling me you didn't call him Sunday and invite him over to your place?" said Phoebe.

"That's exactly what I'm telling you," said Guin, looking directly at the other woman.

"Then who did?"

"I have no idea," said Guin. "But it wasn't me." Suddenly, what Phoebe had said registered. "You say Frank got a call Sunday evening?"

"Yeah, just as we were finishing dinner," said Phoebe. "He took it in the other room. Then he came back and said he had to go. Some problem with a house he was working on."

Guin looked over at the detective.

"It wasn't me," she told him. "You can check my phone. I didn't call Frank Sunday evening."

She held out her phone, but the detective didn't take it.

"Speaking of phones, have you checked Frank's?" Guin asked him.

"Not yet," he replied.

"Why not?" said Guin. "That might tell you who lured him to my house."

"Why bother? She's right here," said Phoebe, looking at Guin.

The detective ignored Phoebe, his eyes focused on Guin, while Guin tried hard not to roll her eyes.

"Just one problem," said the detective.

"Yes?"

"We've been unable to locate his phone."

"It wasn't on him?" said Guin.

"No," replied the detective.

"And you searched the house and his truck?"

The detective gave her a look, the one that said, "What do you think?"

"Where could it be?" she asked him. Then she turned to Phoebe. "Do you know where Frank's phone is?"

"Don't look at me," said Phoebe. "He had it with him when he left. I saw him talking on it as he went to his truck."

"Did he call you after he left?" Guin asked her.

"No," Phoebe replied.

"And you didn't worry when he didn't come home?"

"I was asleep," said Phoebe.

"What about the next morning?"

Phoebe looked uncomfortable.

"Answer the question," said the detective.

"Maybe I was a little worried," Phoebe said. "But I thought Frank had just left early. He often gets up before me."

She's lying, thought Guin. *But why? What isn't she saying?*

Guin was about to ask Phoebe another question, but she was interrupted by the detective.

"Would you excuse us a minute, Ms. Costanza? I'd like to speak with Ms. Jones for a minute in private. If you would just stay here, I'll be right back."

Phoebe glared at Guin.

"Whatever," she said.

"Thank you," said the detective. "Ms. Jones?"

He led her out of his office and down the hall to another room. As soon as the door closed, Guin whipped around.

"Is that why you asked me here, so that crazy woman could accuse me of seducing and then murdering her boyfriend?"

"No," the detective calmly replied. "We brought her in for some additional questioning and she insisted we bring you in, too."

"So now you're taking orders from suspects?"

The detective didn't answer.

"Look, as I said in your office, I didn't call Frank that Sunday. You can check my phone."

She pulled out her phone again and shoved it at the detective.

"That won't be necessary," he said.

Guin put it away.

"So any idea who did call him Sunday?"

"That's what we're trying to find out."

"Good luck."

"There are other ways of finding out who called him, even without his phone," said the detective, enigmatically.

"So, do you believe what Phoebe said, about the drugs?"

The detective gave her another look.

Guin sighed.

"Well, if you're not going to talk to me, I'll be going."

She made to leave, but the detective stopped her, placing a hand on her arm. Guin looked down.

"About the other night, at the Sandbar," began the detective.

"Yes?" said Guin.

He let his hand drop and rubbed his face.

"It's complicated."

"Well, why don't you uncomplicate it for me?"

"Have dinner with me."

"Excuse me?" said Guin. "Did you just invite me to have dinner with you, after not hearing a peep from you in nearly six months?"

The detective looked pained.

"I can explain."

"Then explain it to me here," said Guin, stubbornly.

"Just have dinner with me, Guin, please."

Guin paused at the sound of the detective saying her name.

"Say six o'clock at my place?"

Guin stared at him.

"Let me get this straight: You want me to have dinner with you at six o'clock at your place tonight?"

"Actually, tomorrow."

Guin shook her head. She couldn't believe what she was hearing.

"Won't your girlfriend object to you having me over? Or will she be there, too?"

"She has plans tomorrow."

"You're serious."

The detective nodded.

"Fine. I'll be at your place at six tomorrow."

"Thank you," said the detective.

He opened the door.

Guin looked from him to the open door, then left.

He followed her back down the hall, stopping outside his office.

"I'll see you tomorrow," he said.

CHAPTER 12

Guin checked her phone shortly after she got up Sunday. Still no word from either the Millers or the plumber. It was possible they were both away, but wouldn't they check their email? If she hadn't heard back from either of them by the next day, she would call or send follow-up emails.

She looked out of the window, but it was too dark to see. But it didn't seem like it was raining. She pulled up the forecast on her phone. Not too hot and no rain till later.

"May as well hit the beach," she announced to Fauna, who was curled up at the foot of the bed.

Guin headed to the bathroom, then ducked into her closet, emerging a few minutes later dressed in her beachcombing attire, her hair pulled back in a ponytail. She gave Fauna some food, then grabbed her fanny pack, keys, and her shelling bag and headed out.

Guin had thought about driving over to one of the beaches along West Gulf Drive, but Bowman's was closer, so she went there.

The first rays of sunlight were starting to light up the sky, and she stopped to admire the pink-hued clouds, which looked like cotton candy, as she walked across the bridge and down to the water. Fortunately, there weren't that many people on the beach, though that would change in another hour or two as the day-trippers descended on Sanibel and the beaches.

As she took a look around, trying to decide which way to go, she recognized a familiar figure wearing a Shell Ambassador t-shirt.

"Lenny!" she called.

The man turned and smiled.

"Guin! Long time, no see!"

Guin walked over to the man, whose skin was tanned and wrinkled from days spent in the Florida sun, and smiled up at him.

"Find anything good?"

"Eh," he replied. "Not so much."

"But it's a beautiful morning!"

"If you like it warm and humid," Lenny replied.

Guin grinned. Lenny, a former middle school science teacher from New York City, was a bit of a curmudgeon. But Guin didn't mind. She found it endearing. The two had met on the beach shortly after Guin had moved to Sanibel, and they had bonded over seashells and their love of (and despair over) the New York Mets.

"What've you been up to, kid?" Lenny asked her.

"Oh, the usual: work, mostly."

"Ginny got you slaving away? Wouldn't think there would be that much to write about this time of year."

"You'd be surprised," said Guin.

"How's the house coming along? You about ready to move in?"

"Sadly, no."

"That contractor still giving you problems?"

"You could say that. He's dead."

Lenny stared at her.

"Dead? What happened?"

"Drug overdose, at least according to the autopsy report. Passed out in my bathtub."

Lenny continued to stare.

"I think my hearing's going, kid. I could have sworn you said the guy was in your bathtub."

"Your hearing's fine, Len. That's what I said."

"He OD'd in your tub? Did you know he had a drug problem?"

"Not that I was aware of," said Guin. "But I have a feeling he didn't take the drugs willingly."

"You think someone fed him the stuff and left him to die in your tub?"

"Something like that."

"But why?" said Lenny.

"That's the million-dollar question."

"You okay?"

"Not really," said Guin. "I had no great love for Frank, but he was finally starting to get stuff done around the house."

"You'll find someone else."

"Actually, I think I have."

"Who'd you hire?"

"My colleague, Glen."

"Glen?" said Lenny.

"He's a freelance photographer. Works for the paper. He was with me at the Shell Show."

"Don't remember him," said Lenny. "And he thinks he can fix your house?"

Lenny looked dubious.

"He used to be a carpenter," said Guin. "Before he worked on Wall Street."

Lenny raised an eyebrow.

"A jack of all trades. Just be careful."

"I will. I'm meeting him over at the house this afternoon to give him a key."

"Is it safe to be over there?"

"We were there yesterday. The cops were gone, and the detective didn't say I couldn't go."

Lenny gave her a look.

"What?" said Guin.

"Just be careful. If the guy was murdered, his killer is still out there."

Guin knew that, but she hadn't really thought about it. Until now.

"I'll be fine, Len."

Though even as she said it, she felt less confident.

"So, do the cops have any idea who might have offed him?"

"If so, they haven't said anything to me. Though the detective brought me in for questioning."

"You?"

"Well, the body was found at my house."

Lenny shook his head.

"What's the world coming to?"

"Come, let's walk," said Guin.

They headed down the beach, neither saying anything for several minutes. When they reached Silver Key, they stopped.

"I know you," said Lenny, turning to face her. "And I know you'll want to investigate. But I'm begging you, let the police handle this one."

"I'm merely going to ask a few questions," Guin replied.

Lenny gave her another look.

"I'll be fine, Lenny. I've learned a lot about crime investigations over the last couple of years."

"Though clearly not enough," he replied.

"What's that supposed to mean?"

"It means, sometimes you should let the police take care of finding murderers. That's what we pay them for. You can write about it later."

"This isn't about some article, Len. It's about finding out why my contractor was killed in my house. Now, can we please change the subject? What's up with you? You been playing bridge? Get away at all?"

"No bridge. Annie's been away. [Annie was Lenny's bridge partner.] But I went up to New York over Labor Day to see some of my old buddies."

"That sounds nice," said Guin.

"It was. Though every time I go to New York, it's like a whole new place. Have you seen Times Square?" He shook his head. "I got accosted by a giant Elmo and some naked guy in a cowboy hat, strumming a guitar."

"The Naked Cowboy."

"The Naked Cowboy?" said Lenny.

"That's the name he goes by," Guin explained. "He's kind of a Times Square fixture."

Lenny shook his head.

"I think I preferred it when it was rundown."

Guin smiled.

"I hear you. But it's supposedly a lot safer now."

Lenny made a face.

"You call being accosted by a guy in his underwear safe?"

Guin laughed.

"Okay, forget about Times Square. Let's see if we missed any shells."

"I should get back," said Guin, as they approached the entrance to the beach. "I need to type up my day-tripper article."

"Day-tripper article?"

"Yeah, it's a new series the paper is doing, places to day-trip from Sanibel. First stop, Boca Grande."

"Never been," said Lenny.

"Really?" said Guin, surprised.

"Never thought it worth checking out."

"Well, you should go. You can take the boat from Captiva. Invite Annie."

"I'll think about it."

Guin stopped at the entrance to the beach.

"You coming?"

"Nah, I'm going to hang out here a bit longer, see if anyone needs help identifying any shells."

Guin smiled. Teaching kids (and their parents) about shells and the local ecology was Lenny's passion. He loved seeing their eyes light up when he showed them a live horse conch or a sea star.

"Well, see ya, Len," said Guin.

"Good luck with the house," Lenny called. "And be careful!"

CHAPTER 13

Guin had arrived at the house at three and had given Glen the duplicate key she had made. He had asked her if she was okay with him working late, and she had told him he could work whenever. Then she had left.

It was now five, and Guin was standing in her walk-in closet, wondering what to wear to her dinner with the detective. She held up her skintight dress, the one that left little to the imagination. Then she put it back. Next, she pulled out a t-shirt and a pair of capris. Too casual, she thought, and put them back.

She continued to take out different items of clothing, eyeing each one, then putting them back. Why was this so hard?

Finally, she settled on a pair of skinny jeans and a lowcut white blouse. She eyed herself in the full-length mirror, turning from side to side. Then she went into the bathroom to apply a little makeup.

She had pulled her hair up on top of her head and wondered if she should leave it up or wear it down. Down won out.

She hurried back into her bedroom to check the time. She was running late. Well, the detective could wait.

She grabbed her bag and her keys and slipped on a pair of high-heeled sandals. Then she dashed out the door, being careful not to trip and fall down the stairs.

Guin rang the doorbell and the detective let her in. He was wearing an apron, one of those funny ones that made you look like you had a muscled beach body, and Guin couldn't help smiling. It was so not him.

"It was a gift," he said, as if reading her mind.

She followed him into the kitchen and noticed a big pot on the stove. She sniffed.

"Smells good," she said. "You making tomato sauce?"

He nodded.

"With meatballs. My grandmother's special recipe."

Guin went over to the stove and looked into the pot, breathing in the tomato-y aroma and closing her eyes.

"I didn't know the Irish were famous for spaghetti and meatballs."

"She was Italian," said the detective. "Made the best meatballs in the neighborhood. Tomato sauce, too. She was a great cook. I used to love to sit in her kitchen and watch her."

Guin tried to picture the detective as a child, sitting in his grandmother's kitchen. It made her smile.

"Anything I can do?"

"You wanna open the wine?" he said, placing a handful of pasta into the now boiling water and then stirring the tomato sauce. "There's a bottle on the counter."

He jerked his head in the direction of the bottle.

"Corkscrew?"

"In the drawer underneath," said the detective.

Guin retrieved the corkscrew and opened the bottle.

"Wine glasses?"

"Over there," he said, pointing at a cabinet.

Guin took out two glasses and placed them on the counter.

"You want me to pour you a glass?"

"Just hand me the bottle," said the detective.

She handed him the bottle, and he poured some wine into the sauce. Then he handed her back the bottle.

"Dinner should be ready in a few," he informed her.

Guin watched as the detective placed a salad bowl and some grated parmesan cheese on the table. Then he went back into the kitchen and brought over two heaping bowls of spaghetti and meatballs.

"Have a seat," he commanded.

Guin sat and watched as the detective went back into the kitchen and brought out a loaf of bread he had been warming in the oven, along with the wine. Finally, he took a seat.

"Thank you for coming over," he said.

"Thank you for inviting me," Guin replied.

"Please, eat," said the detective.

Guin rolled her fork in the pasta and took a bite.

"Mmm…" she said. "It's really good."

The detective looked pleased.

She took another bite, then looked over at the detective.

"Aren't you going to eat?"

"In a minute."

He took a sip of his wine.

"I've been meaning to talk to you, about what happened."

"Oh?" said Guin, taking a sip of her wine.

"Yeah," said the detective.

Guin waited.

"So after our trip to Port St. Lucie," he began. "I received a message from an old friend. She said she was moving back to Fort Myers, and she wanted to get together."

"By any chance was this 'friend' the woman I saw you with at the Sandbar the other night?"

The detective nodded.

"And would this old friend be a girlfriend?"

"It's complicated," said the detective.

"So you said," said Guin. "But how complicated can it be? Either you're dating her or you're not."

"I've known Maggie for forever," said the detective. "She was married to my partner, Tommy. Molly and I would get together with Tommy and Mags regularly, before Molly and I split up. Anyway, they wound up moving down here after Tommy got injured in the line of duty and took early retirement."

He paused. Clearly, this was hard for him, but Guin didn't care.

"Tommy took retirement hard. He was used to being a cop and didn't know what to do with himself. He started drinking, pretty heavily, and screwing around. Maggie didn't know a lot of people here. She was pretty upset and didn't have anyone to turn to, except for me."

"So what, you comforted her?"

The detective nodded.

"I see," said Guin. "So what happened?"

"Tommy cleaned up his act, got sober. She went back to him. Then they moved to the East Coast, to get a fresh start."

"So why did she come back to Fort Myers? Did he have a relapse?

"No, he died. Heart attack."

"Oh," said Guin. She wouldn't wish that on anyone.

"Yeah, it wasn't a huge surprise, but it was still a shock," said the detective. "The funeral was right before we went to Spring Training."

"Did you go?" asked Guin.

The detective nodded.

"So Maggie sees you at the funeral, then decides to move back to Fort Myers, take up where you left off?"

The detective nodded again.

"Did you tell her about us?" asked Guin.

"No," said the detective, not looking at Guin. "She had just lost her husband, and I didn't want to upset her."

"I see," said Guin, balling up her napkin.

She glanced around.

"So is she living here with you?"

She didn't see signs of a woman living there, but you never knew.

"No," said the detective. "She got her own place."

"But you two are seeing each other."

The detective nodded.

"You going to marry her?" asked Guin, squeezing her balled-up napkin in her lap.

"God, no!" said the detective.

Guin relaxed her grip on her napkin.

"So why did you invite me over? You could have told me all of this at your office or over coffee—or better yet, last summer. Why go to all the trouble of cooking me dinner?"

"Because I care about you," the detective said, looking at her. "And I wanted to say I was sorry. If things were different…"

"If things were different what?" said Guin.

"Your food is getting cold," said the detective.

"I don't care about the food," Guin snapped. "I want to hear your answer. If things were different what? You and I would be together? If you really cared about me, you would have told Maggie you were seeing someone."

The detective looked down.

Guin put her napkin on the table and stood up.

"I'm going," she said.

"Stay and finish dinner," said the detective.

"I lost my appetite."

"Please, Guin."

Again, at the use of her name, she paused. But her mind was made up.

"I'm going," she said.

She went to look for her bag, the detective following her. He put a hand on her arm, and she froze.

A part of her wanted him to stop her, to tell her it had all been a mistake, that he was going to tell Maggie it was over. But she knew that was ridiculous.

"Just give me some more time," he said.

For a second, she softened. Then she stood up straighter and removed the detective's hand from her arm.

"Sorry, *Bill.* Time's up. Now, if you'll excuse me."

The detective stepped back and watched Guin leave.

Guin ran down the stairs and unlocked the Mini, climbing in. She put her hands on the steering wheel and squeezed it. Then she let out a scream.

She fished her phone out of her bag and saw that Glen had texted her, asking her to give him a call. She punched in his number.

"Hi," he said. "Thanks for giving me a call."

"What's up?" Guin asked. "Is everything okay?"

"Everything's fine," he replied. "I just got back from your place and wanted to go over a few things with you. You got a few minutes?"

"I have a better idea. You want to grab a drink or maybe a bite? I'm in Fort Myers."

"You are?" he said. "In that case, sure, if you're free."

"I'm very free," said Guin, gazing up at the detective's apartment. "Where should we meet?"

"There's a little Italian place by my house."

"I'd prefer not to have Italian, if that's all right with you," said Guin.

"How about Mexican? I know a place that makes killer margaritas."

"Sounds perfect," said Guin. "Give me the name and I'll meet you over there."

"I'll text it to you," said Glen.

She received his text a few seconds later and saw that the restaurant was only 10 minutes away.

"I can meet you there in fifteen. Does that work?"

"Works for me," said Glen.

"Excellent," said Guin. "See you in a few."

CHAPTER 14

Glen was at the restaurant when Guin arrived. They sat and ordered drinks and tacos, and Glen took out the spreadsheet he had prepared. Guin was impressed.

"Of course, I still need to talk to my guys, so don't kill me if I'm slightly off. But I don't anticipate going over this amount," he said, pointing to a number.

"That seems totally fair," said Guin, looking at the spreadsheet. "And I promise not to kill you if you go a bit over. One dead contractor is more than enough."

She smiled, then began laughing, though she knew it wasn't funny. It must have been the margarita. But then Glen began laughing, and before Guin knew it, she had tears streaming down her face.

She wiped her eyes and stopped laughing a minute later.

"You want some dessert?" Glen asked. "Their tres leches cake can't be beat."

"You have a serious sweet tooth," said Guin. "How on earth do you stay so slim?"

"I was blessed with a good metabolism, I guess. I also don't gorge. As my granny used to say, everything in moderation."

Guin's grandmother used to tell her the same thing. Yet another thing she and Glen had in common.

Guin declined dessert, ordering a coffee instead, and

Glen passed on the tres leches cake.

When they were done, Glen walked her to her car. Guin thought he might kiss her. But he just smiled and opened the door for her and then said goodbye.

When she got home, she found a text message from him.

"Thanks for having dinner with me. :-)" he had written. "We should do it more often. I'll be working at the house this week. Let me know when you want to stop by."

Guin smiled. She had had fun, too. She thought about writing him back but turned off her phone instead.

Guin woke up the next morning feeling well-rested, which was a bit surprising. Normally when she drank, she didn't sleep so well. She looked at the clock and saw it was nearly seven. She turned on her phone and checked the weather. It was 74 degrees out and partly sunny.

"Hmm… Should I go shelling or finish up my article?" she asked Fauna, who was curled up next to her.

Fauna looked up at her, yawned, then closed her eyes.

Guin got out of bed and looked out the window.

"I'm thinking beach."

She went into her closet and threw on a pair of shorts and a t-shirt, then went into the bathroom and applied some sunblock.

On her way out, she poured some food into Fauna's bowl. Then she left.

Guin drove up to Blind Pass and parked in the lot. Then she made her way down to the water, where there were several people fishing.

She said hello to the fishermen, then headed east. The tide was pretty high, and there weren't a lot of shells. Twenty minutes later, disappointed, she turned around and headed back to her car. At least she got a walk in.

When she got back to the condo, she made herself a pot of coffee, then took her mug to her desk. She was surprised at how quickly she was able to finish the Boca Grande piece, or at least the first draft. She would need to review it before sending it to Ginny, but she was pleased with what she had written. Hopefully, Glen had good photos to go with it. Though he had taken so many, he probably had enough to publish a coffee table book. Just in case, she sent him her draft along with a note.

She had just taken out her phone to take a social media break when a call came in. It was Craig.

"Hey," she said. "What's up?"

"I have some new information."

"About?" said Guin.

"About your late contractor."

"Lay it on me."

"It seems you weren't Funt and the Son's only unhappy client."

"Tell me something I don't know," said Guin. "I was over at the building department and found two complaints."

"Well, I guarantee you he pissed off more than just a couple of people."

"Oh?" said Guin. "Why do you say that?"

"I got it from a very reliable source that Funt had a habit of abandoning projects then cutting deals with people."

"What kinds of deals?" said Guin.

"Deals as in, you want me to go away or give you some of your money back, you sign a non-disparagement agreement."

"Is that like a non-disclosure?"

"Pretty much," said Craig. "Not only were you forbidden from lodging a complaint, you had to remove any negative reviews."

"Wow," said Guin. "And people agreed to this?"

"If they wanted to get rid of him."

"How is that legal?"

"Lots of contractors do it, at least here in Florida," said Craig.

"Wonderful," said Guin. "So how did you find out about this? If your source signed a non-disparagement or non-disclosure agreement, couldn't Funt sue?"

"As you recall, Funt's dead."

"What about his estate?"

"Do you know how much lawyers cost?"

"As a matter of fact, I do," said Guin. "So, who's this source, and how does he know Funt screwed other people?"

"He's a friend whose neighbor got royally screwed by Funt. He remembered when Funt was working on the place how the neighbor constantly complained about him. I asked if I could speak to the neighbor, and the neighbor agreed. He told me about the whole non-disparagement thing and said he had since found several other people Funt had bamboozled."

"So do you think one of these unhappy clients could have killed him?"

"It's possible."

"What about your friend's neighbor?"

"Irv? Doubtful. He must be closing in on eighty."

"You said there are others. How do I find them?"

"Well, you could always ask over at the Sanibel building department, see if anyone filed a complaint and later withdrew it."

"Will they really tell me that?" asked Guin.

"Can't hurt to ask. After all, the man's dead."

"Okay," said Guin. "I guess I've got nothing to lose."

"Another thing," said Craig. "Word on the street is that Funt owed a lot of money."

"To whom?"

"The kind of people you don't want to be owing money to."

"We talking loan shark?"

"Worse," said Craig.

"Who's worse than a loan shark?"

There was silence on the other end of the line.

"The mob?" said Guin.

Again, there was silence.

"What aren't you telling me, Craig?"

"Just leave it alone, Guin."

"You know I can't do that. Come on, I'm going to find out eventually."

"You hear any more from Detective O'Loughlin?" Craig asked.

Guin sighed. Clearly, Craig was not going to reveal who had loaned Funt money. So she told him about her run-in with Phoebe Costanza in the detective's office.

"She sounds like a real piece of work," said Craig.

"She is," said Guin. "Also, I have a weird feeling she was putting on a show, just to make me look bad."

"What makes you say that?"

"Just a feeling. It was like a scene from the *Real Housewives*."

"Well, she did just lose her boyfriend and meal ticket."

"Yeah, but I have a feeling there's more to her story than she's letting on. After all, we only have her word for Funt getting a call Sunday night. For all we know, she could have killed him and dumped the body at my place."

"Okay, I'll play along. Assuming she did kill him, why dump the body at your place?"

"Because she wanted to frame me."

"Frame you? Why?"

"Like I said, she thinks I was getting it on with her boyfriend."

"Seriously?" said Craig.

"She seemed pretty convinced. But maybe it was just an

act to throw the blame onto me."

"Well, it's an interesting theory," said Craig. "But it's got a bunch of holes."

"I know," said Guin. "But maybe we can fill them."

"You know I'll help any way I can."

"I know, and I appreciate it."

"Well, I'll let you go," he said. "I just wanted to give you the latest."

"Thanks," said Guin.

They then said goodbye and ended the call.

Guin had gone back over to the building department and was standing in front of Irma.

"Hi again," she said.

"You call Clint?"

"I did, but he didn't return my call. However, I think I found someone else to help me with the house."

"Well, if he doesn't work out, give Clint a try," said Irma. "He's probably just away and not checking his voicemail."

"I'll do that," said Guin.

"So, what can I do you for today?"

"Actually, I have a favor to ask you."

"Another one?" said Irma.

Guin ignored the comment.

"I was wondering if you or Heidi knew if anyone had filed a complaint against Funt and the Son Construction or Frank Funt, Jr., and then took it back."

"Took it back?" said Irma.

"You know, withdrew the complaint."

Irma looked thoughtful.

"I hear people do that, withdraw complaints," said Guin, "as part of settlement agreements with their contractor. But if they filed a complaint in the first place, you guys would still have it somewhere, right?"

"Well, if they withdrew the complaint, that means they didn't want anyone seeing it," said Irma.

"I understand that," said Guin. "But Frank Funt—Junior, that is—is dead, and the person who killed him could have been one of those people who filed a complaint and then withdrew it."

"Wait a minute. You say he was murdered?"

"The police haven't ruled it as murder yet, but it looks that way," said Guin.

Irma whistled.

"I'll need to speak with Heidi or Bob."

"Okay," said Guin.

She waited, but Irma didn't move.

"Heidi's not in right now," Irma said.

"What about Bob?"

"I guess I can see, but he may be busy."

"I'd really appreciate it," said Guin.

Irma got up and slowly made her way across the room to an office. She knocked on the door, then disappeared inside. A couple of minutes later, she came back out.

"Bob said he'll see you in a few."

"Thank you, Irma," said Guin.

She moved away from the desk and waited off to the side. A few minutes later, Bob emerged.

"You the young lady Irma was telling me about?"

Guin nodded.

"Well, come on in. But I only have a minute."

Guin followed Bob into his office.

"So, how can I help you?" he said, after taking a seat behind his desk.

"Well," said Guin, not sure how to start. "I'm trying to find out if anyone filed a complaint against Funt and the Son Construction or Frank Funt, Junior, and then withdrew it."

"I see," said Bob.

"Can you help me?"

"That depends," said Bob.

"On what?" asked Guin.

"On a few things," said Bob.

"Like what?"

"Like on whether the people who filed the complaint gave permission."

"But I don't even know who those people are," said Guin. "That's why I need to see the complaints."

"Sorry, I can't help you. Gotta have permission."

"You can't give me one name?"

"You can always ask Mr. Funt."

"He's dead."

"Old Frank died?" said Bob.

"No, his son, Frank Funt, Jr."

"Huh," said Bob.

This was getting exasperating.

"So you're saying you can't help me?"

"I'd like to, Miss. But my hands are tied. Like I said, you can always ask Old Frank. All complaints get sent to the contractor named on the complaint. So he'd have a copy."

"Thanks," said Guin.

"Anything else I can help you with?"

"No," said Guin. "Thank you for your time."

"My pleasure," said Bob, seeing her out.

Guin left and thought about walking over to the police department, which was a short distance away. But she wasn't sure if she wanted to see the detective.

She took out her phone and checked her messages. There was a text from Glen, letting her know he had received her email and was working over at the house. Did she want to stop by?

"Sure," she typed. "Be right over."

CHAPTER 15

Guin arrived at the house a few minutes later. She knocked on the door, which was unlocked, then went inside.

"Hello?" she called.

"Over here," said Glen.

He was standing on a stepstool in the kitchen, dressed only in a pair of shorts.

"What are you doing?" she asked him, trying to avoid looking at his tanned and toned chest.

"Adjusting your cabinets."

"Ah."

Glen climbed down off the stepstool.

"I have my laptop with me, if you want me to go through your article before the guys arrive."

"They're coming today?" said Guin. "How did you get them here so quickly?"

"I told them what happened, and they all felt really bad. Plus, it's kind of slow right now, and I think they were happy to get the work."

"Well, thank you," said Guin.

Glen retrieved his bag and pulled out his laptop.

"Let's see now," he said, placing it on a nearby counter.

He found Guin's email and opened her article. As he scrolled through it, he nodded his head and said "yup" several times.

"No problem," he said, when he was done. "Let me just pull up the folder and we can go through my photos."

He opened a file marked "Boca Grande" and angled his laptop so Guin could see.

"These are great!" she said, as Glen clicked through the images. "Oh, I really like that one of the beach! Did you take that by Thor's place?"

"I did," said Glen.

They went through the photos twice, with Glen marking their favorites.

"I'll edit these, then send them off to Ginny."

"Great," said Guin. "And I'll finish editing the article."

"We make a good team," said Glen.

He smiled at Guin, and she smiled back at him. He really was rather good looking, and sweet, and under different circumstances, she could see herself falling for him. But she wasn't ready to jump into another relationship, especially with someone she had a professional relationship with.

"Well, it looks as though you have things well in hand here," she said, glancing around.

"I'll have a better handle on things after the guys take a look. You want to stop by later this week, check on the progress?"

"Sure," said Guin. "Just send me a text."

"Will do."

They stood there, looking at each other, for another minute, Guin again trying not to stare at Glen's naked chest or his toned arms.

She reached into her bag, fumbling for her keys.

"Well, I should go," she said. "Don't work too late."

"I'll try not to," said Glen.

He smiled at her, and Guin suddenly felt warm. Must be the lack of AC, she told herself.

Guin was thinking about the house (and Glen, if she was being honest) as she drove home. Would Glen and his team finish on time? She wished she knew what exactly Frank had done or hadn't. If only she knew more about construction. Then she remembered what Bob had said.

As soon as she got back to the condo, she went to her computer and typed in "Frank Funt, Sr., address and phone number, Fort Myers." She found a Frank Funt living in a retirement community just across the Causeway. It had to be him. But she couldn't find a phone number. She debated what to do, then decided she would just pay him a visit.

The next morning, Guin got up, did a quick walk around the neighborhood, then showered and got dressed. She thought about baking something to give to Mr. Funt, as a kind of condolence gesture, and peeked in the refrigerator and pantry. Well, she could always make him a batch of chocolate chip cookies.

She grabbed what she needed, placing everything on the counter, and began mixing the ingredients. She had made so many batches of chocolate chip cookies over the years, she could make them blindfolded.

As soon as they were out of the oven and had cooled a bit, she placed half the cookies in a pretty metal tin. Then she popped the tin in a little shopping bag and headed to Fort Myers.

There was a gate at the entrance to the retirement community with a guard. Guin smiled up at him and said she was there to see Mr. Frank Funt.

"Name?" asked the guard.

"Guinivere Jones," Guin replied.

The guard looked down at his clipboard.

"Is he expecting you? I don't see your name on the list."

"I have something for him," said Guin, holding up the bag.

The guard eyed it suspiciously.

"They're cookies," said Guin, removing the tin.

A car honked, and the guard made a face.

"Could you just call Mr. Funt?" Guin asked. "Tell him I'm here about his son, Frank, Jr."

He eyed her one more time, then picked up the phone.

"Hi, Mr. Funt. It's Ernie at the gate. I've got a Ms. Jones here to see you. She says she knew your son and brought you something."

The guard nodded his head, then looked over at Guin.

"Yeah, she's okay looking."

Guin kept her eyes straight ahead.

"Okay, Mr. Funt," the guard said and hung up the phone. He turned to Guin. "He said to let you through."

Guin mentally breathed a sigh of relief.

The guard gave her directions to Frank, Sr.'s building and raised the gate.

"Thank you, Ernie," she said, waving to him as she went by.

Guin didn't know what to expect as she drove to Frank Funt, Sr.'s building. She had never met the man, only the son, and she wondered how old he was. She knew he was retired and that Frank, Jr., had probably been in his late forties. But the father could have been anywhere between seventy and a hundred.

She parked the purple Mini in one of the visitor spots, then found Frank, Sr.'s unit. It was located on the first floor. She rang the doorbell and a minute later it was opened by a tall, thin man with steel gray hair. He had a slight stoop, but he was still a good head taller than Guin. She looked for a resemblance between the man in front of her and the man she knew, but she couldn't find any. Maybe Frank, Jr., took after his mother.

"You Miss Jones?" said the man, eyeing her.

"I am," said Guin. "May I come in? These are for you, by the way." She held out the tin. "They're chocolate chip cookies. I made them myself."

Frank, Sr., took the tin but didn't invite Guin in.

"Ernie said you knew my son."

"I did," said Guin.

"You one of his chippies? Because if you're here looking for money, there's none to be had, not from me at any rate."

"I don't want your money, Mr. Funt. I just want to talk to you about Frank, Jr."

"How'd you know Frank?"

"He was doing some work for me."

Guin noticed a couple standing a little ways away, staring at them.

"May I come in?" she asked Mr. Funt. "I promise not to take up too much of your time."

"All right," he said, begrudgingly.

He opened the door and gestured for her to come in.

"Thank you," said Guin.

He led her into the living area and indicated for her to have a seat.

She sat on the couch and Frank, Sr., seated himself on one of the chairs.

They then stared at each other for several seconds.

"I'm sorry for your loss," Guin began. "I can't imagine what it's like losing a child."

Frank, Sr., grunted.

"That boy was always getting himself into trouble."

"Oh?" said Guin.

"Always looking to make a quick buck and trying to

ingratiate himself with those people."

"Those people?" said Guin.

"Rich people."

Guin waited for him to go on.

"Rich people only want people like Frank for one thing."

"And what's that?" asked Guin.

"To handle all the nasty stuff they don't want to handle themselves."

Guin didn't know what to say.

"The problem is, Frank, he sees all them toys rich people got, and he thinks, I wanna get me a nice car, and some fancy clothes, and a big house."

"So did he make a lot of money renovating houses?" Guin asked.

Frank, Sr., shrugged.

"You'd have to ask that office manager of his."

"You mean Phoebe?"

He nodded.

"I wasn't involved in the day-to-day stuff after they took over."

"About that," said Guin. "I understand you sold Frank the business. Is that correct?"

"That's right," said Frank, Sr. "Though he was behind in his payments."

"He didn't pay you in full for it?"

"He was on the installment plan."

"I see," said Guin. "And how many installments did he have left?"

"Too many."

"So what happens to the business now? Will Phoebe run it?"

"That witch?" said Frank, Sr., making a face.

"I take it you're not a fan," said Guin.

"You could say that."

"Was she the office manager when Frank took over?"

"No, she was a Frank hire. I told him it was a bad idea, but he stopped listening to me a long time ago."

"One more question."

Frank, Sr., looked at her.

"Did Frank have a drug problem?"

"A drug problem? Like, did he smoke weed?"

"Actually, I was thinking more along the lines of opioids, painkillers."

"That detective feller asked me the same thing."

"And what did you tell him?" asked Guin.

"I told him that Frank broke his leg falling off a roof a couple of years back and that the doctor gave him some pills to help with the pain. Don't recall what they were, but Frank was no junkie."

So, thought Guin, either Frank, Sr., was in denial about his son, or he didn't know about his drug habit. Or else someone had given Frank, Jr., those drugs and made it look like an overdose.

"Any idea who might've wanted to kill Frank?"

"That detective asked me that, too," said Frank, Sr. "Say, you a cop or something?"

"No, I'm just looking to find out the truth about Frank's death," said Guin. "So what did you tell the detective?"

"I told him to look into those people Frank was doing favors for."

"You mean his clients?"

Frank, Sr., nodded.

"Any ones in particular?"

"I don't know who all he'd done stuff for recently. You'd have to ask the witch. But I'd check out the real rich ones."

"Speaking of his clients," said Guin. "I understand several of them had filed complaints against Funt and the Son."

Frank, Sr., made a face.

"There's no pleasing some folks."

"Do you happen to have copies of those complaints? They might tell us who bore a grudge against Frank."

"I'd like to help you, but I gave everything to Frank and the witch when I sold the business."

"Speaking of the business, what happens to it now that Frank's dead, if he didn't leave it to Phoebe?"

"It goes back to me. Per the agreement Frank and I signed, if he missed three or more payments or something happened to him, the business reverted to the original owner, me."

Very interesting, Guin thought. Though she couldn't imagine Frank, Sr., knocking off his son, even if it was to get his business back.

"And are you planning on running it?" Guin asked.

"Me? I'm too old. Construction is a young man's game."

"So you're going to sell it?"

"If I get the right price."

Guin got up.

"Well, thank you for your time, Mr. Funt."

She reached into her bag and pulled out her card case.

"Here's my card. If you think of anything, anything at all, regarding Frank, feel free to give me a call or email me."

He took her card and looked at it.

"You're a reporter?" He was looking at her suspiciously again. "Did you just say that you knew Frank so I'd gab about him?"

"No," said Guin. "I did know him. And I meant what I said about finding out the truth about his death."

Frank, Sr., eyed her.

"You didn't sleep with him, did you?"

"Absolutely not!" said Guin. She composed herself and put on her professional smile. "Thank you again for your time, Mr. Funt. I'll see myself out."

She headed to the door, then stopped.

"If you don't mind, may I have your phone number and email address?"

"Why do you want 'em?"

"In case I have any more questions or information to share."

"I guess there's no harm," said Frank, Sr. "Just don't go giving them out."

"I promise," said Guin.

He gave her his contact information, and Guin left.

CHAPTER 16

Guin had typed up her notes from her talk with Frank Funt, Sr., and was researching a new article Ginny had assigned her when her phone started vibrating. The caller ID said Leakey Plumbing. Guin immediately swiped to answer.

"Guinivere Jones."

"This is Larry Leakey. You left me a message."

"Mr. Leakey!" said Guin. "Thank you so much for calling me back. Do you have a minute to answer some questions about Funt and the Son Construction?"

"What do you want to know?"

Guin put him on speakerphone, so she could type.

"I understand you filed a complaint against Funt and the Son Construction with the Sanibel building department."

"That's correct," said Mr. Leakey.

"And just to be clear, you worked with the son, Frank Funt, Jr., not his father?"

"That's right," said Mr. Leakey. "I never met the old man."

"And per the complaint, Frank, Jr., owed you money."

"He did."

"How much?" asked Guin.

"I don't recall the exact figure, but it was a lot."

"Is that why you filed the complaint?"

"Look, I don't like filing complaints against fellow

contractors, but the guy gave me no choice. I tried to get him to pay up. I sent him invoices and called and emailed. But he kept making excuses and blowing me off. I finally had enough. So I filed a complaint."

"Had you done a lot of work for Funt and the Son?"

"I'd done a few jobs for them. The first one went okay. Then on the second one, Frank made all sorts of excuses. He finally paid me a couple of months later, when he wanted me to help him again. I should have known better."

"What happened?"

"He screwed me over, that's what. I did the job—it was a big re-pipe, not cheap, you know? And he wouldn't pay up. Made all sorts of excuses. Then he says he's not paying because I did a bad job. I said, are you kidding me? But he refused to give me a dime. So I filed a complaint with the building department and the Better Business Bureau."

"Did you ever get your money?" asked Guin.

"Nope."

"Did you sue him or take him to small claims court?"

The plumber laughed.

"Yeah, good luck with that."

"And when was that last job?"

"Six, seven months ago?"

"And did you ever hear from Funt after that?"

"Actually, if you can believe it, he left me a message a few weeks ago. Said he had a rush job and would pay me double."

"Did you call him back?"

"Are you crazy? A leopard doesn't change its spots."

"And you say you haven't heard from or seen him in months."

"That's right," said Mr. Leakey.

"Do you know if Funt stiffed any other subs?"

"No, but it wouldn't surprise me. Guys like Funt, they're always looking to do stuff on the cheap. And if they can screw you, they will."

There was a faint beeping in the background.

"I need to go," said Mr. Leakey.

"Well, thank you for speaking with me," said Guin. "And if you think of anything or anyone else who might have had an issue with Funt and the Son, please let me know."

"Got it," said the plumber.

"Oh, and one more thing," Guin began.

But Larry Leakey had already hung up.

Guin reviewed her interview with Larry Leaky, then went back to her article. She had lost track of the time when her stomach started to grumble. She glanced at the clock on her monitor. It was a little after six. And she hadn't eaten lunch.

She got up and went to the kitchen and opened the refrigerator. There wasn't much there. She made a mental note to go grocery shopping in the morning, then changed her mind and grabbed her bag and her keys.

As she was about leave, Fauna came running up to her, meowing.

"I'll be back soon," Guin told the feline.

Fauna continued to meow, then trotted to the kitchen.

"Let me guess," said Guin. "You're hungry."

She sighed and filled Fauna's bowl with dry food. The black cat gave her a disapproving look.

"Sorry, kitty cat. That's what I got."

Reluctantly, Fauna lowered her head and began to eat.

Guin watched for a few seconds, then went to get herself some food.

There were a handful of people shopping at Bailey's. No doubt people on their way home from work. Guin grabbed some vegetables and fruit, a package of chicken thighs, a couple of small strip steaks, a dozen eggs, cheddar cheese, and a pint of Queenie's toasted coconut ice cream. Then she went to check out.

She had been mulling what she was going to make for dinner and was about to make a left onto Sanibel-Captiva Road when she changed her mind and went right. Less than a minute later, she was parked in front of the Pecking Order, a hole-in-the-wall that served the best fried chicken in Southwest Florida. As she got out, she noticed a couple making out in front of a dark, empty storefront a few feet away.

Get a room, Guin thought.

She was about to open the door to go into the Pecking Order when the door was flung open and a woman poked her head out.

"Hey, Phoebe," the woman called. "Your order's ready!"

No, it couldn't be.

Just in case, Guin ducked behind a column as the woman she had seen making out disentangled herself from her partner and went to collect her order. It *was* Phoebe Costanza. But who was the man with her? Guin didn't recognize him.

Fortunately, Phoebe didn't see her as she entered the restaurant.

A few seconds later, she emerged with her bag of fried chicken and went back over to the man, who put an arm around her. Then the two of them headed to a pickup truck parked at the end of the parking lot. It was dark out, but the truck was parked under a light, and Guin could just make out the name on the side, Sunshine Builders.

Once they had gone, Guin went into the Pecking Order and ordered two pieces of chicken with coleslaw and a biscuit.

"It'll just be a few minutes," said the woman behind the counter.

"That's fine," said Guin. "So, um, the woman who was just in here, Phoebe, you know her?"

"Not personally," said the woman.

"But you've seen her here before?"

The woman shrugged.

"Yeah, so?"

"What about the guy she was with? You see him before?"

"Tony?" said the woman. "He's a regular. Must come here two, three times a week."

"They come here together?"

"Why all the questions?" asked the woman.

"Sorry," said Guin. "Occupational hazard. I'm a reporter."

"A reporter, huh?"

Guin handed her a card.

The woman glanced at it, then looked back at Guin.

"Order up!" called the man in the kitchen.

The woman took the box of food, placed it in a bag, and handed the bag to Guin.

"Thanks," said Guin. "So had you seen Phoebe here with Tony before?"

"Why do you want to know?"

"Just curious," said Guin. "I thought Phoebe was seeing someone."

"You a friend?"

"An acquaintance. I knew the guy she was seeing. Or who I thought she was seeing."

"Well, I don't know about that other guy, but I've seen her here with Tony a few times."

"Before this week?"

The woman nodded.

Guin wanted to ask her another question, but just then a

family of four walked in.

"Thanks for your help," Guin called as she left. But the woman behind the counter was too busy helping the family to notice.

🌴

Guin ate dinner in the living room. She had turned on the TV to watch *Jeopardy!* and was playing along. When the show was over, she took her plate to the kitchen and washed it. Then she went back to her office/bedroom. She was seated in front of her computer when her phone started to vibrate. It was Craig.

"Hey," she said. "Any more news?"

"That's why I'm calling. I got a rather interesting piece of information I thought I'd pass along."

"Shoot," said Guin.

"It seems Frank, Jr., was in talks to sell Funt and the Son."

"Oh?" said Guin. "But he only bought it a few years ago," and was still paying it off, she added to herself. "Why was he selling it?"

"Probably needed the money to pay off his loan."

"You mean the loan he got to buy the business in the first place?"

Craig didn't say anything.

"So who was he hoping to sell it to?"

"Sunshine Builders. They're based on Sanibel, but they do work all over."

Guin couldn't believe it.

"Sunshine wouldn't happen to be run by a guy named Tony, would it?"

"As a matter of fact, it is," said Craig. "Tony Del Sole. Why?"

"I just saw him outside the Pecking Order, making out

with Phoebe Costanza, Frank Funt's supposed girlfriend."

Craig whistled.

"She didn't waste any time, did she?"

"The thing of it is, the woman at the Pecking Order said this wasn't the first time she'd seen the two of them together."

"Hmm," said Craig.

"Do you think there could be a connection?" asked Guin.

"It's possible."

"And you say you heard that Frank was in talks to sell Funt and the Son to Sunshine?"

"That's right, but I don't think the deal had gone through."

"Interesting. Frank's father didn't mention anything about Frank selling the business."

"You talked to Mr. Funt?"

"Actually, I saw him, this morning. I drove over to his retirement community."

"What did he have to say?"

"Not a whole lot, just that Frank had a habit of getting himself into trouble."

"Did he happen to say what kind of trouble?"

"He wasn't specific. Though he mentioned that Frank had kind of an obsession with rich people and would do anything to get in good with them."

"Like selling them opioids?"

"That's what I was thinking."

"You ask him if Frank was an addict?"

"Not in so many words. Though I asked him if he knew if Frank ever took painkillers."

"And what did he say?"

"Just that Frank broke his leg a while back and that the doctor had prescribed him something or other to help with the pain. But he swore that Frank didn't have a problem."

"Hmm," said Craig. "So did I ever mention the accident, the one that killed Jimbo's kid, Melissa?"

"No," said Guin. "Though I knew that Jimbo had lost a daughter."

"It happened a few years ago, a couple of months before that article you sent me."

"What happened?"

"Melissa and her boyfriend, Logan, were home from college over winter break and had gone to Fort Myers Beach with a couple of their friends. On their way home, the car they were in got into an accident. It was dark, and the car was going too fast and flipped over. Turns out the kid driving it was high as a kite. Melissa and Logan didn't make it."

"Oh, that's awful," said Guin.

"It was. Jimbo and Terry—that's Melissa's mom, Jimbo's ex—were heartbroken."

"I bet. So what happened to the kid who was driving? And what does the accident have to do with Funt?"

"I was getting to that," said Craig. "The driver lived and was convicted on DUI manslaughter. But he got a lighter sentence for cooperating."

"Cooperating?"

"The DA wanted to know where he got the drugs."

"Let me guess: Frank Funt, Jr."

Craig nodded.

"The kid said he had gotten the stuff from one of the guys who'd been working on his house. He didn't remember the guy's name, just the name of the company, because he thought it was dumb. But when they showed him photos, he pointed to Funt."

"So did they arrest Funt?"

"They did, but there wasn't enough evidence to hold him."

"Seriously? What about that drug bust?"

"That happened a couple of months after. And his lawyer got him off."

"Unbelievable," said Guin. "Jimbo and the other parents must have been furious."

"They were, or at least Jimbo was. I can't speak for the others. Didn't know them."

"You don't think Jimbo or one of the other parents could have killed Frank, do you?"

"The accident was nearly four years ago, and there was no hard proof that Funt was responsible."

"Still, you should talk to Jimbo."

Craig sighed.

"Fine, I'll go have a talk with him."

"If you don't want to, I can," said Guin.

"No, I'll do it," said Craig. "I didn't get the John Jay College/Harry Frank Guggenheim Award for Excellence in Criminal Justice Reporting for avoiding the hard questions."

Guin smiled.

"Let me know what you find out. And good luck."

"Thanks," said Craig.

They said goodbye, then ended the call.

CHAPTER 17

That night, a storm blew through, rattling the windows and waking Guin up. She eventually went back to sleep, but she woke up feeling anxious. It was dark in the room, and when Guin looked at her alarm clock, she saw it was a little before six. She turned on her phone and checked the weather. It was going to be another warm, humid day. But it wasn't supposed to rain until later. If she wanted to get a walk in, now was the time. And there was a good chance the storm had blown in lots of shells.

She stared down at her phone. Should she text Shelly, see if she wanted to go beachcombing?

Guin sent her a text, then went to the bathroom. When she got back, there was a message waiting.

"Would LOVE to go shelling!" Shelly had replied. "When and where?"

Guin smiled.

"How about West Gulf Drive, Beach Access #4, in 30 minutes?"

"I'm there!" Shelly wrote back. "See you then!"

Guin made her bed, then pulled on some clothes. It would take her 20 minutes to get over to Beach Access #4. She thought about making coffee but decided to wait. She quickly fed Fauna, then grabbed her beach bag and her keys and left.

Guin parked the Mini and texted Shelly to meet her on the beach. It was already quite warm, but she didn't mind. There was a gentle breeze blowing and looking around at the palm trees and the Gulf, she knew there was no place she'd rather be. She closed her eyes and inhaled, breathing in the scent of the saltwater. She slowly raised her arms over her head, taking another deep breath in, then she gently lowered them as she exhaled.

The sun was just starting to light up the sky, and Guin loved how rosy and soft the clouds looked, like an Impressionist painting. Sunrise was her favorite time of day, though the sunsets on Sanibel were also pretty spectacular.

A few minutes later, Shelly appeared.

They hugged and stared out at the Gulf.

"I never get tired of this view," said Shelly.

"I know," said Guin.

"So, which way should we go this morning?"

"I'm thinking right," said Guin. "Pretty sure I can see some shell piles that way."

"Let's do it!"

They walked west, neither speaking as they searched the shoreline (assuming a posture known as the Sanibel Stoop). Guin spied something and bent down.

"Whatcha got?"

"A nice lace murex," said Guin, holding it up.

"Very nice," said Shelly, approvingly.

They continued on.

"Hey, look!" said Shelly, pointing at something rolling in the water. She ran in and held up her find.

"Ooh, an alphabet cone!" said Guin. "Nice!"

Shelly grinned.

"Now, if only I could find a junonia."

"You and me both," said Guin. "Though I'd be thrilled to find a true tulip, or a king's crown conch, or a Scotch bonnet."

At the mention of a Scotch bonnet, Shelly turned to Guin.

"That poor girl," she said, remembering the young woman who had been found on the beach that spring, clutching a Scotch bonnet in her hand.[2]

"I know," said Guin. "I still have nightmares about it."

They continued to walk in silence, picking up and discarding shells as they went.

"Whoa," said Shelly, stopping.

In front of them was an enormous shell pile that stretched for several yards.

"Wow," said Guin. "Wish I had a shovel."

They stood there staring at the shell pile for several seconds.

"I don't even know how to approach it."

"Just start digging," said Shelly, scrambling up. She began combing through the pile, moving shells around with her feet. "Come on!" she called.

Guin eyed the pile. Shell piles were not her favorite. Having to comb through thousands of shells in order to find a few good ones seemed like a Sisyphean task. She could be there all day. She looked up at her friend. Well, maybe just for a few minutes...

"Coming."

She picked a spot on the pile and began to dig with her hands and feet.

"That's the spirit!" said Shelly. "Look!" she said, holding up another alphabet cone.

"It's clearly your lucky day," said Guin.

She continued to dig.

"Oh wow," she said, a few minutes later. "A true tulip! Finally!"

---

[2] See Book 5, *Shell Shocked*.

She held up the shell for Shelly to see.

"Told you!" said Shelly. "And I love the orange color!"

They continued to dig for another hour, until Guin's back couldn't take being hunched over any longer.

"Hey, Shell, I think I'm done."

Shelly glanced at the shell pile, then back at Guin.

"It's okay if you want to stay," said Guin.

"You sure?" said Shelly. "I do need to get going on my Christmas collection."

"No problem," said Guin.

"Before you go, you hear anything more about your contractor?"

"A bit."

"Anything you can share?"

Guin hesitated.

"I don't want to say anything until I know more."

"You speak with Detective O'Loughlin?"

"Yeah."

Shelly put her hands on her hips.

"What is going on with you two? Last spring, you were all happy happy happy. Now you make a face whenever I mention his name."

Guin sighed.

"He's seeing someone."

"What?!" said Shelly. "No! Who? And how'd you find out?"

"I ran into them, at the Sandbar, after you left."

"And you didn't tell me?" said Shelly, indignantly.

"It's complicated."

"So who is she?"

"An old friend, the widow of his former partner."

Shelly rolled her eyes.

"How cliché."

"They apparently go way back."

"But what about the two of you? I thought after what happened on Hutchinson Island, you two were a thing."

"I did, too," said Guin. "But..." She shrugged. "It's probably for the best. Better to keep things strictly professional."

Shelly gave her a look.

"Personally, I think you're giving up way too easily."

"What am I supposed to do, Shell? No, better to remain single. I can't deal with men right now."

"Well, when you're ready to start dating again, let me know. Steve has a new colleague he brought home the other night. Recently divorced. Not bad looking. Seemed like a nice guy."

"Thanks, Shell. But..."

Shelly held up a hand.

"I got it. So we're having our first Sunday barbecue of the season this weekend. Can I count you in?"

Steve and Shelly were famous for their Sunday barbecues.

"As long as you don't try to set me up or invite the detective."

"Promise," said Shelly, crossing her heart.

"Okay," said Guin. "If I'm free, I'll be there. You know how I love Steve's famous brats."

"Well then," said Shelly, smiling. "You will have to come. Steve just got his shipment from Wisconsin."

"Let me check my calendar and get back to you." Though she was pretty sure she was free.

"Do that."

"Okay, I'm off," said Guin. "Happy hunting."

She waved goodbye, and Shelly went back to her digging.

CHAPTER 18

Guin was taking a break to check her phone. When she unlocked it, she saw she had a voicemail. It was from an Abe Miller, saying he had received her email about Funt & the Son Construction and was welcome to give him a call. She immediately called him back.

"Hello?" said a tentative male voice.

"Mr. Miller?" said Guin.

"Speaking," said the man.

"This is Guin Jones, Mr. Miller. I had emailed you about Funt and the Son Construction and just got your voicemail."

"Sorry it took so long to reply," said Mr. Miller. "My wife and I were on a cruise and weren't checking our email."

"Totally understandable," said Guin. "I appreciate you giving me a call. So, are you back on Sanibel?"

"No, we're in Ithaca, New York. We won't be back on Sanibel until the end of the month."

"Ah," said Guin. "Well, do you have a few minutes to chat and answer some questions?"

"Sure," he said. "Fire away."

Guin had planned to ask the Millers where they were at the time of Funt's death, but if they had just gotten back from a cruise and were in Ithaca, they couldn't have killed him. Though it was possible they could have hired someone to.

"So where was your cruise?" Guin asked.

"Around the Mediterranean. Gloria, that is Mrs. Miller, and I were celebrating our fiftieth wedding anniversary."

"Congratulations!" said Guin. "My mother and stepfather are about to go on a Mediterranean cruise."

"Which company they going with?" asked Mr. Miller.

"I'm not sure," said Guin. "She just said it was a smaller ship." (She left out the part about it being very exclusive.)

"Ah," said Mr. Miller. "We went with Viking. This is our third trip with them. Good company."

"Good to know," said Guin. "How long were you gone for?"

"Nearly three weeks. We got back a couple of days ago."

"So, about Funt and the Son," said Guin. "According to the complaint you filed with the Sanibel building department, you hired them around a year ago and then you fired them several months later."

"That's right."

"Can you tell me why?"

"If you read the complaint, you know that they gutted our place and then disappeared with our money."

"I did read that, and I can't imagine how awful that must have been." Though Guin could, as something similar had happened to her. "But would you mind going into a little more detail? How did you find them?"

"There isn't a whole lot more to say," said Mr. Miller. "My wife heard about Funt and the Son from some friends of hers. They had hired them to do a bunch of renovation work several years before. Had only good things to say about them. We didn't realize that the father had retired and that the son was now running the business."

"I see," said Guin. "So you hired them and then what?"

"Well, first the son asked for a big deposit."

"How big?"

"Fifty percent, but we said no way."

"What did you give him?

"Twenty-five percent, which I still thought was too much, but Funt said that was standard practice on Sanibel and Captiva."

"Then what happened?"

"Nothing," said Mr. Miller. "A big, fat goose egg. Weeks went by, and we heard nothing from Funt. We kept asking him when he was going to file a permit."

"And what did he say?"

"Some nonsense about the FEMA 50/50 Rule."

"The FEMA 50/50 Rule?"

"Because Florida is one big flood zone, you're only allowed to renovate your property up to fifty percent of the appraised value," Mr. Miller explained. "We didn't think there was a problem as our property was appraised for more than twice the renovation budget. Pretty sure it was just an excuse for him to drag his feet."

"So then what happened?"

"He finally got the permit around Thanksgiving. And I told him Gloria and I were going back up north for Christmas—to see the grandkids—and we expected to see people working at the house before we left."

"So were you renting a place down here?"

"No, we owned a condo over in the Sanctuary. A little two-bedroom we had bought. But with all the kids having kids, we needed a bigger place. That's why we bought the house."

"Got it," said Guin. "So did he send a crew over?"

"He did, and they destroyed the place. It looked like a hurricane had blown through or a bomb had gone off."

"That bad?"

"Worse," said Mr. Miller. "Gloria was hysterical, didn't want to leave, she was so worried about the house. You should have seen it, Ms. Jones. There was dust and debris everywhere, and they had taken big chunks out of the walls."

"So it wasn't supposed to be a gut renovation?"

"No," said Mr. Miller. "We were just updating the place."

"I'm so very sorry," said Guin.

"Hey, it wasn't your fault. We should have never hired Funt or kept a closer eye on those workmen of his. But what did we know? But the real piece de resistance came just after Christmas. We got home to find the building department had slapped a stop-work order on the house."

"Do you know why they did that?"

"The genius had never picked up the permit, and the little bit of work he did do, aside from demolishing the place, was apparently not to code."

"That's awful," said Guin, wishing she had spoken with Mr. Miller before she had started her own renovation project. She would have never hired Funt had she known. "So, what did you do?"

"I called the building department and spoke to Bob. He was sympathetic but said there was nothing he could do. It was up to the contractor to fix the mess."

"I assume you called Funt to complain."

"You're darn right I did," said Mr. Miller. "But he wouldn't answer his phone. Finally had to hire a lawyer. That got his attention. At first he was all apologetic. Then he blamed it on his guys. Said his project manager quit, but that he personally would sort things out with the building department. Ha! That was the last I heard from him."

"So, what did you do?"

"We called the lawyer back."

"Was the lawyer able to help?"

"He helped us terminate Funt, but we never got our money back. In addition to the deposit, he had asked us to pay upfront for a lot of the materials, which we stupidly did, though we never saw a thing."

"I'm so sorry," said Guin. As bad as her situation was, she realized it could have been much worse. "So did you sue Funt?"

"We took him to arbitration," said Mr. Miller. "That's what the lawyer advised. Though he warned us that even if we won, if Funt was broke, we wouldn't see a dime. Still, we decided to go ahead. It seemed like a slam-dunk case and arbitration was cheaper than suing the guy."

"What happened at the arbitration hearing?"

Mr. Miller gave a rueful laugh.

"It never happened. Less than twenty-four hours before we were supposed to go in front of the arbitrator, some lawyer calls our lawyer, saying he's representing Funt and gets the hearing postponed."

"Ouch," said Guin.

"Tell me about it. Gloria was furious."

"So what happened?"

"We wound up settling, though it barely covered the lawyer's fees. Funt's lawyer claimed Funt had no money. All he could offer was pennies on the dollar."

"And you took it?" said Guin.

"Gloria was a wreck. She just wanted to move on. So we agreed. Though we refused to sign the non-disparagement clause his lawyer inserted into the settlement."

"Those seem to be quite popular around here," said Guin.

"'Cause they're all crooks, every one of them," said Mr. Miller.

"So what happened to your house? Were you able to find someone to finish it?"

"We did. We hired Beautiful Homes. Cost me a bundle, and it took forever, but they did a good job. They just finished up."

Guin wished she had hired Beautiful Homes.

"And did you ever see or hear from Funt afterward?"

"Nope. I'm not a violent man, Ms. Jones, but if I had ever run into Funt, I would have been tempted to take a swing at him. Can't say I'm sorry he's dead."

Guin understood how Abe Miller felt.

"Well, thank you for your time, Mr. Miller. I'll let you go."

"That's it?" he replied.

"Unless there's something you wanted to add?"

"You should talk to Funt's project manager."

"The one who quit?"

"Yeah. We only met him a couple of times, but I'd look him up if you're looking for dirt on Funt. He seemed like an okay guy. Maybe he'll tell you why he quit."

"Do you happen to recall his name?"

"Yeah, Nick DiDio."

"Did you ever try to contact him?"

"We thought about it, but he wasn't really involved in our job, and the lawyer said to lay off."

"Do you happen to know if Mr. DiDio lives around here?"

"I think he lives over in Cape Coral. I remember hearing him mention how bad traffic was getting from there to Sanibel."

"Well, thanks again for your time, Mr. Miller."

"No problem," he said. "Good luck to you."

"Actually, I do have one more question," said Guin.

"Yes?"

"Would it be okay to call or email you if I have any additional questions?"

"Feel free," said Mr. Miller. "And please, call me Abe."

Guin smiled.

"Thanks, Abe."

They said goodbye, then ended the call.

Guin stared out the window, gazing at the trees. Well, it seemed the Millers were in the clear. But now she had a new person of interest: Nick DiDio. She wondered if the detective had spoken with him. Well, there was only one way to find out.

"Ms. Jones."

Guin was surprised he had answered. She'd been expecting to get his voicemail.

"Detective," she replied. She could feel her heart beating. "What do you know about a Nick DiDio?"

"DiDio?" said the detective.

"Funt's former project manager."

The detective didn't say anything.

"I just spoke with Abe Miller. He and his wife had hired Funt to renovate their house last year. The project went sideways, and they fired him. He told me to reach out to Funt's former project manager, a guy named Nick DiDio. Said DiDio quit just after they started on their house. Didn't know why. And Funt wouldn't say."

Again, the detective didn't say anything.

"You still there?"

"I'm here," replied the detective.

"So?" said Guin.

"So, what?" said the detective.

"So, did you speak with Nick DiDio? Sounds like he and Funt had a falling out. Maybe Nick bore a grudge."

"If everyone who bore a grudge against a contractor killed him, there would be no contractors."

Guin paused. That was probably true.

"Whatever," she said. "So, did you speak with DiDio?"

"We have."

Guin was surprised the detective actually answered her. "And?"

"And you know I can't discuss it."

Guin rolled her eyes.

"Did you arrest him?"

There was silence.

"Come on, detective, give me something!"

"No, we did not arrest Mr. DiDio."

"Thank you," said Guin. "Have you arrested anyone? It's been over a week, and I haven't heard of any arrests. Unless you really believe Funt died of a self-inflicted drug overdose."

"I could always arrest you, if it would make you happy."

Guin wasn't sure if he was kidding.

"Unlike on TV, Ms. Jones, murder cases take more than a few days to solve. And the task becomes that much harder when there is little or no evidence and no eyewitnesses."

"What do you mean little or no evidence? What about a syringe or a pill container?"

"The place was clean."

"That should be proof that someone gave him the drugs!"

The detective didn't say anything.

"What about fingerprints? There must have been fingerprints in the bathroom."

"Only yours."

Neither said anything for several seconds.

"Come on! You don't really think I killed him, do you? Where would I have even gotten the drugs, let alone gotten him to take them?"

Guin paced around her bedroom.

"So, do you have any suspects, other than me?"

"We're investigating."

"Yeah, yeah, yeah," she said. "Well, if you're not going to tell me anything, I'll just continue to investigate on my own."

"I would prefer that you leave the investigating to the police," said the detective.

"Fine. Let me know if you find out anything. Oh, that's right. I'm on a need-to-know basis. Well, goodbye, detective. Thanks for the help. Hope you find the killer before he kills someone else. And I hope you and Maggie live happily ever after."

"Guin, wait."

Guin stopped pacing.

"About the other night. I wish you'd let me explain."

"What's left to explain? You made your choice, and I have to accept it."

"Please," said the detective.

Guin's throat felt dry.

"Could you just meet me someplace, just for a few minutes?"

"Fine," said Guin. "As long as it's not your place."

"How about Doc Ford's?"

"When?"

"You free later?"

Guin thought about lying.

"I guess I could spare a few minutes. What time?"

"Five-thirty?"

"See you then."

CHAPTER 19

Guin typed "Nick DiDio" into her search engine and watched as the screen populated. There were far too many results, so she typed in "Nick DiDio Cape Coral." That narrowed things down considerably. Though she still found two Nicholas DiDios in Cape Coral. Possibly they were related.

She hunted for phone numbers and found one. She was about to try it when she received a text from Ginny. She wanted to know if Guin would do a write-up on a new book. It was a work of historical fiction set on Sanibel, written by a local author.

"What happened to Nicole?" asked Guin. (Nicole was the paper's regular book reviewer.)

"She's on vacation," Ginny typed. "And I need the write-up before she gets back."

"What's the book called?" Guin texted.

Instead of texting her back, Ginny called her.

"Hey," said Guin.

"Hey yourself."

"I assume this is about the book."

"It is," said Ginny.

"So what's the hurry?"

"The author is giving a talk here in a few weeks, and I want the article to appear beforehand."

"That doesn't give me much time."

"You can handle it."

"So who's the author?"

"Caroline Simms."

Guin swallowed.

"As in…?"

"Yes, as in the wife of the head of the Island Trust Company," said Ginny. "She sits on a number of boards and does a lot of charitable work on the island, as you no doubt know. And this is her first novel."

Guin sent up a silent prayer. She had a bad feeling about this. She had seen Caroline Simms at various charitable events on the island, and she had spoken with her, but she didn't know much about her.

"And does this novel have a title?" she asked Ginny.

"*The Belle of Sanibel*."

Guin didn't say anything for several seconds.

"You're kidding, right?"

"I'm deadly serious," replied Ginny.

"*The Belle of Sanibel*? Seriously? It sounds like a bad romance novel."

"It's historical fiction," Ginny corrected.

"Have you read it?"

"No, I've been too busy."

Guin knew an excuse when she heard one.

"Look, the write-up doesn't have to be that long. Just read the book, interview Caroline, then bang out a few paragraphs."

"When do you want it again?"

"Can you get something to me by Tuesday?"

"As in next Tuesday?" said Guin. "That's less than a week away, and I don't even have a copy!"

"I have a copy for you if you want to swing by, or…"

Guin could hear Ginny speaking with someone.

"Actually, Glen just walked in, and he said he could drop

it off on his way up to Captiva later."

"What's Glen doing there?" asked Guin.

"I invited him out for lunch," Ginny replied. "Will you be at home later?"

"You invited Glen to have lunch with you?"

Ginny never invited freelancers out for lunch, at least as far as she knew.

"Shall I have him drop off the book later?" Ginny asked.

"Sure," said Guin. "What time does he think he'll swing by?"

Guin could hear Ginny speaking to Glen in the background.

"Say around two-thirty? He says he has to be at South Seas at three-thirty."

"That's fine," said Guin. "Just tell him to text me when he's on his way."

"Will do," said Ginny. "Now, if you will excuse me, I must be off. Ciao!"

"Ciao," said Guin.

They ended the call and Guin made a face. *The Belle of Sanibel?* Really? *Try to think positively, Guin*, she told herself. She sighed. Well, maybe it wouldn't be so bad. Though she had a feeling it would be.

Guin stared out the window. Why of all people had Ginny picked *her* to review Caroline Simms's new novel? She sighed again, then turned back to her monitor. She found the phone number for one of the Nicholas DiDios and picked up her phone.

She entered the number, and a male voice answered.

"Hello?"

"Hello," said Guin. "Is this Nicholas DiDio?"

"It is," said the man. "Who's this?"

"My name's Guinivere Jones," said Guin. "I'm calling to find out if you are the Nicholas DiDio who worked for Funt and the Son Construction."

"Why do you want to know?" asked the man.

"It's for a story I'm working on," said Guin. "I'm a reporter with the *Sanibel-Captiva Sun-Times*."

"A reporter, eh?" said the man. "What kind of story are you doing?"

"I'm looking into the death of Frank Funt, Jr., and I'm trying to find out what kind of person he was."

"I'll tell you what kind of person he was," said the man. "He was a crook. Promised Nicky he'd make him a partner, then reneged. Didn't pay him, either."

"Is Nicky your son?" asked Guin.

"That's right. He worked for Funt and the Son for years, for Frank, Sr. Then Frank, Jr., took over and threw Nicky under the bus."

"How so?"

"The old man had told Nicky he was going to make him a partner. Then he sold the business to his son, and Frank, Jr., said his dad has said no such thing."

"I see," said Guin.

"Then he starts blaming Nicky for all sorts of stuff and stops paying him. Finally, Nicky had enough and walked."

"Did he get another contracting job?"

"He did," said Mr. DiDio. "Went to work for Tony Del Sole over at Sunshine."

Did all roads lead to Sunshine? Guin wondered.

"By any chance is Nicky around?" asked Guin. "I'd love to speak with him."

"He's at work," said Mr. DiDio.

"Do you have a number where I could reach him?"

"What did you say your name was again?"

"Guin Jones. I'm with the *Sanibel-Captiva Sun-Times*."

"That's right," said Mr. DiDio.

"About Nicky," said Guin. "Could I get his number?"

"Give me a second. It's around here somewhere."

Guin waited.

"Ah, here we go."

He read off a number to her.

"Thank you, Mr. DiDio."

"Just be sure to tell your readers that Frank Funt, Jr., was a no-good bum."

"Thanks again for your help," said Guin.

She ended the call and was about to call the younger DiDio when she stopped. What exactly was she going to say to him?

She grabbed a piece of paper and a pen and started writing some questions.

Guin had meant to call Nicky DiDio right after lunch, but she had decided to look up Caroline Simms instead. She was so engrossed in her research that she almost missed a text from Glen, letting her know he was on his way.

She still had around 15 minutes until Glen arrived, so she turned back to her screen and continued reading. Caroline Simms came from an old Southern family and had met William Simms while in college. The two had gotten married shortly afterward and had two children, a girl and a boy. The latter had gone on to become the star quarterback for the University of Central Florida Knights and then had gone to work in the family business after graduation.

As for Mrs. Simms, she was heavily involved in charitable work on the island and in Fort Myers and had served on the boards of the Sanibel Historical Museum and Village, the local food pantry (known as F.I.S.H.), and Golisano Children's Hospital in Fort Myers, among other nonprofits.

As Guin was reading, her phone began vibrating again. It was Glen, letting her know he was downstairs.

"Be right down," she texted him back.

She got up and went down the stairs.

"Special delivery," said Glen, holding out the book and smiling.

"Thanks," said Guin, taking it.

She looked down at the cover and had to stop herself from rolling her eyes.

"I know," said Glen. "I just hope the inside is better than the outside."

"You and me both," said Guin.

"Well, I have to run. Got a photoshoot up on Captiva."

"Anything interesting?"

"Doing a Thanksgiving shoot for South Seas."

"But Thanksgiving isn't for nearly two months."

"Yeah, but you know resorts: Gotta plan ahead. And two months isn't really that long."

True, thought Guin. Back in the old days, before the Internet, magazines prepared stories and shot them months ahead of time. Businesses, too. How times had changed. Though not completely.

"Well, have fun."

"You want to grab a drink after or a bite to eat? I'm not sure how long I'll be there, but I have to come back this way."

"Sorry, can't tonight. I've got plans."

"Well, if your plans fall through, send me a text. I may be out on Captiva till late."

"Will do," said Guin. "But don't count on it."

"I won't," said Glen.

"So, how are things going at the house?"

"Good," he said. "You should stop by."

"I will."

They stood there awkwardly.

"Well, gotta go," Glen finally said. "Have fun with your book!"

He got into his BMW and slowly backed out of the driveway.

Guin looked down at the book in her hands. It certainly didn't look like a historical novel, unless the women and men back in the 1880s on Sanibel were a whole lot buxomer and buff and scantily clad than she remembered.

CHAPTER 20

Guin had meant to phone Nicky DiDio yet again, but she had begun reading *The Belle of Sanibel* instead and couldn't seem to put it down. While she wouldn't call it great literature, it wasn't as bad as she had feared.

While Ginny had referred to the book as a work of historical fiction, it read more like a romance novel with some history sprinkled in. The main character, Isabelle (Belle, for short), lived on Sanibel in the late nineteenth century, along with her father and three older brothers. As one of only a few young women on the island, and quite beautiful, she was constantly being courted by the local males. But she wasn't interested in any of them. Instead, her heart belonged to one Juan Valdés, a wealthy and mysterious Cuban who owned a nearby fishery. Though Belle was unaware of Juan's true identity.

Juan had encountered Belle on one of his visits to the island and had immediately been smitten by the fair maiden. He had followed her, discovering where she lived, and began sending her gifts anonymously, saying they were from a secret admirer. Intrigued, Belle began asking if anyone knew who had been leaving gifts for her, which arrived before dawn on her doorstep.

Unable to ascertain who her secret admirer was, she stayed up all night one evening, hiding behind the bench on her porch, determined to catch the gift giver. But when she did, Juan said he was only the messenger and had no idea who the sender was.

The two wound up talking, and Juan told Belle he would try to discover the identity of her secret admirer. All he asked in return was that she meet him the next evening down by the beach. Belle was hesitant at first, but her sense of curiosity won out, and she met Juan down by the boat dock the following evening. And the night after that and the night after that.

After a fortnight of secret meetings, not all of them at night, Belle and Juan declared their love for each other, though Belle still had no idea who her secret admirer was or Juan's true identity.

Guin put the book down. She couldn't imagine prim and proper Caroline Simms writing such a novel. She just didn't seem the romantic type. She stared out past the lanai, to the trees ringing the golf course below, and watched as a flock of birds flew by. Then she picked up the book to continue reading.

She had only read a few more pages when her phone started buzzing. It was her calendar, reminding her that she had an appointment with the detective at five-thirty. Good thing she had set that reminder, otherwise she might have forgotten.

She went into the bedroom, placing the book on her nightstand, then headed to her closet.

She stood there, looking at her clothes, wondering what to wear.

"Screw it," she said, picking out a form-fitting dress with a low neckline.

She wriggled into it, then smoothed it over her body. She looked at her reflection in the mirror. Not bad, she thought. She went into the bathroom and ran a comb through her tangle of strawberry blonde curls and applied some makeup.

As she left, she glanced at herself in the full-length mirror again. She was ridiculously overdressed for Doc Ford's, but she didn't care. She wanted the detective to realize he had made the wrong choice.

She grabbed a pair of high-heeled sandals and headed to the front door.

"Goodbye, kitty cat!" she called. "I'll be back in a bit."

Doc Ford's wasn't busy, and Guin had no trouble finding a seat at the bar.

"What can I get you?" asked the bartender. "We're having a special on mojitos tonight."

"Fine, give me a mojito," said Guin, ignoring the looks of the men seated nearby.

(She knew she was overdressed, but it was too late to change now.)

The bartender nodded and went to make her drink.

Guin glanced around. There was no sign of the detective. Could he have forgotten? Or could something have come up? She checked her phone. There were no messages.

The bartender brought over her mojito.

"Thanks," said Guin.

"Can I get you something to eat?" he asked her.

"I'm good," she said. "I'm waiting for a friend."

"Well, if you need anything, just holler."

Guin sipped her drink and glanced around every few seconds. Twenty minutes went by and there was still no sign of or word from the detective.

"Can I get you a refill?" asked the bartender.

Guin looked down. How had that happened? She had nearly finished her mojito.

"Not right now," she said. "Though could I trouble you for a glass of water?"

"Coming right up."

He took a glass from under the bar and filled it with water.

"Here you go."

"Thanks," said Guin.

She took several sips and was debating how long she should wait for the detective when her phone started to vibrate.

"Hello?" she said, thinking it was the detective.

"Hey, I know you said you had plans, but I got done early and was thinking maybe we could grab a quick drink."

It was Glen.

"Why not?" said Guin. "I just happen to be at Doc Ford's on Sanibel. Come on over!"

"I can be there in twenty, if you don't mind waiting."

"No problem," said Guin. "I've waited this long. What's another twenty minutes?"

"Um, okay," said Glen. "See you soon."

The bartender came back over.

"You good or you want something else?"

"I'm good," said Guin, feeling a little tipsy. "My friend should be here soon. Then I'll order some food."

The bartender nodded, then moved off to speak with another customer.

Guin read the news on her phone while she waited for Glen. As she was reading, she felt a hand on her shoulder and jumped.

"Didn't mean to startle you," said the detective.

Guin whipped around.

"I got held up at the office."

"You might have called or texted me," said Guin, annoyed.

"Sorry, I lost track of time."

Just then Guin saw Glen enter the restaurant. He waved

and headed over. Then he noticed the detective.

"Am I interrupting something?" he asked, looking from Guin to the detective.

"No," said Guin. "Detective O'Loughlin was just leaving."

"You're welcome to join us, detective," said Glen.

"Thank you. Maybe another time," the detective replied.

He turned to go and Guin watched him. Was she making a mistake?

"What was that about?" asked Glen, taking a seat.

"Can I get you something to drink?" asked the bartender.

"It's mojito night," Guin said.

"Then I'll have a mojito," said Glen.

"I'll have one, too," said Guin. "And could you give us a couple of menus?"

The bartender returned with their drinks and menus a minute later.

"Hmm…" said Guin, looking over the menu. "You know what you want?"

"How about we get some oysters?" Glen suggested.

"Sounds good to me! And how about some fried calamari?"

"Why not?" said Glen. "All that turkey and fixings made me hungry."

"Didn't they feed you?"

"No, the food was strictly for show."

They signaled to the bartender, and he took their order. Then they made small talk, Glen telling her all about his shoot.

The bartender arrived a short time later with their food.

Guin raised the lemon wedge over the oysters.

"Okay?" she asked.

"Be my guest," said Glen.

She squeezed the lemon over the oysters, then speared one with the cocktail fork, dipping it into the cocktail sauce and then swallowing it. She closed her eyes and hummed, enjoying its salty-sweet goodness.

When she opened her eyes, she saw Glen looking at her. "What?"

"You're very sexy when you do that," he said.

Guin felt her cheeks growing warm.

"Don't be embarrassed. I like a woman who enjoys her food."

Glen smiled at her, and Guin felt her cheeks growing warmer.

"And that dress looks amazing on you," he added.

She took a sip of her water, then speared some calamari, making sure to keep her eyes open and not make a sound as she ate it.

Glen laughed, then stuck his fork into the fried squid.

Halfway through their meal (they had decided to order dinner), Guin had forgotten all about the detective.

After finishing their coffee, they paid their bill and left Doc Ford's.

"Thank you," Guin said, after they had stepped outside.

"What for?" Glen asked her.

"I don't know. Just for being you."

"No problem," said Glen, smiling. "It's the only way I know how to be."

Guin smiled back at him. Being with Glen was so easy.

"Well, I should get going," he said. "Got some more work to do."

They slowly walked to the parking lot.

"Where did you park?"

"Just over there," said Guin, pointing a little ways away.

Glen followed her to the Mini.

"Thanks for walking me to my car," Guin said, smiling up at him.

"My pleasure," he replied.

They stood there for several seconds. It was dark out, and you could see the stars and the moon. A breeze rustled Guin's hair, blowing a curl across her face. Glen reached out and gently took the errant curl between his fingers, holding it for a few seconds before placing it behind her ear. Guin looked up at him.

She opened her mouth to speak, and Glen slowly lowered his head. The next thing Guin knew, they were kissing.

It had been months since Guin had been kissed, and she hadn't realized how much she had missed it. Glen's kiss was at first tentative but grew more passionate as Guin kissed him back. After only a minute, though, he pulled away, leaving Guin confused.

"I should go," he said.

"Okay," said Guin.

They stood there for several more seconds.

"Whoever it was who stood you up is an idiot."

"Who says I got stood up?" said Guin.

He glanced down at her dress, then back up at her face.

"I should get going," he repeated.

"Okay," said Guin.

Again, neither moved nor said anything.

"Well, goodnight," Glen finally said. "I'll text you tomorrow about the house."

He turned and made his way across the parking lot.

CHAPTER 21

Guin woke up the next morning with a pounding headache.

"Ugh," she said, sitting up and holding her head. "I'm such a lightweight."

Fauna walked across Guin's legs and started rubbing herself against Guin's torso. Guin stroked the cat, then gently moved her aside and got up. She went to the bathroom, splashed some cold water on her face, then swallowed two ibuprofen.

She made her way to the kitchen and started boiling water for coffee. While she was waiting for the water to boil, she opened a can of cat food and scooped the contents into Fauna's bowl. Then she leaned against the counter. The sun was still below the horizon, but the sky was starting to lighten, and it looked to be a clear day. Guin thought about going for a beach walk, but she had work to do. That is if you called reading a bodice ripper work. She also was determined to call Nicky DiDio and wanted to speak with Craig.

She finished fixing her coffee, then took a sip, closing her eyes. Was there anything better than the aroma of freshly brewed coffee? Perhaps only the smell of sea air.

She glanced at the clock on the microwave.

"Screw it," she said. "Just a quick beach walk. Then I'll get to work."

She took another sip of her coffee, then hurried down

the hall to her bedroom. Ten minutes later, she was out the door.

She drove over to Bowman's Beach and parked. There were only a few cars in the lot. A good sign. She jumped out of the Mini and hastily applied bug spray, to ward off the noseeums. Then she walked down to the beach.

As she made her way, she thought about Lenny. She had meant to arrange a lunch date with him, but she had yet to follow up. Now she felt guilty.

"I'll call him as soon as I get home and see if he's available for brunch this weekend," she vowed.

She made her way down to the wrack line and began searching for shells. She had been walking for almost half an hour when she looked up and noticed a familiar figure a couple of yards ahead of her.

"Lenny!" she called, waving to him.

He waved back and Guin walked quickly over to him.

"I was just thinking about you!" she said. "Were your ears burning?"

"And here I thought it was bug bites," he replied.

Guin smiled.

"I'm sorry about not calling you."

Lenny waved a hand.

"I know you're busy. It's okay."

"It's not okay," said Guin. "And I want to make it up to you. How about brunch this Saturday or Sunday?"

"Don't you have plans?"

"Nope. I'm all yours."

"I'll need to check my calendar," he replied.

"Okay," said Guin. "Give me a call or send me a text and let me know if you can squeeze me in."

They walked down the beach together, neither saying

anything for several minutes.

"So how are things? Any news?"

Guin sighed.

"No. And the detective's been zero help, as usual."

"Speaking of the detective, what's up with the two of you?"

"Nothing," said Guin.

She had told Lenny of her feelings for the detective that spring and how the detective had stopped communicating with her.

"Actually, he's seeing someone."

"Sorry about that, kid. But as the saying goes, there are plenty of fish in the sea."

"Maybe in the sea," said Guin, "but not on Sanibel."

"What about that photographer fellow, the cute one?"

"Glen?"

"You know some other cute photographer?"

"He's just a friend, Len."

They continued walking.

"You want my advice?" asked Lenny.

"Sure, why not?"

"Tell the detective how you feel about him."

Guin made a face.

"What good would that do?"

"You never know," said Lenny.

"It's pointless, Len. He's made his choice."

"Has he asked this woman to marry him?"

"Not that I know of."

"Then fight for him."

Guin made another face.

"Look, Guinivere, you don't get a lot of chances for happiness in this life. If the detective is the guy for you, you need to tell him."

"But…"

"No buts. Next time you see him, tell him how you feel."

"Maybe," said Guin.

Guin got home from the beach a little before nine and took a quick shower. Then she checked her messages. There was a text from Craig, asking her to call him.

She immediately dialed his number.

"What's up?"

"And a good morning to you, too," he replied.

"Sorry, good morning," said Guin. "What's up?"

"First, you've gotta promise me you won't go digging if I tell you something."

"You know I can't promise that," said Guin.

Craig sighed.

"I mean it, Guin. What I'm going to say to you, you have to leave it alone, or let me handle it."

"Then why are you telling me?" said Guin, slightly annoyed.

"Because I rather you heard it from me and let me handle it."

Guin rolled her eyes.

"So you going to tell me this piece of news or what?"

There was silence on the other end of the line for several seconds.

"Fine. You'd probably find out about it anyway. Funt owed a bunch of money to Big Lou."

"The guy who does all those commercials on the radio?" said Guin, confused.

"Different Big Lou, though he's on meds, too."

Craig chuckled at his little joke.

"So who's this other Big Lou?"

"Lou Antinori, Southwest Florida's very own drug kingpin."

"Is that what it says on his business card?"

"Very funny," said Craig. "No. Officially, he's a developer. Owns a bunch of real estate and contracting businesses around Florida, mostly in the Fort Myers area."

"So what kind of drugs are we talking about?"

"You name it, he's got it or can get it."

"Does that include opioids?"

"Opioids, coke, dope, you name it. If there's a market for it, he'll sell it to you, for the right price."

"And you say Funt owed him money?"

"Apparently a lot of money."

"And you think Big Lou killed him?"

"I don't have any proof, but not only did Funt owe him money, he was supposedly selling Lou's stuff behind Lou's back."

"Sounds like a motive for murder to me," said Guin. "Do the police know?"

"Where do you think I heard it from?"

Guin was dying to know who Craig's source was, but she knew he wouldn't tell her.

"So are they going to arrest him?"

"Doubtful."

"Why not?"

"First, they need to prove Lou did it or that he was behind the hit, if in fact it was a hit."

"And they can't?"

"Big Lou says he knows nothing about it."

"Of course he does," said Guin. "So how do I talk to Big Lou?"

"*You* don't," said Craig.

"Come on, Craig! You can't tell me this stuff and not expect me to want to talk to the guy! Frank was found in my house, remember?"

"Which is why I hesitated to tell you. I didn't want you

charging over there and asking him a bunch of nosy questions. Big Lou isn't exactly fond of reporters. And I don't think he'd take kindly to being asked if he sold drugs or murdered someone."

"Come on, Craig. You know me. It's not like I'd say to him, 'Hey, Lou, you order a hit on Frank Funt?'"

"Let me talk to him."

"Last I checked, you were also a reporter."

"A fishing reporter."

"Seriously?" said Guin. "We both know you're an award-winning crime reporter, as you and Ginny often remind me."

"Yeah, but I'm officially a fishing reporter now, and Big Lou loves to fish."

"Of course he does," said Guin.

One of these days she needed to learn how to fish. But the thought of spending all day on a boat, waiting for a bite, only to throw whatever she caught back in the water, had no appeal to her. Not when she could be taking a boat to the Ten Thousand Islands and looking for shells.

"So, where is Big Lou anyway?"

"I'm not saying."

"You know I'm going to find out," said Guin. "May as well just tell me."

"I mean it, Guin. You don't want to mess with Big Lou. Let me handle it."

"At least let me come with you."

"I'll think about it," said Craig. "So, any news on your end?"

"I spoke with Nicholas DiDio, the father of Funt's former project manager."

"And?"

"And he confirmed that Funt and his son, Nicky, had a falling out."

"You speak with the son?"

"Not yet," said Guin. "I'm going to call him right after I hang up with you. His father said he works over at Sunshine now"

"Interesting," said Craig.

"I thought so," said Guin. "Speaking of Sunshine, I want to speak with Tony Del Sole, find out what he knew about Frank and Funt and the Son Construction."

"Let me know if you need my help. These contractors can be hard to pin down, and a lot of them don't like dealing with women."

"I think I can handle him," said Guin. "Just let me know if you hear from Big Lou or anything else."

"Will do," said Craig.

"Hey, I almost forgot, you speak with Jimbo?"

"Not yet."

"My offer still stands if you get cold feet."

"My feet are never cold," said Craig.

"Okay," said Guin. "I need to go. I have a call coming in. Talk to you later?"

Craig mumbled something, and they ended the call.

Guin saw she had a new voicemail and called in.

"Hey, I just wanted to say I'm sorry about last night." It was Glen. "I know I was out of line. You just looked so amazing in that dress and well... Anyway, still friends? And let me know when you want to stop by the house. I think you'll be pleased with the progress."

Guin smiled, then sent him a text: "Still friends."

Glen replied with a smiley face.

There was also a text message from Shelly.

"You coming to the BBQ Sunday?"

Guin had forgotten to officially reply.

She gazed down at her calendar. It was empty, as usual.

"I'll be there," she wrote.

CHAPTER 22

Guin dialed Nicky DiDio's number.

"Nick DiDio."

"Hi there," said Guin. "My name's Guinivere Jones. I'm a reporter with the *San-Cap Sun-Times*, and I'm doing a story on Frank Funt, Jr. I understand you used to work for Funt and the Son Construction, and I was hoping you could spare me a few minutes of your time."

"I'm kinda busy."

"It will only take a few minutes."

"Fine. You've got a minute. Go."

"Actually, I was hoping we could meet in person. Do you have some time later today? I could meet you over at Sunshine Builders."

"Look, I already spoke to the cops. I've got nothing further to say about Frank."

"Did they ask you who might want Frank out of the way?"

"Yeah, and I'll tell you what I told them: Frank was a screwup. He could be charming as hell one minute, then moody the next. He made people all sorts of promises, and he rarely kept them. And he was no good with money. And yeah, there were probably a dozen people who wanted to kill him, or wring his neck, myself included. But I had nothing to do with his death."

"Got it," said Guin. "Still, if I could meet with you for just a few minutes…"

Nick sighed.

"Fine. Meet me over at Sunshine at four. But I can only give you a few minutes. I've got an appointment at five."

"I understand," said Guin. "Thank you, Mr. DiDio."

"And call me Nick. Mr. DiDio is my father."

"Thank you, Nick. See you at four."

They ended the call and Guin looked down at Fauna, who had curled up in her lap and fallen asleep. She smiled down at the sleeping feline and stroked her back. Then she looked up at her computer monitor. There were several things she could be working on, but she knew Ginny wanted that book review ASAP. So she gently removed Fauna and retrieved her copy of *The Belle of Sanibel.*

Guin couldn't believe it was nearly one o'clock. She had been so busy reading the book, she had no idea it was past noon. Though now that she was aware of it, she realized she was hungry. She made her way to the kitchen and opened the refrigerator. Even though she had just gone shopping, she didn't like any of her options.

What she was craving was one of Jean-Luc's signature sandwiches. Without a second thought, she grabbed her bag and her keys and headed out the door.

"*Bonjour!*" called Jean-Luc, as soon as he saw Guin.

"*Bonjour!*" replied Guin. "How was your vacation?"

"Very good," said Jean-Luc, the owner of Jean-Luc's Bakery, the best (and only) French boulangerie, patisserie, and sandwich shop on Sanibel.

Jean-Luc hailed from France and had gone back there for

six weeks over the summer, closing the shop and leaving Guin and his other regulars longing for his buttery croissants and decadent pastries. But now he was back, and in a couple of months there would be a line out the door. For now, though, Guin was the only customer in the shop.

"And what can I get for you today, Ms. Guinivere?" he asked Guin, in his charming French accent.

Guin looked at the case, which held a variety of readymade sandwiches and pastries.

"Everything looks so good. Say, is that one of those crepe thingies?" she said, spying a round griddle.

"*Oui*," said Jean-Luc. "I brought her back with me from France. I thought I'd try my hand at making crepes."

Guin could feel herself salivating. She loved crepes.

"Would you like me to make one for you? They are not officially on the menu, but…"

"Yes, please!" said Guin.

"What would you like in it?"

"What are my choices?"

Before Jean-Luc could answer, the bell above the door jingled.

"*Bonjour*, detective!" called Jean-Luc.

Guin froze.

"I was just about to make this fair lady a crepe. Would you like one, too?"

Guin turned to look at Detective O'Loughlin.

"I'm fine with a sandwich," replied the detective, looking at Jean-Luc.

"These crepes, they are like a sandwich," explained Jean-Luc. "They are savory crepes, or as we say in France, *crêpes salés*. They are also referred to as galettes. You make them with buckwheat and fill them with ham and cheese and egg or whatever you desire."

"Sounds delicious," said Guin.

"Fine," said the detective. "You can make me one of those savory things."

"*Bon*! I will make you both the traditional *jambon-fromage*, a ham-and-cheese galette, with I think some spinach and onion. Does that sound good?"

Guin nodded vigorously.

She watched as Jean-Luc spread the buckwheat batter evenly across the griddle, then placed the chopped bits of ham and cheese on top after he had flipped it over, finally adding the sautéed spinach and onion before folding the crepe and sliding it onto a plate.

"*Et voilà!*" said Jean-Luc, handing the plate to Guin.

"*Merci!*" said Guin, closing her eyes and smelling it.

"And now for you, detective!" said Jean-Luc, repeating the process.

"Thanks," said the detective, after Jean-Luc handed him a plate.

"And what can I get the two of you to drink?"

"A LaCroix for me," said Guin.

"Make that two," said the detective.

Jean-Luc handed them their sparkling waters, and Guin asked him how much for the meal.

"The crepes are on the house," said Jean-Luc, "as I am still practicing."

"You don't have to do that!" said Guin.

Jean-Luc waved her off.

The detective stepped up and handed him some money. "For the drinks."

"*Merci*, detective," said Jean-Luc.

"I was going to pay for that," said Guin.

Jean-Luc handed the detective his change.

"Keep it," said the detective.

"*Merci encore!*" said Jean-Luc.

"You have a minute?" the detective asked Guin.

"I will be in the back," said Jean-Luc.

He winked at Guin, then disappeared.

"Sure," said Guin.

They took a seat by the window, under the fan.

"About the other night," began the detective. "I'm sorry I was late and didn't text you."

Guin ate her galette, staring down at her plate.

"Guin, please."

Guin stopped eating and looked up.

"What exactly is it you want me to say?"

"That you accept my apology," said the detective.

"Fine, I accept your apology," said Guin, cutting into her galette and popping a piece into her mouth.

She watched as the detective cut a large piece of his galette and began to chew.

"Not bad, right?"

The detective nodded.

They ate in silence, until they were nearly done with their food.

"So," said Guin, taking a sip of her sparkling water. "Was there anything else you wanted to get off your chest?"

The detective looked at her. As usual, his expression was hard to read.

"You know I care about you," he finally said.

"You sure have a funny way of showing it."

The detective rubbed his face.

"You're not going to make this easy for me, are you?"

"Nope."

Guin took another sip of her LaCroix.

"I did think that after our outing, things would be different between us. But then Maggie called, and I…"

He stared down at his plate, at a loss for words.

"Do you love her?"

"Maggie?" he said, sounding surprised.

"Unless there's some other former girlfriend you haven't told me about."

"No, just Maggie."

Again there was a pause.

"So answer the question: Are you in love with her, with Maggie?"

"No," he said. "But I care about her."

"Like you care about me."

"No," said the detective. "It's different."

"Different good or different bad?"

"Just different."

"So if you're not in love with her, why are you with her?"

"Like I said, I care about her. And she's alone down here."

"She's not a child, detective, nor a stray cat. She can take care of herself. Didn't you say she had family up north?"

"Yes, but…"

"I'm done," said Guin, getting up.

The detective was about to say something when the bell above the door jangled and an older couple entered.

"*Bonjour*, Monsieur and Madame MacDonald!" called Jean-Luc. "So nice to see you! Did you just return to the island?"

"So nice to see you, too, Jean-Luc!" said Mrs. MacDonald. "We've missed you!"

"She means we've missed those chocolate croissants of yours," said Mr. MacDonald.

Jean-Luc smiled.

"I should go, too," said the detective.

As they turned to leave, Jean-Luc called out to them.

"Leaving without dessert?"

Guin paused.

"I saved a mocha eclair just for you!"

Guin felt torn.

"I will put it in a box for you, and you can eat it later!"

Guin turned and went over to the counter.

"You know I can't turn down a mocha éclair."

"I do," said Jean-Luc, a mischievous grin on his face.

He removed the mocha eclair from the display case and placed it in a little white box.

"Here you go!" he said, handing it to her.

"*Merci*," said Guin.

She reached into her bag and pulled out her wallet, handing him some money.

"*Merci à vous*," said Jean-Luc. "*Bonne journée!*"

Guin hurried out the door, hoping to catch the detective. He was standing next to his car, on his phone. Guin waited until he got off. He didn't look happy.

"What's up?" she asked.

"I need to go," he replied.

"Anything serious?"

"Police business."

"Before you go, I should tell you, I spoke with Nick DiDio, Funt's former project manager a little while ago. I'm meeting with him at four."

"I doubt that," said the detective.

"Oh?" said Guin, slightly annoyed. "Why, did you arrest him?"

"No. DiDio fell off a roof a little while ago and was taken to the hospital. So he's not going to be speaking to anyone for a while."

"Oh no!" said Guin. "Is he going to be okay?"

"I don't know."

He opened the door to his car.

"Will you let me know if he's all right?" asked Guin. "Which hospital did they take him to?"

"I have to go," said the detective.

This time Guin didn't stop him.

CHAPTER 23

Guin knew it was foolish, and she might even get arrested, but she had to follow the detective, if only to find out which hospital Nick DiDio had been brought to. Chances are it was the one closest to Sanibel, but she couldn't be sure.

She followed the detective along Periwinkle, wishing her purple Mini wasn't so noticeable. Fortunately, there was a car between them, but he had to know she was following him. She just hoped he didn't put on his siren.

As if on cue, he did, veering into the left lane, causing cars on both sides of Periwinkle to pull over. For a second, Guin thought about speeding up and following him, but she knew that would be stupid. Instead, she waited until traffic began moving again. Fortunately, as it wasn't yet rush hour, it didn't take her long to get to the Causeway.

As the Health Park was the closest medical facility to Sanibel, she pulled in there. Sure enough, she spotted the detective's car in one of the spots reserved for emergency vehicles. She pulled into a nearby spot and made her way inside. There was no sign of the detective, just a woman speaking with the receptionist.

Guin waited patiently for the woman to finish, then she approached the desk.

"May I help you?" asked the receptionist.

"Yes," said Guin, adopting an expression of nervous

concern. "My boyfriend was just brought here in serious condition. He fell off a roof."

She knew it was a gamble to pretend she was Nick's girlfriend (and a lie), but she had used a similar tactic before, and it had worked.

"I'm so sorry," said the woman behind the desk. "What's your boyfriend's name?"

"Nick," said Guin. "Nick DiDio."

The woman looked up at her.

"Did you say Nicholas DiDio?"

"That's right," said Guin.

"And you say you're his girlfriend?"

Guin nodded.

The receptionist had an odd look on her face.

"Is something the matter?" asked Guin.

"It's just that there was another lady here, just a few minutes ago, saying *she* was Mr. DiDio's girlfriend."

Guin could have kicked herself. Of course he could have a girlfriend, or a wife. Why hadn't she thought of that?

"Do you recall her name?"

"I believe it was Phoebe," said the woman.

"Phoebe?!" said Guin, unable to hide her shock. "Was her last name Costanza?"

"That's right," said the woman. "Do you know her?"

Guin nodded.

"And she said she was Mr. DiDio's *girlfriend*?"

"That's what she said. And I told her what I'm going to tell you: No visitors. Just immediate family."

"But…" said Guin.

"Sorry, those are the rules," said the woman.

"Can you at least tell me how he is? Is he going to be okay?"

The woman looked over at her computer and typed something.

"He just got out of surgery. If you want, you can give me your information, and I can ask one of the doctors to contact you."

"That would be wonderful," said Guin.

"Here," said the woman, handing Guin a clipboard with a form. "Fill this out."

"Thank you," said Guin.

She stood to the side and filled it out. Then she handed the clipboard back to the receptionist.

"Tell the doctor he can call or text me."

"It could be a while," said the woman. "But I'm sure someone will contact you."

"Thank you," said Guin. "Is there someplace I can wait?"

"It might be best if you returned later."

"Please?" said Guin, giving the woman an imploring look.

The receptionist sighed.

"There's a waiting area upstairs, third floor. Take the elevator over there," she said, pointing.

She handed Guin a visitor badge.

"Thank you," said Guin.

She donned the badge and walked quickly to the elevators.

One of the cars opened a few seconds later, and a half-dozen or so people got out. Guin looked to see if Phoebe or the detective were among them. They were not. She got in and pressed the button for the third floor. There was no sign of the detective or Phoebe in the waiting area. She found a quiet alcove and called Craig.

After several rings, he picked up.

"Hey, I'm at the hospital," she whispered.

"Are you okay?" Craig whispered back.

"I'm fine," Guin replied, still keeping her voice low. "Nick DiDio, Funt's former project manager, had an accident. Fell off a roof and was brought to the Health Park.

I'm trying to find out what happened."

"Be careful," said Craig.

Guin looked around.

"I am. I'm just worried there's a connection."

"A connection?"

"I spoke with DiDio earlier today," said Guin, continuing to keep an eye out for the detective and Phoebe. "He was going to meet with me this afternoon, over at Sunshine. Then shortly after, boom! He falls off a roof and winds up in the hospital."

"It could be just a coincidence," said Craig.

"It could be, but get this: When I got here, the woman at the front desk said there had been another woman asking to see DiDio. And you'll never guess who: Phoebe Costanza!"

Craig whistled.

"Right?" said Guin.

"You think she was involved?"

"I don't know. But it seems suspicious. First Funt, now DiDio? There's gotta be a connection."

"Didn't you tell me you saw her with Tony Del Sole?"

"I did, over at the Pecking Order."

There was silence for several seconds.

"You think she was seeing all three of them?"

"It's possible," said Craig.

"Huh," said Guin. "I wonder if Nick or Tony were the jealous type. Maybe one of them found out about Phoebe and Frank and bumped Frank off."

"That seems a bit extreme, don't you think? Is this Phoebe worth killing for?"

Well, when he put it that way.

"Or maybe Phoebe got rid of Frank," said Guin, her wheels turning. "Maybe she and Nick were in it together. And then Tony found out and made sure something happened to Nick!"

"Or maybe Phoebe and Tony were in cahoots," said Craig.

"But what was in it for Phoebe?" said Guin. "Maybe Phoebe's one of those black widow types. You know, women who get men to fall in love with them and make them the beneficiary of their life insurance policy, then knock them off, making it look like an accident."

"I think you've seen too many of those cable movies," said Craig.

"Maybe," said Guin. "But we should find out if Funt had a life insurance policy and if Phoebe was the beneficiary."

"I'll make some inquiries," said Craig.

"Thanks. Though what's her connection to DiDio?"

Suddenly she spied the detective.

"Hey, Craig, I've gotta go. Call you later?"

"I'll be here," he replied.

Guin ended the call and shoved her phone back into her bag.

"Detective!" she called, a little too loudly, quickly walking over to where he was standing.

He was with a uniformed policeman, who Guin didn't recognize. The detective frowned.

"Could I speak with you for a minute?" she asked him.

The detective looked at the officer.

"Would you excuse us for a minute?"

The uniformed officer nodded.

The detective took Guin's arm and ushered her to the opposite side of the waiting room.

"Please tell me you didn't follow me here."

"Just tell me, is Nick DiDio going to be okay?"

"He's in critical condition."

"So what happened? You said he fell off a roof? That seems a bit odd."

The detective ran a hand over his face.

"According to one of the guys working at the site, DiDio was inspecting something up on the roof. Next thing anybody knew, he was lying on the ground, unconscious."

"So was it an accident?"

"That's what they said."

"But from your tone and the look on your face, I take it you don't believe that," said Guin.

The detective didn't answer.

"Is he badly injured?"

"He's lucky to be alive."

"Does his father know?"

The detective looked at her.

"I spoke with Mr. DiDio the other day, when I was looking for Nick," Guin explained.

"He's been contacted," said the detective.

"What about Phoebe Costanza? I heard she was here, claiming to be Nick's girlfriend."

The detective raised an eyebrow.

"Do you happen to know if Funt had a will or a life insurance policy?" Guin continued.

"And why do you want to know that?" asked the detective.

"Did he leave anything to Phoebe?"

The detective didn't reply.

"Can you tell me anything?" Guin asked, frustrated. "What about Tony Del Sole?"

"What about him?"

"Did you check to see if he was okay?"

"I know I'm going to regret asking this," said the detective, "but why do you think the police should check on Mr. Del Sole?"

"Well, if Phoebe knocked off Frank, who she was dating, and then tried to get rid of Nick, who she was also seeing, Tony Del Sole could be next!"

"And why would Ms. Costanza be getting rid of contractors?"

"Isn't it obvious?" said Guin. "To get their money!"

"You have a very active imagination," said the detective.

"Come on!" said Guin. "It makes perfect sense."

"To you, maybe," said the detective. "If it makes you feel any better, we spoke to Mr. Del Sole a little while ago. He seemed perfectly fine."

"Sure, for now," said Guin. "Did you ask him if he had a life insurance policy, and if Phoebe was the beneficiary?"

The detective rubbed his face.

"Fine. Don't ask," said Guin. "But what about Funt? Did you check to see if he had a policy?"

"We did," replied the detective.

"And?"

"It lapsed," said the detective. "Due to nonpayment."

"Oh," said Guin. Well, so much for her theory.

"But was Phoebe the beneficiary? Maybe she didn't know it had lapsed."

"Ms. Costanza was not the beneficiary."

"Who was?" asked Guin.

"His father."

"His father?"

The detective nodded.

"Huh," said Guin. "So Phoebe got nothing?"

"Not a cent, at least in terms of life insurance."

Guin was about to ask the detective another question, but before she could the uniformed officer came over and whispered something in the detective's ear.

The detective nodded and looked over at Guin.

"I need to go."

"But I have more questions," said Guin.

"They'll have to wait."

Guin opened her mouth to speak but was silenced with a look from the detective.

"Fine," she said.

She watched as the officer escorted the detective over to where an elderly man was standing.

CHAPTER 24

Guin watched as the detective spoke to the elderly man. It had to be Nick DiDio's father. She was tempted to sneak a bit closer, to try to overhear them, but she knew that if the detective caught her, he'd shoo her away—or have her removed from the hospital. Instead, she bided her time, tucked away in a corner of the waiting area.

As she was surreptitiously watching the detective, her phone began to vibrate. It was a text from her brother, Lance.

"I'll call you later," she replied, then shoved the phone back in her pocket.

Ten minutes went by, and she was feeling restless. How long could they talk for? And she really needed to use the bathroom. She bit her lip. She wanted to speak with the man, if he was, in fact, Nick DiDio's father. But her bladder was about to burst.

She hurried to the restroom, but when she returned the detective and the man were both gone. Though the uniformed officer was still there.

Guin went up to him.

"Excuse me," she said. "That man Detective O'Loughlin was speaking with, did you happen to see where he went?"

"I'm sorry, ma'am, I'm not allowed to say," said the officer.

"I see," said Guin. "Can you at least tell me where the

detective went? Did he take the man with him?"

"Sorry, ma'am, I—."

"Let me guess, you can't say."

The officer nodded.

She turned and headed to the desk.

"Excuse me," Guin said to the woman seated there. "I'm trying to find out how my boyfriend, Nicky DiDio, is doing. I heard he just got out of surgery. Can you help me?"

She did her best to look like a worried girlfriend.

"Here's a form," said the woman. "Fill it out and give it back to me."

Guin was about to say she had already filled out a form downstairs, but she just took the clipboard and pen and thanked the woman. She took a seat nearby and proceeded to fill out the form as best she could.

"Here," she said, a few minutes later, handing over the clipboard.

The woman took it and quickly reviewed the form, looking up at Guin a bit suspiciously.

"We just started dating a few weeks ago," Guin explained. "We're still getting to know each other."

The woman didn't say anything, but Guin knew that look.

"I'd really appreciate it if someone would just let me know how he is and when I can see him," Guin said, sweetly.

"Someone will be in touch," stated the woman.

"Thank you," said Guin.

She smiled, then stepped away from the desk.

She glanced around the room one more time but didn't see the elderly man or the detective, just the uniformed officer. She thought about waiting a bit longer but finally decided to go. If there was news, hopefully someone from the hospital would call her.

Around six-thirty, Guin made herself some chicken and green beans. When her food was ready, she took her plate to the living room, sat down on the couch, and turned on *The Great British Baking Show* on Netflix. She had only taken a couple of bites when her brother's number flashed up on her caller ID.

"Hey, there," she said, pausing the television. "Can I call you back in a bit? I'm eating dinner."

"I'm heading out in ten. Owen and I are having dinner with one of his artists. Can I call you when I get back?"

"As long as it's not too late."

"I know: No calls after ten o'clock."

Guin smiled.

"If you get home too late, just call me in the morning."

"Fine, though I have a busy day tomorrow."

"Whatever," said Guin. "Have fun at dinner!"

They ended the call and Guin pressed play on the remote.

The bakers were making cookies, or biscuits, as they were called in England. And, as she watched, Guin felt an overwhelming desire to bake cookies herself. She continued watching the episode until the end, then she took her plate into the kitchen and took out the ingredients for making chocolate chip cookies, which she always kept on hand, chocolate chip cookies being one of her favorite things to make and eat.

She preheated the oven to 375 degrees, then began to measure and stir. A short time later, the cookies were ready. She placed them on a cooling rack and took one. She closed her eyes as the warm chocolate coated her tongue. They were so good. She reached for another one but stopped herself.

"I should give some of these away," she said aloud.

It was nearly ten o'clock, and Guin was in bed reading *The Belle of Sanibel* when her phone started to vibrate.

It was Lance.

"Hey," she said, picking up.

"Did I wake you?" he asked.

"No, I'm still up. How was dinner?"

"It was all right. At least this artist was amusing."

Lance's husband, Owen, ran a gallery in Chelsea and was always entertaining artists.

"So, what's up?" asked Guin. "Anything new to report?"

"No, just checking in. Mom told me what happened, with the contractor. Frankly, I'm a bit insulted."

"Insulted?" said Guin.

"That you didn't tell me first."

"Sorry," said Guin. "I've been a bit distracted."

She tried to remember what she had told her mother about Frank, but she couldn't remember. So much had happened.

"So, do they know how he died?"

"Supposedly a drug overdose. Opioids."

"Wow, it seems like opioid abuse is everywhere, even on Sanibel."

"Yeah," said Guin.

"So, you find someone to finish your house?"

"I did."

"Good guy?"

"I think so."

"Well, let me know how it goes. Will they be done before you have to move?"

"I hope so."

"Anything else going on that I should know about?"

Guin looked up at the ceiling. There were so many things she wanted to tell Lance, but she didn't want to worry him. Nor did she want a lecture.

"Nope," she said, looking back down.

"Okay," he said. "You know if you ever want to talk, about anything, I'm here for you."

"I know," said Guin. "Miss you."

"I miss you, too," said Lance. "You going to come home for Thanksgiving?"

It was the same question every fall since she had moved to Sanibel. In previous years, she had begrudgingly returned home. But this year there wasn't anything or anyone keeping her on Sanibel over the holiday. And she thought it might be nice to spend some time with her brother.

"I'm thinking about it," said Guin.

"Well you know it would make your mother very happy to have both of us there."

"I know," said Guin.

She let out a yawn.

"I'll let you get some sleep."

"Thanks," said Guin.

She let out another yawn.

"I'll give you a call next week."

"Sounds good. And Guin?"

"Yes, Lance?"

"I love you. And I really do hope you'll come home for Thanksgiving. You know you can always stay with us if you don't want to crash with Mom and Philip."

"I know," said Guin. "And I love you, too. Say hi to Owen for me."

"Will do," said Lance.

They said goodnight, then ended the call.

Guin woke up Friday morning and turned on her phone. When she got back from the bathroom, she saw her message light was flashing. There was a text from Craig, asking her to call him.

"Good morning," she said, as soon as he picked up. "What's up?"

"I got some more information."

"You speak to Big Lou?"

"Not yet. He's away until tomorrow. But I asked his assistant to have him call me."

"So what's the news?"

"According to my source in the medical examiner's office, the opioids found in Funt's system were administered at different times."

"What does that mean?"

"It means that more than one person may have been responsible for Funt's death."

As Guin was processing that information, Craig continued.

"My source said the oxycodone had probably been taken orally, earlier in the day. But the fentanyl had likely been administered intravenously, a short time before he died."

"Could Funt have injected himself with the fentanyl?" asked Guin.

"It's possible. But why would he give himself such a large dose, especially if he had already taken oxycodone? Unless he was trying to kill himself."

"So chances are, someone injected him with the fentanyl, to make it look like a drug overdose. That would explain the track mark on his arm."

"There's more," said Craig.

"More?"

"There were contusions on his body."

"Where?"

"Around his neck and groin. Sounds like he was kneed, then put in a headlock."

"Huh," said Guin. "So you think there was more than one person involved? One person incapacitated him while someone else shot him up?"

"It's possible," said Craig.

"Did your source reveal anything else?"

"No, just what was in the final autopsy report."

The autopsy report, which Guin had asked the detective for but never received.

"Well, thanks for letting me know."

She tried to envision what had happened.

"I can hear those wheels turning," said Craig.

"Sorry. I was just trying to visualize the scene. Whoever did it had to have been pretty strong."

"Agreed," said Craig.

"Though that still leaves a lot of suspects."

Guin heard someone talking to Craig in the background, no doubt Betty.

"That was Betty. She wanted to know if you were free for dinner tonight. She's making cinnamon chicken."

"I'd love to join you!" said Guin. "And, as it happens, I just baked a mess of chocolate chip cookies."

"I can't remember when I last had a freshly baked chocolate chip cookie," said Craig. "Bring 'em on over!"

"Just make sure it's okay with Betty," said Guin, knowing that Betty had Craig on a strict low-sugar diet.

"It'll be fine," he said.

"Just ask her. I don't want to be the cause of any marital fights."

Craig grumbled.

"I need to go," said Guin. "Thanks for the info. Let me know if you get through to Big Lou."

"Will do," said Craig. "And dinner's at six."

"I'll be there," said Guin.

CHAPTER 25

Guin brewed coffee and made herself breakfast. When she was done, she brushed her teeth and got dressed. The whole time she kept thinking about the new information Craig had given her.

"I think it's time I had a little chat with Phoebe Costanza," she told Fauna, who was lounging on the bed.

The cat looked up at Guin, then closed her eyes and went back to sleep. Guin shook her head. Ah, to be a cat.

She retrieved Phoebe's number from her contact list and pressed the green call button. The phone rang several times. Finally, Phoebe picked up.

"What do you want?" she asked Guin.

"I just want to talk, Phoebe. Is there someplace we could meet?"

"What's there to talk about?"

"Well, Frank for one."

"I already talked to the cops."

"I know," said Guin. "But don't you want to know who killed Frank?"

"I know who killed Frank."

"You do?"

"I'm talking to her right now."

Guin silently counted to eight.

"Look, Phoebe, I swear to you, I had nothing to do with

Frank's death, but I have some information that might help us figure out who did kill him."

"What kind of information?"

"Meet me for lunch, and I'll tell you."

"Where?"

"How about Gramma Dot's? That's near your and Frank's place, right?"

"When are we talking about?"

"Say today at noon?"

"I guess that's okay," said Phoebe. "But I've got an appointment off-island at one-thirty."

"No problem," said Guin. "See you at noon."

"You're paying, right?"

Guin sighed inwardly.

"Sure."

They ended the call, and Guin began to formulate her plan.

Before Guin knew it, it was time to meet Phoebe. She was running late, but, fortunately, traffic wasn't bad, and she made good time to the Sanibel Marina, where Gramma Dot's was located.

When she got there, just a few minutes after twelve, she asked for a table for two outside. A waitress came over after she had been seated, and Guin ordered an Arnold Palmer. As she waited, she stared at all the boats, a handful of which were for sale or rent.

Phoebe showed up ten minutes later, not apologizing for her tardiness.

"So, what do you want?" she asked Guin.

"Won't you have a seat?" Guin said, gesturing to the chair opposite her.

Phoebe pulled out the chair and sat. A few seconds later,

their server came over.

"Can I get you something to drink?" she asked Phoebe.

"Iced tea, unsweetened," she replied. "So?" she said to Guin, after the server had departed. "What was so important?"

"Why don't we decide what we're going to have first, then we can talk," said Guin.

"Fine by me," said Phoebe.

They stared at their menus, then put them down. Neither said a word. A couple of minutes later, the waitress returned with Phoebe's iced tea.

"You two know what you want?" she asked them.

"I'll have the coconut curried lobster salad," said Phoebe.

"Make that two," said Guin.

She handed the server her menu and Phoebe did the same.

"Thanks," said the woman.

Phoebe took a noisy sip of her iced tea.

"So did Frank take painkillers?" Guin asked her.

"The detective asked me the same question."

"And what did you tell him?"

"That he took OxyContin when his leg was bothering him."

"And had it been bothering him recently?"

"Frank's leg was always bothering him."

"So did he have a prescription?"

Phoebe looked at Guin.

"How else would he get the pills?"

"There are other ways to get prescription drugs," Guin replied.

Phoebe didn't say anything.

"Did he ever take fentanyl?"

"Like I told that detective, Frank didn't exactly consult with me about his medical issues or what stuff he took."

"Do you know if Frank ever shared his pills?"

"What do you mean by 'share'? You accusing Frank of being a dealer?"

"I was just wondering if maybe Frank occasionally gave or sold people some of his pills. Like, if you told me you had a headache, I'd offer you one of my ibuprofen caplets."

Phoebe looked like she was mulling it over. Finally, she spoke.

"I couldn't say."

"Any idea who might have borne a grudge against Frank?"

"You want the short list or the long list?"

"The short list is fine."

"That plumber, for one" said Phoebe.

"You mean Mr. Leakey?"

"Yeah, he's the one. Bad name for a plumber, don't you think? Anyway, he was always getting into it with Frank, accused Frank of welching on him, which was absurd."

"I see," said Guin. "Anyone else?"

"That couple, the Millers. They were badmouthing Frank all over the island, saying he destroyed their house."

"I doubt the Millers had anything to do with Frank's death," said Guin. "They're both in their seventies."

"Oh yeah?" said Phoebe. "So's my pops, and he could take Frank in an arm-wrestling match."

Guin tried to picture Abe Miller arm-wrestling Funt but couldn't.

"What about Nick DiDio?"

"Nicky? Nicky and Frank had their issues, but Nicky would never hurt Frank."

Guin noticed the suddenly tender tone in Phoebe's voice.

"I understand he and Frank had a big falling out, and that Frank owed him money," said Guin.

"It was all just a big misunderstanding," said Phoebe.

"Speaking of Nicky," Guin continued, "I understand you

were at the hospital the other day, checking on him."

"How'd you know Nicky was in the hospital?"

"The question is, why were you there?"

"Nicky and I go way back," said Phoebe. "We grew up together. Mr. DiDio and my dad were in the Navy together. As soon as Mr. DiDio heard about Nicky, he called my dad, and Pops called me."

"You told the woman at the front desk you were Nick's girlfriend."

"You spying on me?" said Phoebe.

"No," said Guin. "And you didn't answer the question. Are you and Nick dating?"

Phoebe shook her head.

"Nicky's like a brother to me. It would be weird if we dated. But I figured it was better to say I was his girlfriend than just his friend. Though I should have told them I was his sister."

"And being his friend, you weren't conflicted when he and Frank got into it?"

"Sure, I was. But it wasn't any of my business."

Guin looked skeptical.

"I know what you're thinking, but when it came to Frank and Nicky, I stayed out of it."

"So why did Nicky quit?"

"Like I said, it was a misunderstanding. And he was better off not working for Frank. Frank always had to be the one in charge, you know?"

"And did you help him get the job at Sunshine Builders?"

"I may have put in a good word with Tony," she said, sipping her iced tea.

"That would be Tony Del Sole, the owner?"

"Yeah."

"And what's your relationship with Mr. Del Sole?"

"I'm his new office manager."

"His office manager?" said Guin.

Before Phoebe could reply, the waitress came over with their food.

"Here you go!" she said, placing the plates on the table. "Enjoy!"

"Thank you," said Guin, smiling up at her. Phoebe said nothing.

Guin ate her coconut curried lobster salad while Phoebe picked at hers.

"So, are you seeing Tony?" Guin asked her.

Phoebe put down her fork.

"So what if I am? It's a free country."

"Were you seeing him while you were living with Frank?"

"No," Phoebe replied. But Guin didn't believe her.

"Getting back to Frank, did you know he had money troubles?"

Phoebe looked at her.

"Of course I knew. But he told me he had things taken care of."

"Did you know that Frank had borrowed money from Lou Antinori?"

Phoebe seemed taken aback.

"Frank would never borrow money from Big Lou."

"Well, he did."

Before either could say anything, their server returned.

"Are you ladies done?"

"I am," Guin answered. "Phoebe?"

"Yeah, take it away," she said, pushing the plate toward the server.

"Can I get you ladies anything else?"

"I'm good," said Guin.

She looked over at Phoebe.

"Me too," said Phoebe.

Guin asked for the check.

"Just one more thing," said Guin, looking at Phoebe. "You mentioned that you thought Frank was having an affair."

"Yeah, with you."

Guin let the comment go.

"Is it possible he was having an affair with one of his other female clients? Was there anyone he seemed sweet on or seemed sweet on him?"

"Just that broad whose husband runs the Island Trust Company. I think he had a soft spot for her. But she was too old for Frank to bang."

Guin stared at her.

"Are you referring to Caroline Simms?"

"Yeah, she's the one. I think she was sweet on Frank. Probably why that husband of hers fired him."

Guin opened her mouth to say something, but she couldn't think of what to say. It was too preposterous. Then again, she had been surprised by all the love scenes in *The Belle of Sanibel.* Could Frank Funt, Jr., have been the inspiration for Juan? She would have never thought so before, but now…

"Hey, look, it's been fun, but I've gotta go," Phoebe said, getting up. "Let me know if you figure out who killed Frank."

Guin nodded and watched as Phoebe made her way to the parking lot, swinging her hips as she went.

CHAPTER 26

As soon as Guin got home, she called Ginny.

"What's up, Buttercup?"

"I need Caroline Simms's phone number."

"You got questions about the book?"

"Yes," said Guin. Well, it wasn't a total lie.

"Give me a sec."

Guin waited.

"Here you go," said Ginny. "So, how are you liking it?"

"It's not as bad as I thought it would be."

"Now there's a ringing endorsement."

"Don't worry. I'll be nice."

"That's my girl," said Ginny. "Though I would never tell you what to write."

Guin rolled her eyes.

"Hey, can I ask you a personal question, about the Simmses?"

"Shoot," said Ginny.

"Would you say that Mr. and Mrs. Simms were happily married?"

"Define *happily.*"

"You know what I mean."

Ginny sighed.

"Now don't quote me, but it's been rumored that Bill's been known to play the field. Never on Sanibel, mind you, but when he's off-campus, so to speak."

"Does his wife know?"

"Probably."

"Did she threaten to divorce him?"

"Caroline would never do that."

"So what did she do?" asked Guin.

"She had the house remodeled."

"Seriously?" said Guin.

"You should see their house."

"Is it nice?"

"Very."

"Huh," said Guin. "Though I heard she used Funt and the Son Construction."

"Could be. I don't recall. Where'd you hear that?"

"From Phoebe Costanza, Funt's former girlfriend and office manager. She also said that Mrs. Simms had been sweet on Frank and that's why Mr. Simms fired them."

"Caroline, sweet on Frank Funt? I find that hard to believe," said Ginny.

"I thought the same thing, but the more I thought about it... You should read *The Belle of Sanibel*. There are some pretty steamy scenes in there, and the love interest bears a passing resemblance to Frank Funt, Jr."

"You don't say," said Ginny. "Maybe I should take a look at it. It's been ages since I read anything steamy."

"You can have my copy when I'm done," said Guin. "But getting back to Caroline Simms..."

"I guess it's possible she had a dalliance. But I can't imagine her having an affair with the contractor. It seems so..."

"Déclassé?" Guin suggested. "Cliché?"

"Precisely."

"But not impossible."

"No. Still... tread lightly, Guin. You don't want to go

poking a potential hornet's nest."

"I know," she said. "I'll be careful. But I need to talk to Caroline Simms, and her husband."

"Why him?"

"He's the one who fired Funt. I want to find out why."

"Just be careful."

"I will," said Guin.

"Is that everything?" asked Ginny.

"For now," said Guin.

"Okay, just make sure you get me that book review—and don't do anything to piss off Caroline."

"I'll be good," said Guin. "Bye."

"Bye," said Ginny.

Guin ended the call and stared at Caroline Simms's phone number. Should she call her now or wait? As she was deciding, her phone began to vibrate. It was Glen.

"Hey there," she said. "What's up?"

"I was wondering if it would be okay if I crashed at the house this weekend."

"That's fine," said Guin. "But do you really want to do that?"

"It'd save me a bunch of time, and there's water and electricity, so I should be okay."

"What about AC?"

"The AC guys are coming next week, but I'll be fine."

"Well, if you really want to camp out there," said Guin.

"I've camped out in worse places. It'll be fun."

Guin wasn't so sure about that.

"By the way, my buddy Pete's going to come by tomorrow morning. He's the painter I mentioned. You want to stop by, discuss paint colors with him?"

"Sure," said Guin. "But I'm kind of surprised he's working on a Saturday."

"Pete's like me, he works whenever. Especially this time

of year. You've got to take the work when you can get it."

"If you say so," said Guin. "What time should I stop by?"

"Say nine o'clock? Or is that too early?"

"No, that's fine," said Guin.

She was thinking maybe she'd drive over to the house earlier, park the car, then go for a walk along West Gulf Drive beach.

"Great," said Glen. "See you tomorrow."

Guin ended the call and stared at her phone again.

"Well, nothing ventured, nothing gained." (She was full of clichés today.)

She dialed Caroline Simms's number.

"This is Caroline Simms," said a female voice.

"Hi, Mrs. Simms, this is Guinivere Jones, from the *Sanibel-Captiva Sun-Times*."

"Oh, yes, Ms. Jones. Ginny told me you were reviewing my book. How are you enjoying it?"

"Very much," said Guin, crossing her fingers. "Might you have some time this weekend to discuss it? I had a few questions."

"I'm afraid this weekend won't work," said Mrs. Simms. "Mr. Simms and I will be away. Might you be available for breakfast Monday? I could meet you over at the Sanctuary Club."

"That would be fine," said Guin.

She had been hoping to meet with Mrs. Simms sooner, but that clearly wasn't possible. She would just have to work harder Monday to get the article in on time.

"What time?"

"Shall we say nine a.m.?"

"Nine a.m. Monday it is," said Guin. "See you then."

She ended the call and gazed out the window. The Sanctuary Club was just a 15-minute walk from the condo, and it would most likely be empty Monday morning.

Guin continued to stare out the window for another couple of minutes, then she got up and grabbed *The Belle of Sanibel*, taking it with her into the living room.

Once again, Guin had become so engrossed in the book that she had lost track of the time. Good thing she had set a reminder on her phone. Otherwise she might have forgotten about dinner at Craig and Betty's.

Despite the florid language, Guin had found herself unable to put down the book. She found the history of Sanibel quite interesting. Caroline clearly knew her stuff. No surprise as she sat on the board of the Sanibel Historical Museum and Village. And Guin found herself drawn into the love story. Would Belle and Juan Valdés wind up together? She was eager to find out, though she suspected not.

She got up and stretched, leaving the book on the coffee table, and went into her room to change. Even though Craig and Betty were like family, Guin didn't feel it was appropriate to wear shorts and a t-shirt to their house for dinner. So she slipped into a sundress and gave her hair a quick comb. Though it made little difference. Guin had pretty much resigned herself to looking like a poodle since she moved to Sanibel.

She made her way to the kitchen and gave Fauna some food. Then she grabbed her bag and her keys and headed out the door.

"Guinivere, don't you look nice!" said Betty, giving her a kiss on the cheek. "Thanks for coming over."

"Thank you for having me," said Guin.

"Guin!" said Craig, making his way over. "Glad you could make it."

Guin handed Betty the plate of cookies she had brought.

"Craig said it was okay to bring these. I made them last night."

"I'm sure they're delicious," said Betty. "I'll just have to hide them, so Craig doesn't eat them all."

"Now, Betty," said Craig. "I'll make sure to leave you a few."

He winked at Guin and smiled.

"Come, have a seat at the dining table," said Betty. "Dinner will be ready in just a minute."

"Can I help with anything?" asked Guin.

"We've got it," said Craig.

The two of them fussed in the kitchen as Guin sat at the table. A minute later, they brought out the food.

"Looks delicious!" said Guin.

Craig took a seat and Betty served everyone, only sitting when everyone had a plate.

They made small talk during the meal.

"So I hear you found someone to finish your house," said Betty.

"That's right," said Guin. "He's a freelance photographer I work with."

"A photographer?" said Betty, confused.

"He used to be a carpenter, and a painter, and a handyman," Guin explained.

"I see," said Betty.

"You trust him?" asked Craig.

"I do," said Guin. "He already gave me a spreadsheet, and he's supposedly camping out there this weekend, trying to get stuff done before I have to move out of the condo."

"Just be sure to keep an eye on him."

"I will," said Guin. "I'm going over there tomorrow, to pick out paint."

"Well, I hope it finally gets done," said Betty. "Honestly,

the luck you've had." She shook her head.

"I know," said Guin. "But, hopefully, Glen will bring me some good luck. So, what do you two have planned this weekend? You going to do some fishing?" she asked Craig.

"Sunday," said Craig. "And we're going to see a movie tomorrow."

"No poker?"

Craig played in a regular Friday night poker game.

"We took September off," said Craig. "We'll start up again next month when all the snowbirds are back."

"I've been playing poker with him in the meantime," said Betty, "but he says it's not the same."

Craig patted Betty's hand.

"What about you?"

"Shelly invited me over for dinner Sunday. They're having one of their barbeques."

"That'll be nice," said Betty.

They finished their meal and Craig cleared the plates.

"Who's ready for some dessert?" Betty asked when Craig was done.

"I know I am," said Craig.

Betty smiled.

"Can I help?" asked Guin.

"You stay right there," said Betty. "You're the guest."

Guin obeyed, but she thought it ridiculous. She felt more like a member of the family than a guest, and she sensed they felt the same way about her.

"I thought we might have some ice cream with the cookies," said Betty, depositing a tub of vanilla ice cream on the table.

Craig brought over bowls and spoons and they helped themselves.

"Best chocolate chip cookies I've ever had," said Craig, when he had finished his cookie.

He reached for another one, but Betty gave him a warning look.

"I'm glad you like them," said Guin, smiling. "Can I help you clean up?"

"Heavens, no!" said Betty.

"Well then, if you don't need me, I should go. I've got a bunch of reading to do. Thank you again for having me over."

"Our pleasure," said Betty. "You know you're always welcome."

"I know," said Guin, giving each of them a hug.

"Let me know if you learn anything or need me to do some more digging," Craig whispered in her ear.

Guin nodded.

"Well, goodnight," said Guin.

She made her way to the Mini, Craig and Betty watching her as she walked down the driveway. She waved just before she got in the car, then drove off.

CHAPTER 27

Guin arrived at the house a little before eight the next morning and parked in the driveway. She thought about knocking on the door and seeing if Glen was up, but she really wanted to get in a walk.

As she was making her way down the block, she saw a familiar figure walking towards her.

"Jimbo!" Guin called, waving.

Jimbo, who was walking with a woman, stopped.

"I didn't know you lived around here," said Guin, smiling up at him.

Jimbo looked a bit awkward.

"I, uh…" he replied.

"He was visiting me," said the woman. "I'm Sally, Sally Bates," she said, extending a hand. "I live just down the block."

"I'm Guin," said Guin, shaking Sally's hand. "I live over at 2244, or I will once it's finally fixed up."

Jimbo and Sally exchanged a quick look.

"So, you're the one who bought Dusty's place," said Sally.

"Yup," said Guin. "Did you know him well? I hear he was a character."

"He was definitely a character," said Sally. "You've been renovating it, I see."

"I have," said Guin. "Or at least trying to. My contractor didn't do a very good job, and I just hired someone else to finish up."

"That's too bad," said Sally. "Hard to find good help on the islands."

"Hopefully, I have someone good helping me now."

"Who'd you hire?" asked Jimbo.

"My friend Glen. But I had originally hired Funt and the Son. Big mistake."

Jimbo and Sally exchanged another look.

"Anyway, if you see a tall, good-looking blond guy lurking around my house, that's Glen. Though he has a bunch of his buddies helping him out."

"Well, good luck to you," said Sally. "It'll be nice to have another young person in the neighborhood. And lord knows that house needed some fixing up."

Jimbo nodded.

"So," said Guin, looking at the two of them. "How do you two know each other?"

"Our kids went to high school together," said Jimbo.

Sally looped her arm through Jimbo's.

"Actually, we're dating," she said.

"So this must be who you were meeting the other night!" said Guin, smiling at Jimbo.

Jimbo didn't say anything.

"Well, I should get going," said Guin. "Want to get my walk in before I meet with the painter. Nice meeting you, Sally."

"Nice meeting you, too, Guin."

Guin started to go, then stopped and turned around.

"Hey, Sally," she called.

Sally and Jimbo stopped.

"You said you live just over there?" she said, pointing at a nearby house.

"That's right," said Sally.

"You didn't happen to see or hear anything strange over at my place Sunday before last, did you?"

"The Sunday before last?" said Sally. "I'm afraid I don't recall. Why?"

"Oh, no reason," said Guin. "I just thought my contractor might have stopped by. Well, I should go. See you around!"

She began walking again, but something was nagging at her. Had it been her imagination or did Jimbo and Sally know more than they were letting on?

Guin got back to the house a few minutes after nine and saw a van with the name Peter Pan Painters printed on the side, with an image of Peter Pan and Tinkerbell. She smiled and rang the doorbell.

"It's open!" called a familiar voice.

Guin let herself in.

She saw Glen standing in the kitchen with another man, who looked to be around their age. Guin went over to them.

"You must be Peter," said Guin, extending a hand.

"I am," said Peter, shaking it. He was around Guin's height and had an impish air to him.

"I love the name of your business," said Guin.

"Thank you," said Peter.

"Just to be clear, he's not the actual Peter Pan, despite appearances," said Glen, smiling at his friend.

"My last name is Pantoliano," explained Peter. "And people used to call me Peter Pan when I was a kid."

"Ah," said Guin.

"I think he took the name to heart," said Glen. "His mother was always saying to him, 'When are you going to grow up?'"

"Well, I bet your mother thinks you're grown up now.

Running your own business is very adult."

"Unfortunately, she died when I was nineteen, when I was still pretty immature."

"I'm sorry to hear that," said Guin.

She knew what it was like to lose a parent. Her father had also died when she was young.

"But, yeah, I think she would have been proud of what I've accomplished," said Peter.

"How about we talk about your house?" said Glen. "I showed Peter around, and we have some ideas."

"Great!" said Guin. "Lay 'em on me."

They spent the next hour walking around the house, inside and out, discussing paint colors.

"If only Tinkerbell were here," said Guin. "Then she could just wave her wand and the whole house would be done."

"But then I'd be out of a job," said Peter, smiling at her.

Guin smiled back at him.

"So, why don't I send you an email, later, recapping what we discussed?" said Peter. "I'll cc you, Glen."

"Sounds good," said Guin. She turned to Glen. "Do you think you'll be able to finish before the condo closes?"

"It'll be close," he replied. "We may still be working on a few things, but I'm going to do my best to make sure your bedroom and bathroom and the kitchen are done, or at least functional, by then. Should be able to make it, unless I run into problems."

"I hope there aren't any," said Guin. "I've had enough problems with this place to last a lifetime. If only Funt had done a decent job. He should have been finished by now."

"It's really not as bad as it looks," said Glen. "He just cut corners, used cheap materials, and probably didn't supervise his guys properly."

"Oh, is that all?" said Guin, sarcastically.

"But my guys will fix you up. They're pros."

"Okay," said Guin.

"Just have a little faith."

"Easier said than done."

"Well, if you two are done with me, I'll be heading out," said Peter.

"Sorry," said Guin. "Thanks for coming."

"Happy to help out. Call me when you're ready for me, G-Man."

Glen nodded and walked Peter out.

Guin turned and glanced around the house. She took a step towards the guest bathroom, then stopped.

She felt Glen beside her.

"It's going to be okay. I promise," he said, taking her arm. "We're going to re-do the guest bathroom, so there'll be no trace of Funt. I have my guy coming to do the floor next week, and I already ordered a new tub. And like I said, I'm going to camp out here today and tomorrow, get as much stuff done as I can."

Guin turned and looked up at him.

"Thank you."

Suddenly, she had an idea.

"You free Sunday evening?"

"I think so," said Glen. "Why?"

"My friends Shelly and Steve are having a barbeque. They live not too far from here and always have a ton of food—and beer."

"I'll need to double-check my calendar, but it sounds like fun. You sure it's okay?"

"I'll text Shelly right now and ask her," said Guin. "I'm sure it's fine."

She pulled out her phone and sent Shelly a text.

"You okay if I bring a friend to the BBQ Sunday?" she wrote.

"Does this friend happen to work for the SPD?" Shelly typed back.

"No," wrote Guin.

Shelly replied with a frowny face.

"It's my photographer friend, Glen, who's been helping me with the house," typed Guin. "He's working here this weekend, and I thought maybe…"

"Sure, bring him with you," wrote Shelly. "He's the cute one, right?"

"I'll see you Sunday," Guin replied, ignoring Shelly's question.

"That was a lot of typing and some interesting faces," said Glen.

Guin felt her cheeks grow warm.

"Sorry, Shelly just likes to talk, or text, a lot."

"No worries," said Glen. "So, is it okay?"

"Totally," said Guin. "Shall I pick you up here? The barbecue's at six, and it's just a few minutes away."

"Sounds good," said Glen. "I was planning on working here until around then anyway." He paused. "Is it okay if I wear shorts and a t-shirt? I didn't bring much with me."

"Totally fine," said Guin. "Steve and Shelly are very laid back."

"Okay then," said Glen. "So I guess I'll see you tomorrow around six."

"Tomorrow at six it is."

Guin stood in the driveway, looking back at the house. As she was standing there, she could feel her phone vibrating. She pulled it out of her back pocket and looked at the screen. It was a local number, but one she didn't recognize.

"Guin Jones," she said.

"Ms. Jones, this is William Simms."

"Mr. Simms," said Guin, not sure what to say.

"I understand you've been asking questions about Funt and the Son Construction."

"That's right," said Guin.

"And that you arranged a meeting with my wife."

"To discuss her book. I'm reviewing it for the paper."

"As long as you stick to the book," said Mr. Simms.

Guin made a face.

"May I ask why you don't want me asking your wife about Frank Funt?"

"Because I don't want you upsetting her."

"I see," said Guin. "And why would mentioning Mr. Funt upset her?"

There was silence on the other end of the line.

"Mr. Simms?"

"Just leave Funt out of it," he replied.

"You did hire him to renovate your home, did you not?"

"Caroline hired him. The house is her domain."

"But I understand you were the one who fired him."

"The man came into our house, destroyed the place, then tried to extort me for more money."

"I see," said Guin. Clearly, that was Funt's M.O.

"No, I don't think you do," said Mr. Simms. "The man was a crook and should've had his license revoked."

"Then why didn't you file a complaint with the building department?"

"Caroline, Mrs. Simms, wouldn't let me."

"Yet she allowed you to fire him."

"Someone had to."

"But I heard the house was lovely."

"No thanks to Funt. You should have seen the idiots he hired. They wouldn't know which end of a paintbrush was which."

"Is that why you fired them?"

"One of the reasons."

"I see," said Guin. "And did Mrs. Simms share your opinion of Funt and his crew?"

Mr. Simms mumbled something.

"I'm sorry, I didn't catch that."

"I said, I don't know what kind of garbage Funt was feeding her, but he could do no wrong in Caroline's eyes. Every time I'd say something, she'd bring up the accident."

"Accident?" said Guin.

"Caroline came home one morning after playing tennis and supposedly fainted and hit her head. By some miracle, Funt was there and found her lying on the floor. Then he supposedly carried her to the sofa and refused to leave her side until he knew she was okay."

"Very gallant of him," said Guin.

"Very opportunistic, if you ask me. I came home that evening, no clue that anything had happened, and she tells me all about it. I asked her why she didn't call me or have Funt take her to see a doctor, and she said he offered, but she declined. Said he gave her something to help with the pain. That's when I lost it. I called Funt the next day and told him he was done, that I didn't want him setting foot in my house ever again, and that I'd call the cops if he did."

Guin thought that seemed a bit overdramatic.

"How did he respond?"

"He said, 'You may want to talk to your wife. I don't think she wants me gone.' And I said, 'I run the show around here,' and he laughed. I tell you, I could have throttled him."

"So what happened?"

"I called my lawyer and had him draw up a termination agreement."

"And did Funt sign?"

"Only if I agreed to pay him the balance of the contract, though there was still over a hundred thousand dollars of work to be done."

"And did you agree?"

"I did," said Mr. Simms. "It was worth it to get rid of him."

"And was Mrs. Simms upset?"

"At first, but she understood. Now you understand why I don't want you discussing the matter with her."

Guin was about to say something, but Mr. Simms cut her off.

"I have another call," he said. "Good day, Ms. Jones."

CHAPTER 28

Guin called the Sanibel police department and asked to speak with Detective O'Loughlin. She was informed he was out, so left a message asking him to call her back, saying it was urgent. Then she sent him a text for good measure. She stared down at her phone, hoping he might return her call or text right away, but after a minute went by, she tucked her phone away and drove back to the condo.

Fauna was there to greet her and acted as though Guin had been gone for days not hours.

"You sure you're not a dog?" Guin asked her.

The cat meowed indignantly and rubbed herself against Guin's legs.

Guin bent down and scratched Fauna's chin and behind her ears, which elicited loud purrs. Then she straightened up, much to Fauna's dismay.

"Sorry, kitty cat. I need to work."

Guin had no idea how she was going to get Ginny the article about *The Belle of Sanibel* by Tuesday when she had yet to finish the book and still had to interview Caroline Simms, but she had to try. Which meant she needed to hunker down.

She marched into her bedroom and grabbed the book off her night table. Then she went into the living room and settled herself on the couch. Fortunately, the book wasn't too long, and she was nearly two-thirds of the way through it. But she would have to glue herself to the couch for the next twenty-four hours if she was to finish it by Sunday night.

She started reading, then put the book down, getting up to get a glass of water.

"There," she said, making herself comfortable on the couch once more. "Now let's see if Belle and Juan will have their happily ever after."

Guin had been so engrossed in the book that it was only when her stomach began making telltale gurgling sounds that she checked her phone to see what time it was. As she suspected, it was well past lunchtime.

She got up and stretched to restore circulation in her legs. (Fauna had been napping in her lap.) Then she made her way to the kitchen and fixed herself a sandwich, which she ate standing up. When she was done, she washed her plate, then headed back into the living room.

She had left her phone on the coffee table, turned over. When she checked it, she saw she had a voicemail. She hit speed dial and listened to the message. Of course, it was the detective.

She immediately called him back and prayed that he would pick up.

"This better be good," he said.

"Were you out fishing?" she asked him.

"I was. Now what was so urgent you had to leave me a voicemail and a text?"

He was clearly not in a good mood. Though he rarely was.

"Yes, well, I had a very interesting conversation with William Simms, the president of the Island Trust Company."

"I know who he is," said the detective.

"Well, he called to tell me that under no circumstance was I to discuss Frank Funt, Jr., with his wife."

"Did he tell you why?" asked the detective.

"He said he didn't want me upsetting her. It seems she may have been sweet on Funt and was upset when her husband fired him."

"I see," said the detective.

"Also, Simms confessed to wanting to throttle Funt."

"Doesn't mean he killed him."

"No," said Guin. "But you should have heard him on the phone. He became very angry when I asked him about Funt and his wife."

Again, there was silence on the other end of the line.

"So have you questioned him?" Guin asked.

"We did."

"You did?"

"I know you may find this hard to believe, Ms. Jones, but while you've been playing Nancy Drew, the Sanibel police department has been conducting a thorough investigation into the suspicious death of your former contractor."

He was definitely not in a good mood.

"So, did Simms and his wife have alibis for the night of the murder?"

"They did."

"Though they could have hired someone," said Guin, thinking out loud.

"I can't believe I even have to say this but assuming they had hired a hitman to take out Funt, which is extremely unlikely, don't you think the hitman would have done a better job disposing of the body?"

He had a point.

"Now would you please stop with the cockamamie theories and leave the detective work to me?"

Yup, he was definitely in a bad mood.

"Is something wrong, detective?"

"I just don't understand you women," he said.

"What don't you understand?"

"First you say you want to get back together. So we get back together. Then you say you don't feel I'm committed to the relationship, that I don't care, when I've done nearly everything you've asked. I give up."

"Uh, I'm assuming by *you* you mean Maggie?"

"Yeah, Maggie, but all you women are the same. You're never happy."

Something was definitely up, thought Guin.

"Did something happen between you and Maggie?"

"All she does is pick, pick, pick. Nothing I do is good enough."

Guin didn't think she had ever heard the detective talk so much or complain. She didn't know what to say. Though a little part of her—okay, a big part—was thrilled to hear that things were not going so well between him and Maggie.

"I'm sorry to hear that," said Guin.

"Whatever," said the detective. "This is why I didn't want to be in a relationship. Women, they always try to change you. They can't leave well enough alone."

Guin thought about defending womankind but decided to change the subject instead.

"So, are you any closer to solving the case? Any idea who killed Funt?"

"We're working on it," said the detective.

"Will you let me know if you arrest anyone?"

"You'll be the first to know."

Was that sarcasm? With the detective, it was hard to tell.

"Well, it's been lovely talking with you, detective. Good luck with everything."

The detective mumbled something and ended the call.

Well, that was an odd conversation, thought Guin.

She gazed out past the lanai, at the trees and the birds flying by. It sounded like things were not going so well between the detective and Maggie. Should she call him back and invite him out for a drink, tell him how she felt? Maybe not right now, as he was clearly in a bad mood, but in a few days?

She continued to stare out the window for another minute. Then she turned and went back to the couch and her book.

Guin was once again immersed in the novel when her phone started vibrating. She tried to ignore it but couldn't. When she flipped it over, she saw that Craig had called and immediately called him back.

"Hey, I saw that you called. What's up?"

"I just left you a message," said Craig. "I spoke with Big Lou."

"What did he have to say?"

"At first he played coy, said he loaned money to a lot of people and could have loaned some money to Funt but didn't remember. I helped refresh his memory, and he fessed up, but he said it was no big deal."

"Did he happen to say how much he loaned Frank?"

"He did not. But he told me that Funt said he needed the money to buy out his father, so I'm guessing Big Lou loaned him at least six figures."

Guin whistled, then paused, another thought popping into her head.

"But Funt Senior said Frank was on the installment plan and hadn't paid for the business yet. If Big Lou loaned him that much money, where did it go?"

Craig shrugged.

"No idea."

"So was Frank paying back the loan?"

"In a manner of speaking."

"What does that mean?" asked Guin.

"Funt wasn't exactly flush, so Big Lou was having him help out with the business."

"The business," said Guin, not following.

Suddenly she got what Craig was implying.

"So Funt was handling drugs for Big Lou?"

"That's what I'm guessing."

"So Big Lou supplied Funt with the drugs, and Funt turned around and sold them to his customers?"

"Big Lou didn't say that explicitly," said Craig. "But it's a fair assumption."

Guin's wheels were turning again.

"So is it possible that Frank slipped up and Big Lou had him killed? We know Funt got caught by the cops at least once. Maybe Big Lou saw him as a liability?"

"It's possible," said Craig. "I did ask Big Lou if he knew anything about Funt's death."

"And?" said Guin.

"And he said he had nothing to do with it."

"Of course he did."

Guin made a face.

"So do *you* think Big Lou could have been involved?"

"Like I said, it's possible. Though if he were, he would make sure there was nothing connecting him to Funt's death. Leaving a body to be found in someone's tub isn't his style."

"But Funt's death was attributed to a drug overdose. And it's possible the drugs found in his system came from Big Lou."

"But how do you prove that?" said Craig.

Guin didn't know the answer, yet.

CHAPTER 29

So who killed Frank Funt and why her place?

The question kept playing over and over again in Guin's brain, like a broken record. There was clearly some piece of the puzzle she was missing, but how or where to find it? If only she could speak with Nick DiDio. She had a feeling he knew something, something important. But he was in the hospital and not allowed to have visitors. Though maybe his condition had improved, and she could try speaking with him again.

She grabbed her phone and called the Health Park, asking to speak to someone who could give her information about Nicholas DiDio. After being transferred several times, she finally reached a woman who said she'd see what she could find out.

As Guin listened to the hold music, she wondered if she would be transferred yet again.

Finally, after ten minutes, the woman came back on the line.

"I'm sorry about that," said the woman. "I have one of Mr. DiDio's doctors on the line. Go ahead, please."

"Hi," said Guin. "Thank you for taking my call. How is he?"

"I'm afraid Mr. DiDio is still in critical condition," said the doctor.

"Is he conscious?"

"No," said the doctor. "We've been keeping him sedated.

He had a pretty bad fall. He sustained damage to both legs and his spine."

"Will he be able to walk?"

"We don't know yet."

Guin didn't know what to say. It would be devastating for Nick if he couldn't walk. And although it wasn't her fault, Guin felt that she was somehow responsible.

"Could you let me know when he regains consciousness? I'd really like to see him. The hospital has my information, but I'd be happy to give it to you. You can call or text me any time, day or night."

The doctor wrote down Guin's number and said she would give Guin a call or text her if there was any change.

"Thank you," said Guin.

Guin finally finished *The Belle of Sanibel* Sunday afternoon. While the plot had been predictable and the prose somewhat cliché and flowery, she had enjoyed the book. She found herself relating to Belle and Juan's tragic romance and had learned more about Sanibel's history and the people who had settled the island.

Although Guin initially had misgivings about reviewing the book, she no longer did. She just hoped her interview with Caroline Simms went well, as she wanted to flesh out the article with insights from the author.

She finished making some notes, then went to change her clothes for the barbeque. She glanced at her reflection, then headed to the kitchen.

She placed the container of remaining chocolate chip cookies into a small shopping bag, gave Fauna some food, then grabbed her keys and her bag and left.

Guin knocked on the door to her house and waited. When no one answered, she began to worry. Had Glen forgotten—or worse, had something happened to him? She tried the door, but it was locked. She banged on it several more times, calling Glen's name and asking if he was all right. Finally, it opened.

Glen was dressed in only a towel, his hair wet and uncombed. Once again, Guin found herself staring at his naked chest.

"Sorry," said Glen. "Guess I lost track of the time. I was in the shower. I'll just be a minute."

"So the shower works?"

"Yup," said Glen. "Though there's no hot water. I left a message for the plumber. He should be here tomorrow."

Guin couldn't help noticing Glen's toned physique and felt herself blushing.

"You want to come in?"

Guin stepped inside and glanced around. She could tell Glen had been busy.

"The boys were here until just a little while ago, which is why I'm running late," he explained. "Feel free to take a look around while I put some clothes on. You may not notice much, but trust me, we made good progress. I'll be back in a minute."

Guin watched as Glen headed to the master bedroom. She wondered what he had slept on as there was no furniture in the house. Then she wandered into the kitchen, looking to see what had been done.

"I'm ready!" said Glen, emerging from the bedroom a few minutes later.

He was dressed in a pair of board shorts and a polo shirt and had combed his ash-blond hair back. For a second, it was as though her ex, Art, was standing there. (The two shared a similar build and coloring.)

"You okay?" Glen asked her.

"Sorry, I was just woolgathering," said Guin.

"Shall we go?"

They stepped outside and Glen locked the door behind them.

Guin looked over at the Mini, then at Glen's silver BMW.

"I'm happy to drive," he said. "Up to you."

"Sure," said Guin. "Go ahead. It's just a few minutes away, over by Middle Gulf."

They got in the BMW and headed over to Shelly and Steve's.

🌴

"Guin!" said Shelly, giving her a big hug. "And I remember you!" she said, turning to Glen. "You're the photographer from the Shell Show."

"That's me," said Glen. "And I remember you. You're the prize-winning artist with the stunning mermaid jewelry."

Shelly grinned.

"Good memory."

She turned to Guin and whispered, "I like this one."

Guin handed her the container of cookies.

"Here."

"Thanks," said Shelly, taking them. "Go help yourselves to beer. The cooler's on the lanai, along with some nibbles. Guin will show you the way."

The doorbell rang and Shelly excused herself.

"Follow me," said Guin, leading Glen out onto the lanai.

Steve was at his post, manning the grill.

"Steve," said Guin, tapping him lightly on the shoulder. "I'd like to introduce you to my friend, Glen."

"Welcome," said Steve, turning towards Glen. "Sorry if I don't shake your hand. Mine are a little full." In his left hand was a beer and in his right was a grill fork.

"No worries," said Glen. "Can I give you a hand?"

"Thanks, I'm good."

"Sometimes I think Steve is secretly an octopus," Guin told Glen in a hushed tone. "We just can't see his other arms."

"Just years of practice, my dear," said Steve. "Help yourselves to a beer and some food. There're fried crab balls, guacamole, shrimp, and some veggies my wife insisted on putting out."

"Thanks," said Guin. She turned to Glen. "The cooler's over there."

They walked over and pulled out two beers, then popped off the tops with a nearby bottle opener.

"Cheers," said Glen, raising his bottle.

"Cheers," said Guin.

They clinked, then took a sip.

"Thanks for inviting me," said Glen.

"My pleasure," said Guin. "I thought feeding you was the least I could do. And Steve's brats are legendary."

"Brats?" said Glen. "I thought you said he was into fishing."

"Steve's from Wisconsin, and as far as he's concerned, you can't have a barbeque without bratwurst. He has a place up there that ships them to him."

"That's hardcore," said Glen.

Guin nodded. "Though there's always fish and other stuff, too."

Shelly stepped onto the lanai, accompanied by a couple.

"Guin, you remember the Astleys."

"Of course!" said Guin, going over and exchanging hugs with Paul and Cindy.

"We haven't seen you at the restaurant in a while," said Paul. "I hope everything's okay."

(Paul and his wife Cindy owned the Beach House, a

restaurant in Fort Myers Beach that Guin used to frequent when she was dating her former beau, Ris Hartwick.)

"I can't believe Shelly didn't tell you," said Guin.

"Tell us what?" said Cindy.

"Ris and I broke up last spring. He moved to Australia."

"Australia?" said Cindy. "I had read about his problems, of course, but Australia?"

"It's a long story," said Guin. "Anyway, let me introduce you to Glen. Glen Anderson, may I present Paul and Cindy Astley."

"Nice to meet you," said Glen.

"So, are you two…" said Cindy, looking from one to the other.

"Oh no!" said Guin. "We're just friends."

"We work together," said Glen, amused by Guin's reaction. "I'm a freelance photographer."

"A freelance photographer, you say? You know," said Cindy, looking at her husband. "We could use some new photographs of the restaurant. We just re-did the place. Updated the decor and re-did the menu. We won't officially be re-opening until the end of October, but we're having a soft opening for friends and family Friday."

She looked at Glen.

"By any chance are you available? I'd love to have you come to the soft opening, so you can get a feel for the place. Then you could come back when we're all done and take photos."

"Thanks," said Glen. "I'd love to check it out."

"Great!" said Cindy. "And, of course, we'd pay you for the photographs."

"Of course," said Glen, smiling.

"So, Glen, what brought you to Sanibel?" asked Paul.

"I'm originally from Fort Myers," Glen replied. "Grew up here, then wound up in the big city."

"New York?" said Paul.

"Yup."

"Glen was an investment banker," said Guin.

"Really?" said Paul.

"Really," said Glen. "But those days are long behind me."

Guin was about to say something when she spied a new guest step out onto the lanai and froze.

"Would you excuse me?" she said to Glen and the Astleys.

"Everything okay?" asked Glen, noticing her expression.

"I just need to have a quick word with Shelly."

"Bill!" said Steve, raising his beer in greeting. "Glad you could make it. Grab yourself a cold one and a crab ball."

Guin grabbed Shelly and hissed into her ear.

"What's he doing here? I thought you said you weren't inviting him."

"I didn't," said Shelly. "Swear. Steve must have. They must have run into each other fishing this morning."

Guin glanced over at the detective and Steve, who were engaged in conversation.

"What am I supposed to do?" said Guin, hiding behind Shelly.

"For starters, try not acting like you're in middle school."

Guin peeked out from behind Shelly and glanced around.

"He's still talking with Steve," said Shelly. "Now stop hiding and behave like the mature woman you are."

"In a minute," said Guin.

"Well, unless you want to totally embarrass yourself, I'd come out now. They're headed this way."

"What?" said Guin.

"Darling, look who's here!" said Steve.

"Oh, there it is!" said Guin, pretending she had been looking for something on the ground. She stood up and smiled at Steve and the detective.

"Why detective, how nice to see you."

"Ms. Jones," said the detective. "What is it you were looking for?"

"I, um…" said Guin. "A button. I thought I lost it. Anyway, I should be getting back to my date. Nice to see you, detective!"

Guin hurried off to find Glen, mortified.

He was still chatting with the Astleys.

"Everything okay?" he asked her.

"Yes," said Guin.

A minute later, Shelly and Steve announced that dinner was ready. It was buffet style, as usual, and Guin and Glen helped themselves, then took a seat at one of the tables. The Astleys joined them.

After dessert, Guin told Glen she wanted to go. They excused themselves and went over to Shelly and Steve.

"We're heading out," Guin announced.

"Thanks for inviting me," said Glen. "Best barbecue I've had in ages. Those brats were phenomenal."

Steve beamed.

"You're welcome back any time, Glen. You fish?"

"I used to," he said. "I'm a bit rusty. Though maybe now that I'm back here, I should take it up again."

"I'd be happy to take you out," said Steve.

"Thanks. I may take you up on that."

Shelly turned to Guin and whispered in her ear.

"I like him."

"Well, we've gotta go," Guin said, ignoring Shelly.

Shelly walked them to the door, then gave Guin a kiss on the cheek.

As they made their way down the walkway, Shelly called out to Guin.

"Going to be some good low tides this week! Text me!"

Guin gave her a thumbs up, then hurriedly got into Glen's car.

CHAPTER 30

"You okay?" asked Glen, after they had parked at Guin's house. "You seemed a little tense at the barbeque."

"Sorry," said Guin. "It's just…" She searched for the right words but couldn't find them.

"It's okay," said Glen. "It was the detective, wasn't it? Did you think he'd come there to arrest you?"

"No," said Guin. She sighed. May as well just spit it out. "The truth is, he's the guy who stood me up the other night, though it turns out he didn't. He was just late."

"O'Loughlin?" said Glen.

"Yeah, him," said Guin. "The detective and I…" Again, she struggled to find the right words. "The detective and I… We didn't actually *date*, per se. I thought there was something there last spring. Then he disappeared. Totally ghosted me. Turns out, he had a girlfriend."

"Ouch," said Glen. "That must have hurt."

"It did."

"So, do you still have feelings for him?"

"I…" said Guin, looking out into the darkness. "I don't know."

Glen placed a hand gently on her arm and Guin turned to look at him.

"I'm here for you, Guin. You know that. If you ever want to talk…"

Guin could tell by Glen's expression that he meant it.

"Thank you," she said. "You've been so great. And I…"

Again, Guin didn't know what to say.

Glen ran his hand gently over Guin's cheek.

"I need to go," he said. "You sure you're okay?"

Guin nodded.

"Thank you for inviting me to the barbeque. Shelly and Steve seem very nice. And, hey, I got a gig! Maybe I should hire you as my agent."

Guin laughed.

"That's better," he said. "I'm just going to run inside and get my stuff, then head out."

"Okay," said Guin. "And thank you."

"What for?"

"For everything. For fixing up my house. For listening to me. For being my friend."

Glen smiled.

"No apology necessary."

He went over to Guin and gave her a kiss on the forehead.

"Now get in that Mini and go home. And get a good night's rest. I'm going to put you to work this week."

"Oh, you are are you?" said Guin, smiling.

"Uh-huh," said Glen. "Now go. I'll talk to you tomorrow."

Guin saluted, then headed over to the Mini.

That night Guin had the strangest dream, though when she thought about it, it wasn't that strange, considering. She dreamed she was living on Sanibel in Belle's time, back in the late 1880s, and her father ran a farm, just like Belle's father did. Just like in the book, her father wanted Guin to marry the son of the man who owned the farm adjacent to theirs, who was a perfectly nice young man but for whom Guin had no romantic feelings.

In the dream, just as in the book, Guin's heart belonged to another man. And that man, in the dream at least, was the detective, or a man who looked like the detective. And Guin was torn: marry the nice, safe neighbor (who in the dream looked like Glen), or marry the mysterious stranger (who looked like the detective) who held her heart?

However, before she was forced to come to a decision, she woke up. She glanced over at her night table, where she had left *The Belle of Sanibel*, after rereading some of it just before she fell asleep. The dream had seemed so real. Clearly, the book had worked its way into her subconscious.

Fauna rubbed her head against Guin's chin and started purring.

Guin glanced at her clock. It was a little before six-thirty. Fauna continued to rub herself against Guin.

"I know what you want," said Guin, stroking Fauna's soft black fur. "But first, I need to go to the bathroom."

"Okay," said Guin, looking at herself in the full-length mirror.

For her breakfast with Caroline Simms at the Sanctuary Club, she had chosen a pretty blue sundress and had put on her heart pendant, a bracelet, and some rings. Although she doubted there would be many people there, she wanted to look her best.

She checked out her reflection one last time, then gathered her things.

She had thought about walking to the clubhouse, as it was less than a mile away. But the morning was warm and Guin had opted to wear heels. So she took the Mini. She arrived five minutes later and parked her car in one of the visitor spots. Then she made her way to the clubhouse.

As she went through the double doors, she stopped to look around. The entrance was beautifully decorated, with two oversized white sofas facing each other, a rug that resembled the sea, and paintings of beach scenes on the walls. Very coastal chic.

"May I help you?" asked the woman at the front desk.

"Yes, I'm meeting Mrs. Simms for breakfast," said Guin.

"You must be Ms. Jones," said the woman. "She's expecting you."

Guin looked down at her watch. She was right on time. Mrs. Simms must have been early.

"It's right through there," said the woman, gesturing towards the dining room.

"Thank you," said Guin.

She had been to the Sanctuary Club a few times, though not recently, and she glanced around to see if anything had changed since her last visit. Everything appeared the same, except for a couple of new names on the men's and women's Club Championship plaques.

Guin made her way to the dining room and immediately spied Caroline Simms, who was chatting with another woman. Guin walked up to the two women and paused.

"Ah, Ms. Jones. Do you know Mrs. Manderly?" asked Mrs. Simms.

"I don't believe I do," said Guin, smiling at the older woman. "Hi, I'm Guin," she said, extending a hand.

Mrs. Manderly shook it.

"Nice to meet you, Guin."

"Don't let that sweet face fool you," Mrs. Simms told Guin. "She's a killer, at least when it comes to bridge. She and her husband won the couples bridge tournament for the second year in a row this past spring. William was most upset. And, of course, blamed me."

"You and William are excellent bridge players," said Mrs. Manderly. "Bruce and I just got lucky."

"Hmm..." said Mrs. Simms.

"Anyway, your guest is here," said Mrs. Manderly. "And I need to get going."

"Give Bruce my best," said Mrs. Simms.

Mrs. Manderly waved as she left the dining room.

"Lovely couple," said Mrs. Simms. "He sold his business a few years ago and they retired here."

"Nice," said Guin.

"Shall we have a seat?" said Mrs. Simms.

They sat at a nearby table and a few seconds later a server came over.

"May I get you something to drink?" the young woman asked them.

"Some coffee for me, please, and some water," said Guin.

"Bring us a pot of coffee, if you please, Josie."

"Yes, Mrs. Simms," said the young woman.

"So, I understand Ginny asked you to read my book and review it. I hope you weren't bored."

"Bored?" said Guin. "Not at all! In fact, I quite enjoyed it."

"You're just being kind," said Mrs. Simms.

"No, really," said Guin. "I found Belle's story fascinating. You clearly did your research."

"Well, I have been on the board of the Sanibel Historical Museum and Village for years. It's nice to think I absorbed something," she said with a smile.

Josie brought over a pot of coffee and poured it into two cups.

"May I get you ladies something to eat?" she asked.

"Do you have a menu?" said Guin.

"Oh, sorry!" said the young woman.

She hurried away and returned a minute later with two menus.

"That's okay," said Mrs. Simms, waving away the menu. "I know what I want."

Guin scanned the menu. She was hungry, but she wanted something that would be easy to eat while they talked.

"I'll have the egg whites with dry whole wheat toast and some fruit," said Mrs. Simms.

Guin glanced across the table. Caroline Simms didn't look like she needed to watch her weight. In fact, if anything, she could stand to gain a few pounds.

"And what would you like, Miss?" said Josie.

"Do try the Bananas Foster French toast," said Mrs. Simms. "I hear it's divine."

Guin again looked over at Mrs. Simms, who was tall and rail thin. While Guin didn't consider herself heavy, she was more generously proportioned than Mrs. Simms and shorter. And she suddenly felt fat. But the Bananas Foster French toast did sound awfully good. And maybe Mrs. Simms was one of those ladies who felt better when others ate more than they did.

"Okay," said Guin. "I'll have the Bananas Foster French toast."

Maybe she'd go for a run later, to help burn off some of the calories.

"Very good," said the young woman.

"Now, where were we?" said Mrs. Simms, after Josie had departed.

"I was saying how much I enjoyed *The Belle of Sanibel*," said Guin.

"Ah, yes," said Mrs. Simms, stirring her coffee.

Guin reached into her purse and pulled out her microcassette recorder.

"Would it be okay if I recorded our conversation?" she asked Mrs. Simms.

Mrs. Simms looked down at the recording device.

"How darling!" she said. "I haven't seen one of those in years."

"I know it's a bit old-fashioned," said Guin. "But I'm not a big fan of those recording apps they have for your phone. Okay for me to use it?"

Guin's fingers hovered over the record button.

"By all means," said Mrs. Simms.

"Thank you," said Guin. "So my first question is, what inspired you to write the book?"

Mrs. Simms answered all of Guin's questions, often going off on tangents. And Guin dreaded having to transcribe the whole interview.

They had taken a break when the food arrived, Guin practically wolfing down her Bananas Foster French toast, so she could get in more questions.

When she had gone through her list, she asked Mrs. Simms if she had anything else she wanted to add.

"No, I think we covered everything," said Mrs. Simms. "I must say, you're quite thorough."

"I try to be," said Guin. "I'm going to transcribe the interview when I get home, but if I have any additional questions, what's the best way to reach you?"

"You can call me, though I have an appointment later this morning and another one this afternoon. It may be best to just email me."

"Will do," said Guin.

"Can I get you ladies anything else?" asked Josie.

"I think we're good, Josie," said Mrs. Simms. "Just a check, please."

"Very good," said the young woman.

Guin had debated throughout breakfast whether or not

to ask Mrs. Simms about Frank Funt, Jr. Her husband had given her a strict order not to, but Guin felt now was her opportunity.

"Before we go," said Guin, "I do have one more question."

"Yes?" said Mrs. Simms.

"I understand you hired Funt and the Son Construction to do some remodeling."

The smile quickly faded.

"And that your husband fired them before the work was completed."

"What does this have to do with my book?" asked Mrs. Simms.

"I'm covering the murder of Frank Funt, Jr. for the paper," Guin said. (Not a total lie, though not exactly the truth.)

"And you think William and I had something to do with it?" Mrs. Simms asked, a horrified expression on her face.

"I'm just trying to speak to some of his customers, to learn more about him," Guin calmly explained, though her heart was racing.

Mrs. Simms fingered her pearls.

"So is it okay if I ask you a few questions about Mr. Funt?" Guin asked.

"Go ahead," said Mrs. Simms. "I've got nothing to hide."

"Thank you," said Guin. "So is it correct that you were the one who hired Funt and the Son Construction?"

"That is correct," said Mrs. Simms.

"But I understand your husband was the one who fired them."

"William wasn't happy with the work they were doing. And once someone gets on his bad side, well…"

"So Frank Funt was on his bad side? Why is that?"

"William is not the most patient man," said Mrs. Simms.

"And he doesn't understand the renovation process, that problems can occur."

"So there were problems with your renovation project?"

Mrs. Simms sighed again.

"Sadly, yes. Frank only discovered them when he removed the walls."

"I see," said Guin. "And did he ask you for more money to fix these problems?"

"He did," said Mrs. Simms. "But it was understandable. There was more work that needed to be done than in the original contract."

"And how did Mr. Simms feel about that?"

"He was unhappy. He didn't like people working in his home, creating a mess and making noise. And he didn't like having to spend more money. He already thought we had paid Frank too much."

Guin noted Mrs. Simms's repeated use of Funt's first name.

"Were they doing a good job, though?" asked Guin.

"Not according to Mr. Simms."

"And is that why he fired them?"

Mrs. Simms nodded.

"He felt Frank was a huckster."

"A huckster?" said Guin.

"A Slick Willie, not to be trusted."

"I see," said Guin. "And what did you think?"

"I felt sorry for Frank. He hadn't had an easy life, but he was trying to make something of himself. His mother died when he was quite young. And he had gotten involved with some gang as a teenager. But he straightened himself out and had become a successful contractor."

Guin raised an eyebrow at that but didn't comment.

"And what did Frank say when your husband accused him of doing shoddy work and trying to bilk you?"

"He said he understood William's qualms, and that it might look like they were making a mess and overcharging, but that was construction for you. There was always some dust and surprises. But he said he would make sure our project was done right."

"And did William, Mr. Simms, buy it?"

"William said he'd give Frank one more chance."

"Then what happened?"

Mrs. Simms sighed a third time.

"I had a little accident. It was nothing really. But William flew off the handle."

Guin waited for her to continue.

"I had been playing tennis all morning. It was quite hot out, and I probably hadn't drunk enough water. When I got home, Frank and his crew were there. I'm not sure what happened. I think I must have fainted. Anyway, when I came to, I was on the couch in the living room and Frank was there by my side.

"I asked him what had happened, and he said he had heard a thunk and found me passed out in the kitchen. He asked me if I was all right, and I told him I thought so. But when I tried to sit up, I felt quite dizzy and my back hurt. He told me to lie back down, and that he'd get me something to ease the pain.

"He returned a few minutes later with a cool washcloth, a glass of water, and some pills. He told me to take one, and I did."

"Did you know what he was giving you?"

"Some kind of painkiller."

"Did you go see a doctor?"

"He asked me if I wanted to, but I was already feeling better, so I told him no. He offered to sit with me, just to make sure I was all right, but I told him to get back to work."

"Did you phone your husband, tell him what happened?"

"No," said Mrs. Simms. "I didn't want to worry him. Besides, as I said, I was feeling much better after a little while, and Frank left me with some pills, in case the pain got worse or didn't go away."

"And what happened when your husband got home? Was he upset?"

"He was furious when I told him what had happened!" said Mrs. Simms. "Said I had probably tripped on something left out by one of the workers, and that the whole thing was Frank's fault, which was ridiculous. But he insisted on speaking with Frank and told me that under no circumstances was I to communicate with him."

"And was that the last time you saw Mr. Funt?"

Mrs. Simms looked down at the table and fingered her pearls.

"Yes," she said, after a pause.

"Excuse me."

It was Josie, their server.

"Here's your check, Mrs. Simms," she said, placing a little leather folder in front of her.

"Thank you, Josie," said Mrs. Simms.

She signed the check, then closed the leather folder.

And now, Ms. Jones, I really must go," said Mrs. Simms, gathering her bag and easing herself out of the booth. "If you have any more questions about the book, you know how to reach me."

CHAPTER 31

On her way home, Guin kept thinking about her interview with Caroline Simms, or rather their conversation about Frank Funt, Jr. Phoebe Costanza had said that Mrs. Simms had been sweet on Funt. And Guin had noticed that Mrs. Simms repeatedly referred to him as Frank. There was also that scene in the book where
Belle slips and falls, and Juan is magically there to catch her and made sure she was okay.

Not for the first time, Guin wondered if Frank Funt, Jr., could have been the inspiration for Juan Valdés. Both men were around six feet tall and solidly built, with swarthy good looks. Though Juan was Cuban and Frank was not.

Had Caroline Simms been attracted to Funt? Quite possibly. Had there been more to their relationship than contractor and client?

Guin felt she needed to speak with William Simms again, this time in person. That way she could read his body language. But she was uncharacteristically nervous about asking him a lot of sensitive questions. She knew Island Trust was a big advertiser. And that Ginny was friendly with the Simmses.

She stared out the window.

She had interviewed heads of Fortune 500 companies and tech startups and had never hesitated to ask them tough questions. But none of them had lived in her small New

England town or wielded the kind of influence the Simmses did on Sanibel.

Guin got out her phone and hit speed dial.

"What's up, Buttercup?" came Ginny's familiar voice. "You have a good chat with Caroline? Did you tell her you loved her book?"

"I did," said Guin. "Though that's not why I'm calling. I want to speak with William Simms."

"So, speak with him," said Ginny.

"The problem is, he may not want to answer some of my questions."

"Just be persistent."

"The thing is, some of the questions I need to ask him are of a sensitive nature, regarding his wife. And I don't want to piss him off. I know the Island Trust Company is a big advertiser."

"Please," said Ginny. "Let me worry about advertising. Besides, where else are they going to run their ads? Now if there's nothing else, let me go. I have work to do. Just be a brave little reporter and call over there and make yourself an appointment."

"What if he won't meet with me?"

Ginny sighed.

"Then call me back. I'll talk to Bill myself."

"Okay," said Guin. "I'll give him a call now. Thank you, Ginny."

"Yeah, yeah, yeah," she said.

They ended the call, or rather Ginny hung up, and Guin called the number for the Island Trust Company.

"Island Trust Company. How may I help you?" came a cheery female voice.

"Hi there," said Guin. "Mr. Simms, please."

"And who may I say is calling?" asked the woman.

"Guinivere Jones. I'm with the *Sanibel-Captiva Sun-Times*."

"One moment, please."

Guin waited.

"I'm sorry, Mr. Simms is on another call," said the woman. "May I take your number and have him call you back?"

"Sure," said Guin.

She gave the woman her number and said that it was important she speak with him.

When the call ended, Guin put her phone back down, turning it over. She stared out the window again. A flock of ibis was pecking its way across the golf course. She watched them for several minutes, then she heard her phone buzzing.

She picked it up but didn't recognize the number. Something told her she should answer, though, so she did.

"Guin Jones," she said.

"Ms. Jones?"

It was a woman.

"Yes, speaking," said Guin.

"This is the Health Park. We had a note to contact you should Mr. DiDio regain consciousness."

"He's awake?" said Guin. "Is he okay?"

"I'm afraid I don't have any additional information," said the caller.

"Can I see him?" Guin asked.

This could be the break she was looking for.

"As long as it's during visiting hours."

"Okay, great," said Guin. "I'll be right there. Thank you!"

Guin grabbed her bag and her keys and raced downstairs.

Guin checked in at the desk and was given directions to Nick DiDio's room. She stood outside for a minute, listening at the door to see if anyone was in there with him, but she couldn't really hear anything. She knocked and heard someone say "come in."

Guin slowly opened the door and glanced around. There were two beds in the large room, divided by a curtain. One of the beds was empty. In the other one was a man lying immobilized, surrounded by machines, his eyes closed. Guin moved closer, then stopped.

"Mr. DiDio?"

The man opened his eyes and turned them towards her.

"My name's Guin, Guin Jones. We spoke on the phone the other day, before your accident, about Frank Funt."

"Come here," he said, his voice barely above a croak. "I can't see so good."

Guin moved closer to the bed. She looked down at Nick. She guessed him to be around her age, early forties. Though it was hard to get an accurate read as he was pretty banged up.

"Have we met?" he said, looking up at her. "I think I would have remembered if we had."

"No," said Guin. "We haven't met. I had called you, about Frank Funt, Jr., and Funt in the Son Construction. We were supposed to meet the other day, before your, uh, accident."

"Accident, huh? That's what they're calling it?"

He made a face.

"They said you fell off a roof."

"I've been doing construction for years," Nick informed her, "and I've never *fallen* off a roof."

Guin didn't know what to say.

"Everything's a bit hazy," he continued. "But I remember getting a call while I was up there, and the next thing I knew, I was lying on the ground, unable to move, the wind knocked out of me. Then everything went black. When I came to, I was lying here in this hospital bed, feeling like I got run over by a truck."

"Ouch," said Guin.

"Yeah, ouch," said Nick. "So, what brings you to my death bed?"

Guin looked horrified.

"Sorry, gallows humor. Though death's gotta be less painful. Anyway, answer the question."

"I just wanted to see if you were okay."

"Why?" he asked, looking directly at her.

"Well," said Guin. "I know it might sound crazy, but I feel partially responsible."

"You push me off that roof?"

"No!" said Guin. "I had no idea where you were. But the accident happened right after I spoke with you about Funt and we had arranged to meet."

"Don't beat yourself up about it," said Nick. "Like they said, it was probably an accident."

Though judging by his face, Guin didn't think he really believed that.

He winced.

"You okay?" she asked.

"No. The pain's pretty bad."

"Should I call for a nurse, have her give you something?"

"As if they would. They keep a pretty tight rein on how much pain meds they give you these days. Don't want you to get addicted."

He chuckled.

"What's so funny?" asked Guin.

"You wanted to know about Funt, right?"

"That's right," said Guin. "But not if it hurts to talk."

"It's okay," said Nick. "You know what the irony of all this is? If that's what you call it."

"What?" said Guin.

"Frank was always popping painkillers. He had a bum leg. Got it falling off a roof. Pretty funny, no? I think he was addicted to the stuff, but he denied it. Said the old man would kill him if he thought he was an addict. That was one of the conditions of the old man selling him the business: no drugs."

"So his father didn't know?"

"Or he was in denial. And now look at me, practically begging for something to ease the pain."

"This is different," said Guin.

"Is it?" said Nick. "How do you think people get addicted to painkillers? Doctors hand out the stuff like lollipops. Or they used to."

"You think doctors are responsible for getting people hooked on painkillers?"

"I think big pharma pays doctors to get people hooked. It's how they make their money."

Guin didn't know what to say. She had never taken opioids, or any illicit drugs, though she read the news and knew that certain drug companies continued to push opioids even after finding out how addictive they were.

"Getting back to Frank," she finally said. "Do you think he might have been selling painkillers and other drugs to his clients?"

"Why do you ask?"

"Just something I heard. I also understand he took out a loan from Big Lou Antinori to buy out his father."

Nick closed his eyes.

"I told Frank that was a big mistake."

"Why's that?"

Nick opened his eyes again and looked at her.

"Big Lou is big trouble, especially for a guy like Frank."

"How so?"

"Frank wasn't very good with money."

"So I've heard," said Guin. "I understand he owed you a bunch."

"Where'd you hear that?"

"From your father."

"You spoke with Pops?"

"I did," said Guin. "And got an earful."

Nick smiled up at her, then frowned.

"Poor Pops. This must be killing him."

"So, is it true? Did Frank owe you a lot of money?"

"Yeah, it's true. Though Frank owed a lot of people money."

"Did he owe Big Lou a lot of money?"

Nick nodded.

"That loan was the last straw for me. No way was I going to be partners with Big Lou."

"But it was just a loan," said Guin. "Frank wasn't selling him a share of the business, was he?"

"Might as well have been. Frank had to put the business up as collateral."

"So you quit?"

"I quit."

"And you went to work for Tony Del Sole."

"I heard he was looking for a project manager."

"Who'd you hear that from, Phoebe?"

"You know Phoebe?" asked Nick.

"We've met," said Guin.

"She's a great gal, isn't she? She's been here every day, bringing me stuff."

Nick was smiling.

"You two ever date?"

"Me and Phoebe?"

Nick looked at Guin as though she had said something crazy.

"Phoebe's like a sister to me."

"Do you know if she's seeing Tony Del Sole?"

"You should ask Phoebe that."

"Did Phoebe help you get the job with Tony?"

"She just told me he was expanding and needed another PM."

"You know anything about Sunshine buying Funt and the Son?"

"I might have heard something."

"Where were you the Sunday before last?" Guin asked him.

"What is this, the inquisition?"

"Sorry," said Guin. "It's the reporter in me. But do you happen to recall where you were two Sundays ago?"

"Listen, lady, I can barely remember what happened two days ago. I have no clue what I was doing the Sunday before last."

Guin was about to ask him another question when the door opened and a nurse walked in.

"Time to check your vitals, Mr. DiDio."

She turned and looked at Guin.

"And you are?"

"Just leaving," said Nick.

"Thank you for your time, Mr. DiDio," Guin said, not wanting to interfere. "I hope you feel better soon."

She left the room, kicking herself for not handling the situation better. As she was walking down the hall, mumbling to herself, she nearly collided with another woman.

"Excuse me," she said. She looked up. "Phoebe!"

"What are *you* doing here?" said Phoebe, scowling at Guin.

"I heard that Nick regained consciousness."

"You better not have done anything to upset him," warned Phoebe.

"Go see for yourself," said Guin. "The nurse is in with him."

Phoebe looked past her, towards Nick's room.

"Just one question," said Guin.

Phoebe waited.

"Where were you when Nick had his accident?"

"At work."

"Can anyone verify that?"

"I don't think I like what you're implying, Ms. Jones. Now, if you'll excuse me, I'm off to see my friend."

Guin watched as Phoebe strode down the hall.

CHAPTER 32

Guin leaned against the Mini, glancing up at the hospital. She wondered what Phoebe and Nick were discussing, and if her name had been mentioned. She pulled out her phone and looked up Sunshine Builders. It was time she had a chat with Tony Del Sole.

She called the number listed on the website. No one answered, so she left a message. Then she called the Sanibel police department and asked to be put through to Detective O'Loughlin. She nearly dropped the phone when he answered.

"This better be important," he said.

"It is," said Guin. "I'm at the hospital. I just saw Nick DiDio."

She thought she heard the detective mumble something.

"I also bumped into Phoebe Costanza. Did you know she's working for Tony Del Sole now, the same Tony Del Sole who was in talks to buy Funt and the Son from Frank, Jr.?"

"I am aware."

"Well, did you know that something may have been going on between Caroline Simms and Funt?"

There was silence for several seconds.

"Anything else, Nancy Drew?"

Guin hated it when he called her that.

"As a matter of fact, yes. But first, I was hoping *you* might share some information."

Guin waited, but the detective didn't say anything.

"Can you at least tell me who's on your list of suspects?"

"Other than you?" replied the detective.

"That's not funny," said Guin. "Look, I know about the autopsy report. Do you honestly believe I could have tackled the guy and then shot him up with fentanyl?"

"You could have had help," said the detective. "We have a witness who heard you arguing with Funt a few days before he died. According to the witness, you threatened to get rid of him."

Guin wondered who the witness was. Probably one of the guys Funt had working on the house.

"Get rid of him as in fire him," she clarified. "Not kill him. And I was nowhere near the house that Sunday night. I was at the condo. You can check the location history on my phone."

The location history! That was it. Why hadn't she thought of that before?

"Speaking of location history, did you check the location history on Phoebe Costanza's and Tony Del Sole's phones? While you're at it, check out Nick DiDio's and William Simms's location histories, too."

"First of all, Ms. Jones, you need a warrant to search someone's phone."

"So, get a warrant."

"It's not that simple," replied the detective.

Guin huffed.

"Well, have you talked to Big Lou? I understand Funt owed him a lot of money."

"Please don't tell me you're investigating Lou Antinori," said the detective.

"I might be. What's it to you?"

"Stay away from Big Lou. I'm serious. Let the police handle it. People who ask too many questions about Mr. Antinori have a habit of disappearing or suffering bodily harm."

Guin suddenly worried about Craig.

"Fine, but give me something, detective. If not for me, for our readers."

"You can tell your readers that the Sanibel police department is continuing to investigate and will have a comment for the press once an arrest has been made."

Guin rolled her eyes.

"So, what's up with you and Maggie? You two straighten things out?"

"Mmph," said the detective.

"I'm sorry, I didn't hear that," said Guin. "Could you repeat what you just said?"

"I need to go."

Guin was about to say something, but the detective had already hung up.

Guin spent the rest of the day working on her article about *The Belle of Sanibel*. She had suffered a bit of writer's block at first, not being used to writing book reviews or author profiles, but once she got going, the words flowed. It was nearly five o'clock when she took a break to go to the bathroom and check her phone.

Tony Del Sole had not returned her call. She thought about calling him again, then decided to wait until the morning, as he no doubt had gone home for the day.

She sat back down at her computer, then glanced out the window. It was still light out, and she didn't feel like working anymore. She got up and changed into a pair of shorts and a t-shirt. Then she grabbed her keys and her fanny pack and headed out the door.

Guin arrived at Blind Pass ten minutes later. There were plenty of free spaces in the parking lot, and she was able to park close to the entrance to the beach.

She walked down to the water and took a deep breath, closing her eyes and slowly inhaling and exhaling.

"I love this time of day, don't you?" said a friendly female voice.

Guin opened her eyes to see her friend Bonnie, the treasurer of the Shell Club.

"Bonnie!" said Guin. "What are you doing up at Blind Pass?"

Bonnie, like Shelly, lived in the area of Sanibel known as Middle Gulf (which Guin's brother teasingly referred to as "Middle Earth"). Though like many shell seekers, she frequented different beaches.

"I was visiting a friend up on Captiva and figured I'd stop by the beach before I drove home. You?"

"I needed a break from an article I was working on."

"What's the article about?" asked Bonnie.

"It's actually a book review."

"What's the book?"

"It's called *The Belle of Sanibel*."

"*The Belle of Sanibel*?"

"It's kind of a romance, set on Sanibel in the eighteen-eighties," said Guin. "It's by a local author."

"Oh, which one?"

"Caroline Simms."

Bonnie put a hand on Guin's arm.

"Caroline Simms wrote a romance novel?"

Guin nodded.

"And it's actually not bad."

Bonnie shook her head.

"You could knock me over with a feather. And you say it's pretty good?"

"A little flowery," said Guin. "But very readable. Steamy, too," she added with a grin.

"I may have to read it," said Bonnie.

"You should," said Guin. "It's a pretty easy read. She's giving a book talk next week over at the Sanctuary Club, if you're interested."

"Maybe," said Bonnie.

"Well, I need to stretch my legs," said Guin.

"No worries," said Bonnie. "I was just leaving. Enjoy your walk." She paused. "Say, you hear anything more about that contractor, Funt?"

Ginny had run a short piece about him in the paper, leaving Guin's name out of it, which Guin had appreciated.

"I know you're not supposed to speak ill of the dead," Bonnie continued. "But I can't help thinking he got what he deserved."

"Why do you say that?"

"You may not know the story since it happened before you moved here, but Funt was responsible for getting two local kids killed. They were in an automobile accident. Turns out, the driver was high on drugs Funt had sold him."

"Actually, I did hear about that and that one of the kids was Jimbo Leidecker's daughter."

Bonnie nodded.

"Melissa. She was with her boyfriend, Logan, and a couple of his friends. They were home from college and had gone over to Fort Myers Beach. I knew Melissa a bit. Sweet girl. She volunteered over at the museum. Just about killed Jimbo and Terry when they lost her."

"Did you know any of the other kids or their parents?"

Bonnie nodded.

"I'm in Zonta with Sally Bates, Logan's mom. She was devastated when Logan died. He was her pride and joy."

Guin had no children, but she could imagine how awful it must have been.

"Wait, did you say Sally Bates?"

"That's right," said Bonnie. "Why?"

"She's my new neighbor, or will be, once I move into my new place."

"I forgot all about that," said Bonnie. "How's the renovation going? Weren't you supposed to move in around now?"

Guin hoped Bonnie wouldn't make the connection between her and Funt. (She couldn't remember if she had told Bonnie who she had hired.)

"Getting there," said Guin. "There were some unforeseen problems, but I should be moving in in a few weeks."

"Well, good luck."

"Thanks," said Guin. "I'll have you over when it's done."

"I'd like that. Well, I should shove off. Nice seeing you, Guin."

"Nice seeing you, too, Bonnie."

Bonnie headed toward the parking lot while Guin headed down the beach in search of shells.

CHAPTER 33

Guin leaned against the kitchen counter, sipping her coffee. No one was returning her calls, which always annoyed her.

"The hell with it," she said, grabbing her phone.

She entered the number for Sunshine Builders.

"Sunshine Builders," said a female voice.

"Phoebe?"

"Yeah," said the voice. "Who's this?"

"Phoebe, it's Guin Jones. Don't hang up!" she said, sensing that Phoebe was on the verge of ending their call. "I need to talk to Tony. Is he there?"

"No, he's on a job."

"Can you give me his cell phone number? It's important."

There was silence for several seconds.

"I know you've been snooping around," said Phoebe. "Asking questions about Frank. But Tony had nothing to do with it."

"Great," said Guin. "Then he has nothing to worry about. His number?"

There was no reply.

"Would you rather I come to the office and wait for him there?" Guin asked her.

"Fine," said Phoebe. "I'll give you his number. But don't expect him to pick up."

She reluctantly gave Guin the number for Tony's mobile phone.

"Thank you," said Guin.

Phoebe mumbled something, which sounded like *bitch*, then ended the call.

"Well, at least she gave me his number."

She entered the number Phoebe gave her into her phone, hoping it wasn't a fake.

"Del Sole here," came a male voice.

"Hi, Mr. Del Sole. This is Guin Jones. I left you a message the other day, about Frank Funt, and—"

"I know who you are, Ms. Jones. And I've got nothing to say about Frank Funt."

"Please, I just want a few minutes of your time."

"I'm busy."

"How about later? I could meet you at your office."

There was a long pause, then he spoke again.

"Fine. Meet me there at four-thirty."

"Great," said Guin.

"But I can only spare you a few minutes."

"Understood. See you at four-thirty."

The call ended, but at least Guin had been able to arrange a meeting with the elusive owner of Sunshine Builders.

"Now let's see who else I can pin down," she said to Fauna.

She entered the number for the Island Trust Company into her phone.

"Island Trust Company," came a familiar female voice.

"Good afternoon," said Guin. "Mr. William Simms, please. Tell him it's Guinivere Jones, and that I will keep calling him until he agrees to see me."

"One moment, please," said the woman.

A minute later, she was put through.

"Ms. Jones," came a deep voice. "I hope this has to do

with my wife's book and not Frank Funt."

Guin thought about lying but decided against it.

"Well, I did have a couple of questions about your wife and her book, but I also wanted to ask you about Frank Funt. I promise it won't take long."

Mr. Simms sighed.

"Ginny called me just a little while ago. Told me I was not to yell at her star reporter, that you were just doing your job and I should be nice."

Guin smiled. She could just picture Ginny in her best schoolmarm voice chastising William Simms.

"So, would it be okay for me to stop by the office later? I promise not to take up too much of your time."

"I have to head out to a meeting in a few. But I could spare you a few minutes now."

"Okay," said Guin, disappointed. She would have much preferred to ask him her questions in person. "Could you hold on a second?"

She put her phone on speaker and raced to grab her microcassette recorder and pop in a tape.

As she did, she could hear Mr. Simms drumming his fingers.

"Okay, I'm back!" she said, recorder in hand. "So is it okay if I record our conversation? It'll save time, and I'm the only one who'll hear it."

"If you must," said Mr. Simms.

"Thank you," said Guin.

She hit "record" and asked him some softball questions about his wife and her book, hoping to butter him up.

"Okay," she said, when they were done. "Now if I could just ask you a few questions about Frank Funt."

"I'm terribly sorry," said Mr. Simms. "But I really must go. Another time, perhaps."

"I—" Guin began, but Mr. Simms cut her off.

"Good day, Ms. Jones. I look forward to reading your article about my wife's book."

He ended the call, leaving Guin clutching her phone, frustrated.

"Grr," she said, gritting her teeth. She stared down at her microcassette recorder. "Well, at least now I can finish the article."

Guin had been so focused on finishing her piece on Caroline Simms and *The Belle of Sanibel* that she hadn't checked her phone in hours. But first, she got up and stretched.

When she removed her phone from the drawer, she saw that she had several messages, including one from Glen, left around an hour before, asking her to call him ASAP. She immediately called him back.

"Hey, it's Guin," she said, as soon as he answered. "I just got your message. What's up?"

"Can you come over here, to the house?"

"Is everything okay? I didn't think you were working there today."

"I had my tile guy working over there. Figured that was okay."

"Of course," said Guin. "Did he find something bad in the bathroom? Please tell me he didn't find a leak or rotted wood."

Or another dead body, Guin thought.

"No, nothing like that. He just found something I think you should take a look at."

"Can you tell me over the phone?"

"I'd rather show it to you. Are you free?"

Guin looked at the clock on her monitor.

"I'll be right over. Just give me a few."

"I'll be here," said Glen.

They ended the call and Guin stared out the window. What could Glen's tile guy have found? Her mind flashed to *Antiques Roadshow* and those home renovation shows on HGTV. Maybe the tile guy had found some old liquor bottles or perhaps a stash of gold coins or some other hidden treasure.

She saved her article, which she wanted to go over one more time before sending it off to Ginny. Then she got her bag and her keys and left.

Guin knocked on the front door, which was locked, and Glen let her in.

"So what's so hush-hush that you couldn't tell me about over the phone?" asked Guin.

"This," said Glen, holding up what looked like an old cookie tin.

Maybe it was buried treasure!

"What's in it?" asked Guin, peering at the tin.

Glen lifted the lid. On top was a sealed envelope.

Guin looked from the envelope to Glen.

"Lift it up," said Glen.

"Okay," said Guin.

She removed the envelope and looked inside the container. There were dozens of small round objects, in white, pink, yellow, green, and blue.

"They look like pills," said Guin, taking a finger and gently touching a couple of them.

"That's my guess, too," said Glen.

"But what are they doing here?"

"I was hoping you might know," said Glen.

"I have no idea," said Guin. "Where did you say your guy found it?"

"Under one of the tiles in the bathroom. I'm surprised

the cops didn't come across it."

Guin was surprised, too.

"Do you think it belonged to Funt? Though it could have belonged to the previous owner."

"It's possible," said Glen. "But considering where it was found, my money's on Funt."

Guin continued to look at the tin.

"Any idea what kind of pills these are?"

"If I had to take a guess, I'd say painkillers. More precisely, opioids."

Guin looked up at him.

"Opioids?"

Glen nodded.

Guin realized she was still holding the envelope. She turned it over. There was nothing written on either side."

"Should we open it? It may tell us who the tin belonged to."

"Do you think that's a good idea?" said Glen. "Maybe we should call the police first. It could be evidence."

"You didn't notify them when you found this?"

Glen shook his head.

"I wanted to speak to you first, in case the tin belonged to you."

"I've never seen it before," said Guin. "And I have no reason to be hiding painkillers in my unfinished bathroom." She looked at the tin again, then at the envelope she was holding in her hand. She placed the envelope back inside the tin and pulled out her phone.

"Sanibel police department," said a female voice.

"Detective O'Loughlin, please. Tell him it's Guin Jones."

"One moment please."

Guin waited.

"I'm sorry, Ms. Jones," said the operator, "but he's busy right now. Would you like to leave a message?"

"This is urgent," said Guin.

"He said he was not to be disturbed unless it was an emergency."

"Tell him this is an emergency."

"Hold, please," said the operator.

Guin waited.

"What's the emergency this time?" said the detective.

"One of the guys working at my house found a tin filled with what we believe are painkillers hidden beneath a tile in the bathroom where Funt was found. There was also an envelope, but it's sealed. And I didn't want to open it without consulting you first."

Though had Guin discovered the tin on her own, she would have probably torn open the envelope and then called the detective had it contained anything relevant to the case.

"Where are you now?" asked the detective.

"At the house."

"Okay, I'll head over there as soon as I wrap things up here. Don't open the envelope or touch anything until I get there."

"And when will that be?"

"Just don't touch anything," repeated the detective. Then he hung up.

A half an hour later, the detective arrived at the house, just as Guin was wondering if he would ever show up.

"Show me where your guy found it," the detective said to Glen.

"Just there," said Glen, pointing to the spot in the guest bathroom.

The detective went over to take a better look.

"And besides you and your tile guy and Ms. Jones, has anyone else touched the tin?"

"Just the guy who put it there," said Glen.

"And you didn't open the envelope?" asked the detective.

"It's still sealed, as you can see," said Guin.

The detective put on a pair of disposable gloves, then gingerly took the envelope out of the tin. He turned it over a couple of times.

"There doesn't appear to be any writing on it," said Guin. "But there's definitely something inside. You can feel it. I'm guessing it's a sheet of paper. Maybe two."

The detective regarded the envelope, holding it up to the light, but it was impossible to see what was inside.

"I'm taking the container and the envelope with me," he said, placing the envelope back inside the tin and then closing it.

"You're not going to open it here?" said Guin.

"It's evidence," said the detective.

"Come on, detective!" said Guin, exasperated. "I could have opened the envelope and not told you about it. I deserve to know what's inside."

"Go on, detective," said Glen. "It is her house, so technically the tin belongs to her."

The detective scowled.

"I'll be right back."

"Where are you going?" said Guin, following him.

"To get a letter opener."

A minute later he returned.

"You keep a letter opener in your car?"

"No, but I keep a Swiss army knife," he said, producing it.

"Ah," said Guin.

The detective flipped up a small blade and proceeded to very carefully tear the top of the envelope. Guin watched and waited as the detective gingerly removed a folded piece of paper from the envelope.

"What does it say?" said Guin, trying to peer over the paper.

"It appears to be a page from a ledger," said the detective.

"A ledger?" said Guin. "Like those things accountants use to use to keep track of transactions?"

"Exactly," said the detective, examining the page.

"Though who uses a ledger these days? Seems very old fashioned. Why not put the information online or on a computer?"

"Maybe the person was worried about getting hacked," suggested Glen. "My dad used to keep a ledger for his business. Actually two ledgers, in case something happened to one of them. I told him he needed to put everything on a computer, but he resisted for a long time. Said the information was safer in the ledgers, which he kept in two different safes, than putting it on the computer."

"In the movies, mob guys always keep two ledgers," Guin said. "One for show and one that showed where the money really came from and went. Not that your father was involved with the mob," she quickly added.

The detective was looking at the piece of paper.

"So what does it say?" asked Guin, trying to take a peek.

"Sorry, confidential," said the detective, folding the piece of paper and putting it back in the envelope.

"Come on!" said Guin. "If not for us, you wouldn't have even known about the tin and the paper," she said, planting her hands on her hips.

"Sorry," repeated the detective. "It's police property now. Evidence."

"Just one little peek. I promise not to tell."

The detective gave her a look.

"Fine. Next time I find a sealed envelope in a hidden

container, I'm looking at it before calling the police," Guin huffed. "Can you at least confirm the container belonged to Funt?"

"We'll need to run a few tests."

"Fine," said Guin again. "Then will you let me know?"

"I need to go," said the detective.

"Will you at least tell me if the pills are painkillers?" asked Guin, following him out.

"Good day, Ms. Jones, Mr. Anderson."

The detective nodded to them, then let himself out.

"Argh!" said Guin, after the door had closed. "We should have opened the envelope and looked inside! Now I have yet another mystery to solve."

"Actually…" said Glen, looking a bit sheepish.

"What?" said Guin, looking at him.

"When you were sparring with the detective, I was able to get a look at the paper. I guess he forgot I was standing just behind him. It appeared to be a list of names with some numbers and notes beside them."

"Were you able to make out any of the names?"

"The handwriting was a bit hard to read, but I did make out a couple."

"And?" said Guin.

"I'm pretty sure one of them was Simms."

CHAPTER 34

"Simms?!" said Guin. "As in William and Caroline Simms?"

They were the only two Simms on the island she knew about. Well, three, including their son, William, Jr., known as Billy, the former star quarterback for the University of Central Florida Knights, who also worked at the Island Trust Company. Could he have been buying drugs from Funt? Though last she heard, he had gone to work in their Tampa office. Still…

"I don't know," said Glen. "It just stood out because of Phil Simms, the former Giants quarterback."

"What was the other name? You said you saw a couple."

"I think it was Smith."

Guin knew of a few Smiths on the island but none she knew well. And there were doubtless many more in Fort Myers.

"But you're sure you saw the name Simms?" she asked him.

"Not a hundred percent, but pretty sure."

"Hmm…" said Guin. "Any idea what the list could be?"

"Maybe a list of clients?" said Glen.

"Quite possibly," said Guin. "Though I'm guessing from the contents of the tin they weren't home renovation clients, or maybe they were and Funt was supplying them with something more than just materials and labor. That is, assuming the tin belonged to Funt."

She looked thoughtful.

"I wish I had pocketed a few of those pills."

"I thought you might feel that way," said Glen.

Guin arched her eyebrows as Glen reached into his pocket.

"I know they're evidence, but…" he said, revealing a handful of pills.

"I could kiss you, Glen Anderson!"

"I figured the detective wouldn't miss them, and I have a buddy who can tell me what they are."

"Of course you do," said Guin.

"It's not what you're thinking," said Glen, seeing Guin's expression. "He's a pharmacist."

"Ah," she Guin.

"I'll drop these off later and tell him I need them analyzed right away."

"What if he asks questions?"

"I'll tell him the truth."

Guin looked at him.

"That one of my guys found them stashed away in a house he's working on."

"Okay," said Guin. "But nothing else."

Glen crossed his heart.

"Promise. Felix and I go way back. He won't say anything."

"Okay," said Guin. "Just let me know what Felix says."

"Will do. And now, I must be going."

"Sorry," said Guin. "I didn't mean to keep you."

"It's fine," he said. "I should still make it to the shoot on time."

"Where's it at?"

"Back up at South Seas."

"Do they need more turkey shots?"

Glen smiled.

"No, I'm taking some pictures of the general manager's daughter and her family. They wanted some family sunset shots."

"Well, have fun! Any idea when you'll be back at the house?

"Hopefully Thursday. If not, definitely this weekend."

"I hate that you're giving up your weekends to work on the place," said Guin, feeling a bit guilty.

"Don't feel bad. I'm enjoying it. I haven't fixed up a place in ages. Feels kinda good to be doing something useful again."

"Hey, you've done plenty of useful stuff! You've been taking care of your mom and dad. And you're a great photographer."

"You know what I mean," said Glen.

"I do," said Guin. "Just don't be so hard on yourself. I wish I was handy."

"I bet you could be," said Glen. "Come by the house this weekend, and I'll put you to work. It'll be fun."

Guin looked skeptical.

"Well, I would like to help. I just worry I'll screw something up."

"I'll make sure you don't," said Glen. "Come by Saturday. I'll text you Friday to confirm. Who knows, you might discover something."

"That's what I'm afraid of," said Guin. "Though it would be nice if we found some Spanish doubloons."

"You never know," said Glen. "Though I wouldn't get your hopes up."

Guin felt her phone vibrating in her back pocket and grabbed it.

"Shoot!" she said, looking at the time.

"Something wrong?" asked Glen.

"I was supposed to meet with Tony Del Sole five minutes ago."

"You can always call him, tell him you're running late."

Guin sighed.

"I suppose."

Glen waved goodbye as Guin dialed Tony's number. The call went straight to voicemail.

Guin decided to drive over to Sunshine Builders, even though Tony hadn't picked up. There were no cars in front when she got there, and the place looked like it was closed. But she got out and tapped on the door just in case. No one answered. She tried to look inside, but the office was dark. She knocked again and waited. Still no answer.

She pulled out her phone and called Tony's cell phone again. Again, it went to voicemail.

"Hey, Mr. Del Sole, this is Guin Jones again. Sorry I was late. I got hung up. I'm at your office now, but no one seems to be here. Could you give me a call at [she gave him her number] when you get this, so we can reschedule? Thanks."

She ended the call and put her phone back in her bag. Then she got in the Mini and headed home.

Guin was fixing her coffee the next morning when her phone started buzzing. She looked down and saw it was Craig.

"Hey there," she said. "Shouldn't you be out fishing or something?"

"Jimbo just called me from the police department."

"What's he doing there? Is he okay?"

"The police showed up at Sally's this morning. Said they wanted to speak with her. They took her in for questioning.

Jimbo was there and went with them."

"Any idea what it's about?"

"I'm not sure. He just told me Sally had been brought in and asked if I could meet him there."

"Huh," said Guin. "So no idea why the police wanted to speak with her?"

"Jimbo said her name was on some list."

Guin instantly made the connection.

"The list!"

"What list?"

"Sorry," said Guin. "Glen's tile guy was working over at my house yesterday, and he found a tin hidden in my bathroom, the one where I found Funt. Inside was an envelope, with some kind of list, and a bunch of pills."

"Did you happen to see this list?" asked Craig.

"No, the envelope was sealed."

"Then how do you know it was a list?"

"We called the detective. He opened the envelope while we were there, and Glen caught a glimpse of what was inside. It was some kind of list, with a bunch of names and numbers on it."

"Did he recognize any of the names?"

"Just a couple."

Craig waited.

"You going to make me guess?"

"Sorry. One of them was Simms. And the other was Smith."

"Hmm…" said Craig. "So you think the tin belonged to Funt and that the list was of his clients?"

"That's what we thought," said Guin.

"And you say there were a bunch of pills in the tin? You think they were drugs?"

"That's what we were thinking. Glen snagged a few and was going to have them analyzed."

"Let me know what he finds out."

"Will do," said Guin. "So if Sally's name was on the list…"

"You want to meet me over at the SPD?"

"I thought you'd never ask," said Guin. "Just give me a few minutes to throw on some clothes, and I'll be right over."

"Okay," said Craig. "I'll see you there."

Guin poured her coffee into a to-go mug, then hurriedly got dressed. She grabbed the mug, her bag, and her keys, and twenty minutes later was pulling into the parking lot by the Sanibel police department.

She saw Craig on his phone a few feet away and tried to get his attention.

"Craig!" she called, waiving.

He held up a finger, indicating he would just be a minute. Guin waited a few feet away. Finally, he was free.

"So, what's going on? Did you talk to Jimbo?"

"Briefly," said Craig. "It doesn't sound good."

"Did you find out why the police were questioning Sally?"

"They believe she was buying drugs from Funt and may have been involved in his murder."

"What?" said Guin, in disbelief. "That's crazy!" Though she realized after she said it that she really didn't know Sally. For all she knew, Sally could be a drug addict and a murderer.

"That's what Jimbo said."

"Did you ask him if it was true, about the drugs?"

"He swore to me that Sally wasn't a user."

"So why was her name on the list?"

"I don't know," said Craig.

"Where's Jimbo now?"

"In talking with O'Loughlin."

"So now what?"

"Jimbo asked me to wait."

"I'll wait with you."

They didn't have to wait too long as Jimbo emerged from the police department ten minutes later, looking haggard.

"How did it go?" asked Craig.

Jimbo shook his head.

"Not good."

"Did they arrest Sally?" asked Guin.

Jimbo turned to look at her.

"I asked Guin to meet me here," said Craig. "So what did the detective say to you?"

"He wanted to know about Sally, if she had a drug problem. I told him that was ridiculous, that she would never take drugs, that her son was killed because of drugs."

"And what did he say after you told him that?" asked Guin.

"He wanted to know why then her name was on some list, supposedly of people who were buying drugs from Funt."

Craig and Guin exchanged a look.

"What?" said Jimbo, looking at them.

"I'm sorry about Sally," said Guin. "A guy working over at my house found the list in a tin that had been stashed in my guest bathroom. It contained a bunch of pills, which we think are opioids."

Jimbo shook his head.

"I told her it was a dumb idea. But she wouldn't listen. Said it was the only way to catch him, to prove he was responsible."

"Prove who was responsible?" said Guin. "For what?"

"Funt," said Jimbo. "For selling drugs to that kid and other kids."

Guin was momentarily confused.

"My daughter Melissa and Sally's son Logan were involved in an accident a few years back," Jimbo explained. "You may have read about it. They were home for winter break and had gone to Fort Myers Beach to some party. On the way home, their car was in an accident. Melissa and Logan were in the backseat, apparently not wearing seatbelts, and were killed. The kid driving and the other kid wound up in the Emergency Room. Turns out the kid driving the car was high as a kite. He had popped some pills at the party, OxyContin or something, in addition to drinking alcohol, and should have never been allowed to drive.

"The cops asked him where he got the pills, if he had a prescription, and he told them he got the pills from some guy working on his house, and that he didn't understand what all the fuss was about, that lots of people took painkillers, no biggie."

"Let me guess: the guy working on his house who sold him the pills was none other than Frank Funt," Guin said.

Jimbo nodded.

"Of course, Funt denied it. Said he had no idea what the kid was talking about. And his lawyer got him off."

"You and the other parents must have been devastated," said Guin.

"We were. Then the guy gets caught a couple of months later trying to sell drugs to an undercover cop."

Jimbo shook his head again.

"I read about that," said Guin. "And I heard he got off."

"Yup. We couldn't believe it."

Guin was going to say something about Funt being lucky. Then an image of him in her tub flashed up.

"So how did Sally's name get on the list?"

Jimbo sighed.

"Sally never got over Logan's death. He was her baby. Real smart kid, too, except maybe when it came to choosing friends. She was livid when Funt got off and wanted to nail him before more kids died."

He paused.

"I thought she had finally moved on, forgotten about Funt, when one day she sees Funt's truck parked at your place. Though we didn't know you were the new owner. Suddenly it all came rushing back: the car accident, losing Logan, Funt's testimony that he had nothing to do with it. That's when she hatched her plan."

"What plan?" said Guin.

"She was going to hire Funt to do some work at her place and get cozy with him. Then she would get him to sell her some drugs."

"Wasn't that a bit risky?" said Craig.

Jimbo nodded.

"That's what I said. But she had it all planned out. She had me rig up cameras around the house, to keep an eye on Funt and record everything. That way, she'd have a record of him selling her drugs."

"But couldn't she also be incriminated?" asked Guin.

"She had written down her plan on a piece of paper and was planning on mailing it to herself, in case anything happened."

"So what happened?" said Craig. "Did she go through with it? Did Funt bite?"

Jimbo nodded.

"He did. Sally couldn't believe how easy it was."

"But how would Sally buying drugs from him prove Funt was responsible for her son's and Melissa's deaths?" asked Guin.

"She planned on getting him to confess."

"Confess?" said Guin.

"To selling drugs to that kid and others like him."

"How?" said Guin. "I can't imagine that's something he'd confess to."

Jimbo grew a bit uncomfortable.

"By seducing him."

"Excuse me?" said Guin.

Jimbo had said it so softly, she wasn't sure she had heard him correctly.

"Sally thought if she buttered him up, flirted with him, told him how clever he was, and then casually asked him about his other clients, he'd tell her," said Jimbo.

"Seriously?" said Guin. It sounded like a ridiculous plan to her.

"Guys like Funt are all ego," said Jimbo. "They love feeling clever and important. Sally was married to a guy just like Funt. That's why she divorced him. She knew just what to say to rope him in."

"She was taking a pretty big risk," said Craig. "What if Funt caught on and got angry, or worse?"

"I was hiding in the other room," said Jimbo, "watching the whole thing on my phone."

Guin looked at Jimbo. He was around Funt's size but older and mild-mannered. She couldn't picture him tackling the contractor.

"So what happened? Did it work?"

Jimbo nodded.

"Sally had gotten pretty friendly with him. So one day when he's finishing up, she asks him if he'd like a drink, says she just bought this really expensive single-malt Scotch and had no one to share it with. She had recalled Funt mentioning that he liked the stuff but that it wasn't cheap. He says, 'Sure, don't mind if I do.' And she keeps pouring him refills while she gets him talking about his work and all of his rich clients.

"Then, when he's had a few, she casually asks him if he worked on the Smiths' place."

"The Smiths?" said Guin, her ears perking up.

"Their kid was one the driving that night," said Jimbo.

"And what did Funt say?"

"He said that he had and then bragged about how they were always asking him to do stuff for them, how he was the man. Then Sally asks if he ever supplied them with painkillers. And Funt says, 'Sure,' and proceeds to brag about it. So now Sally is curious and asks Funt if he ever worries about being arrested."

"And what did he say?" said Guin, who marveled at Sally's audacity.

"He bragged that the cops around here were idiots and couldn't touch him. And that he had friends in high places who would make sure to get him off if need be."

"Did she happen to ask him where he was getting the drugs?" asked Guin.

"She may have. I don't remember."

"And you say Sally was recording the whole exchange?" said Craig.

Jimbo nodded.

"Did she give the footage to the police?" asked Guin.

"No," said Jimbo. "We heard Funt had died a few days later. There was no point."

Craig and Guin exchanged a look.

"I should go back in," said Jimbo.

"Just one more thing," said Guin.

Jimbo waited.

"Where were you and Sally the evening of Sunday, September 23?"

Jimbo rubbed the back of his head.

"I don't recall off the top of my head, why?"

"Try to remember," said Craig.

"Let's see… Sunday, September 23…" He stood there looking thoughtful for a minute. "I think we had gone to see a movie in town."

"Do you happen to recall seeing Funt's truck parked over at Guin's place that evening?" asked Craig.

"Funt's truck?" said Jimbo. "Now that you mention it, I do recall seeing it parked over there. That's right. We saw it and Sally said something like, 'There's the bastard's truck. Well, enjoy it now, you asshole, because you're going to be heading off to jail for a long, long time.' Sorry about the language," he added, looking at Guin.

"Do you happen to recall seeing any other cars or trucks at Guin's that night when you drove by?" asked Craig.

Jimbo looked thoughtful again.

"Now that you mention it, we did see someone pull in, just as we were getting out."

"Any idea what time that was?" said Craig.

Jimbo rubbed the back of his head again.

"I don't know. Maybe ten-thirty? Why?"

"Do you recall anything about the vehicle?" asked Guin.

"No," said Jimbo. "It was dark, and we were tired. Look, I really should get back inside. Thanks for coming."

"Let me know if you need anything," said Craig.

Jimbo nodded, then disappeared back inside the police department.

CHAPTER 35

"Well?" said Guin, looking over at Craig.

"Well, what?" said Craig.

"Who do you think pulled into my place Sunday night? Chances are, that's the killer."

"Maybe," said Craig.

"Maybe?" said Guin.

"We just have Jimbo's word that a vehicle pulled into your place late that night."

"You saying you don't believe Jimbo?"

"I'm saying we need to check out his story," replied Craig.

"Fine," said Guin. "And how do we do that?"

"Didn't you tell me the other day that one of your neighbors had a surveillance camera outside her house? Maybe it caught something."

Guin squeezed Craig's arm.

"Craig, you're a genius. I totally forgot about the Bregmans' camera! I'll go talk to Mrs. Bregman right after I leave. Though," she said, "wouldn't the detective have spoken to them already?" She shook her head. "I can't believe I forgot all about the camera."

"Don't kick yourself," said Craig. "You've had a lot on your mind, and it's not like you've had much of a chance to get to know your new neighbors."

"True," said Guin. "But I should have remembered."

She looked over at the police department.

"What?" said Craig.

"Do you think the detective knows about the other vehicle?"

"Well, you could always ask him."

Guin bit her lip.

"Tell you what," said Craig. "Why don't I go see the detective, and you go have a chat with your neighbor."

"You sure?" said Guin.

"Don't even think about it."

Guin leaned over and gave Craig a quick kiss on the cheek.

"Thanks, Craig! You're the best! Let me know if you find out anything."

Guin parked her car in her driveway and walked over to the Bregmans' house next door. She rang the doorbell and waited. A minute later the door was opened by a woman with short, poofy gray hair who was a little shorter than Guin.

"Yes?" said the woman, looking up at Guin. "Can I help you?"

"Hi, Mrs. Bregman," said Guin. "I don't know if you remember me. I'm Guin, your new neighbor. We met a couple of times."

"Of yes," said Mrs. Bregman, smiling. "How's the construction going?"

"Getting there," said Guin. "That's actually why I'm here."

"Oh?" said Mrs. Bregman.

"You had mentioned a while back that you had a security camera mounted outside."

"Actually, we have two," said Mrs. Bregman. "But you

don't have to worry, dear. We're not nosy. Sam's just worried about porch pirates."

Guin smiled.

"I wasn't worried. I was just curious. What's the range on them? Can they see out to the street?"

"Oh yes, they can see out to the street and just past the property line on both sides."

"And do you keep them on all the time?"

Mrs. Bregman nodded.

"Twenty-four seven. One of Sam's friends, such a nice man, had his car broken into, right in his own driveway, late at night. So Sam insists we keep the cameras running all the time, even though his friend lives over in Fort Myers."

"I see," said Guin. "And how long do you keep the footage?"

"I think Sam said the system automatically stores it for sixty days. Or maybe it was thirty? You can ask him if you like. You thinking of getting one for your place?"

Guin nodded, even though she hadn't been.

"So you would have footage for, say, a week ago Sunday, the twenty-third, say around ten-thirty?"

"Well, that's less than thirty days ago, so I'm sure it's there somewhere. Why?"

"I'm trying to find out who may have been at my house that evening. Another neighbor told me she saw two vehicles parked outside my place late that night."

"Oh goodness, was anything stolen?"

"No, I'm just trying to find out who might have been there."

"Well, Sam and I were away that weekend. But I'm pretty sure the cameras were recording. Would you like me to ask him?"

"That would be great," said Guin. "If it's not too much trouble."

"Oh no," said Mrs. Bregman. "Sam will be thrilled. He loves playing detective."

Guin smiled.

"Well, I appreciate the help."

She reached into her bag and pulled out her card case.

"Here's my card," she said, handing one to Mrs. Bregman. "You can call, text, or email me, whichever is easier."

"Oh, you're a reporter!" said Mrs. Bregman, looking at the card.

"Yes," said Guin.

"What do you write about?"

"Restaurant openings, store openings…" She was about to say *murders*, but she stopped herself. "Events happening around the island. That kind of thing."

"Sounds like fun," said Mrs. Bregman.

"It is," said Guin. "Do you read the paper?"

"I glance at it. But I'll be sure to look for your byline now!"

"Well, thank you for your help, Mrs. Bregman."

"Please, call me Sadie. We're neighbors, after all."

"Thank you, Sadie," said Guin. "And let me know if one of your cameras picked up anything the evening of the twenty-third."

"Will do," said Sadie. "So are you all moved in?"

"Not yet. There's still a lot of work to be done. But I'm hoping to move in a few weeks."

"Well, good luck to you. Let me know when you've settled in. Sam and I will have you over for dinner."

"That would be lovely," said Guin.

She waved goodbye and headed to her car.

Guin felt restless as she drove back to the condo. She wanted to phone Craig, to see if he was able to speak with the detective, but she knew she should wait. He would no doubt phone her if he had learned anything. She checked her phone again for messages after she had parked, hoping to have heard back from Tony Del Sole, but there was nothing from him either. She was about to put her phone back in her bag when it began to buzz. She looked at the caller ID and saw it was her mother.

Guin thought about letting the call go through to voicemail, then swiped to answer.

"Hey, Mom," she said. "Is everything okay?"

"You would know if you bothered to call me once in a while."

Guin rolled her eyes.

"We're about to leave on our cruise," continued her mother. "And I wanted to check in with you, to make sure you had our itinerary and knew how to reach us."

"I got it," said Guin, vaguely remembering the email. "But I'm sure everything will be fine."

"Just keep it handy," said her mother. "You never know. So, did Alfred ever call you? I spoke with his mother, and she said she'd ask him if he knew of anyone who could help you with your house."

"I didn't hear anything from Alfred, but I found someone to help me."

"Did you check his references?"

"He's a friend, Mom."

"Does that mean you didn't check his references?"

Guin counted to eight.

"He's a good guy, Mom. He's already done a bunch of stuff."

"Just keep an eye on him," said her mother. "You can never be too careful with these contractors. They're always looking for ways to cut corners."

"Yes, Mom. But I don't think Glen's like that."

"How do you know this Glen anyway?"

"He works for the paper. He's a photographer."

"A photographer? I thought you said he was your contractor."

"He renovates homes in his spare time, or he used to. His day job is photography. He's very good. You should see his work."

"Does he have a license?"

"To take people's photographs?"

"Don't get smart with me, young lady. You know what I meant."

Guin stared at a hibiscus bush.

"No, Mother, he doesn't have a contractor license, but the guys he has doing the plumbing and electrical work are licensed."

"Just be careful," said her mother. "You remember what happened to Mrs. Bellingham. She hired that man to renovate her place in Greenwich without checking to see if he had a license, and the next thing she knew, her place was a shambles."

Guin prayed for strength.

"I trust Glen," she repeated.

Her mother made a disapproving noise.

"So, you excited about your trip?" Guin asked.

"I don't know about excited," said her mother.

"You leave next week, yes?"

"That's right."

"And you'll be gone for two weeks?"

"Seventeen days. Really, Guinivere. Didn't you read the email I sent you?"

"I did," said Guin. "I just got the number of days wrong. So, have you started packing?"

"Of course," her mother replied. "Though I'm going to wait to put in my dresses. Don't want them to get all wrinkled. Though I understand there's a dry cleaner on board."

"Well, have fun," said Guin. "Send me a postcard."

"I will. Though, do they even sell postcards anymore? I do miss those days. Just do me a favor and check in once in a while. And keep an eye on that contractor or photographer or whatever he is."

"I will. I'm going over there this weekend to help out."

"Help out?"

Her mother sounded horrified.

"Glen thought it might be fun."

"Fun? Just make sure you have insurance."

"Goodbye, Mother."

"And remember, if you get into any trouble with the house, call Alfred!"

Guin rolled her eyes.

"I got it, Mom. Now please stop worrying about me and go have fun on your cruise. And give my love to Philip."

Her mother had started to stay something when Guin heard the telltale beep of another call coming in.

"Hey, Mom. I've got another call coming in. Love you!"

She ended the call with her mother, as her mother was in mid-sentence, and picked up the other call.

"Hello?" she said.

"It's me," said Craig.

"Any news?" asked Guin.

"Nothing good."

"What's up?"

"They're keeping Sally at the police department for further questioning. Jimbo too."

"Did they arrest them?"

"Not yet," said Craig.

"Did you speak with the detective?"

"Briefly."

"He say anything about the other vehicle?"

"Just that they were investigating."

So much for Craig doing better than she would have.

"You speak with your neighbor?" Craig asked.

"I did. They weren't home that weekend, but their surveillance camera should have been recording. I'm waiting for them to get back to me."

"Okay, let me know what you find out."

"I will, and let me know if you hear anything on your end."

Craig said he would, and they ended the call.

As Guin climbed the stairs to her unit, she kept thinking about the vehicle Jimbo said he saw pulling into her driveway. Who did it belong to, and was whoever drove it Frank Funt's killer? Hopefully, she would get some answers soon.

CHAPTER 36

It was early afternoon and Guin was feeling restless—and hungry. Although she had been out earlier, she decided to drive over to Jean-Luc's to pick up a sandwich. On her way, she passed the Island Trust Company. Impulsively, she turned around and pulled in.

"May I help you?" asked the woman seated at the front desk.

"Yes," said Guin. "I'd like to see Mr. Simms."

"Do you have an appointment?"

"No, but I really need to speak with him."

The woman looked skeptical.

"Please, would you call him and tell him Guinivere Jones is here?"

The woman mulled it over for a few seconds, then picked up the phone.

"Mr. Simms, I have a Ms. Jones here to see you. She says it's urgent."

Guin waited while the woman listened and nodded her head.

"Yes, Mr. Simms," she said. "I'll do that."

The woman at the desk turned back to Guin.

"I'm sorry, Ms. Jones, but Mr. Simms is very busy right now. He asked that you come back another time."

"Tell him this can't wait."

"I'm sorry, Ms. Jones," said the woman. "He was pretty adamant. If you'd care to make an appointment…"

"Well, I can be pretty adamant, too," Guin replied. "Tell him I will just wait here until he is free."

She crossed her arms over her chest.

After what seemed like several minutes, the woman sighed and picked up the phone again.

"Sorry to bother you again, Mr. Simms. But Ms. Jones says she's not leaving until she speaks with you."

She looked up at Guin and Guin nodded.

"All right, I'll tell her," said the woman.

She hung up and looked at Guin.

"He says he'll see you in ten minutes. But he can only spare you a few minutes as he's very busy right now."

"I understand," said Guin. "Thank you."

"You can have a seat over there," said the woman, pointing to a couple of chairs.

Guin went to take a seat, then stopped.

"So does Billy Simms work out of the Tampa office now?" she asked the receptionist.

"Yes," said the woman. "He moved up there at the beginning of the year."

"Thank you," said Guin.

So it was unlikely that the younger Simms was the Simms on Funt's client list.

She took a seat and picked up a magazine.

She was on her third magazine when the woman at the front desk finally called to her.

"Mr. Simms will see you now, Ms. Jones."

"Thank you," said Guin, getting up.

"His office is just over there."

She pointed to an office down the hall, and Guin headed that way. The door was closed, so Guin knocked.

"Come in," called Mr. Simms.

Guin opened the door and stepped inside, closing the door behind her.

"Now what is it you needed to see me about?" Mr. Simms asked her.

He hadn't invited her to sit, so Guin remained standing.

"A man working on my house found a tin hidden in my bathroom," she replied.

"Let me guess: It contained rare gold coins, and you'd like to invest them."

Mr. Simms grinned as he said it, but Guin didn't smile back.

"Not exactly. It contained dozens of pills, which I'm guessing are opioids, and a list of names."

Mr. Simms was no longer grinning.

"I don't see what that has to do with me," he said.

"Your name was on the list."

They continued to eye each other.

"Was it now?" said Mr. Simms.

"Yes," said Guin. "And I believe everyone on that list was a client of Frank Funt."

"Well, as you know, we were clients of his."

"I don't think they were just remodeling clients."

"I'm sorry, Ms. Jones, but I don't follow. And I really am rather busy. So if you would excuse me?"

He bent his head down to study something on his desk, but Guin didn't move.

"The police believe the list is composed of people Funt sold drugs to."

Mr. Simms slowly looked up.

"Then you must have the wrong Simms. I can assure you, Mr. Jones, I have never purchased drugs from that man."

"What about your wife?" asked Guin.

Was that a frown on Mr. Simms's face?

"Just so you know," Guin continued. "The police have

been questioning everyone whose name appears on the list. It's only a matter of time until they question you and Mrs. Simms. After all, there's a good chance someone on that list killed Frank Funt."

Guin had no idea if the police were indeed questioning everyone whose name was on that list, but it was a fair assumption.

"So, is there anything you'd like to tell me?"

"I never bought a single pill from that man," Mr. Simms growled.

"I'm sorry, I didn't hear that," said Guin.

"I said, I never bought any pills from Frank Funt—and I didn't kill him," Mr. Simms practically shouted. "Though Lord knows I wanted to," he added, more softly.

Guin waited, sensing Mr. Simms had more to say.

Mr. Simms shook his head and looked down at his desk.

"Caroline should have never hired him. It was all my fault. I didn't know about the son taking over. I should have, but I was too busy and trusted her friends."

He looked up at Guin.

"Around five years ago, Caroline, Mrs. Simms, had a skiing accident," he explained. "She broke her leg. She was in constant pain, so the doctor gave her some pills. The leg took a long time to heal, and she became addicted to whatever it was he had given her. She denied it, of course, but I knew something was wrong. So did the children. The pills had become a crutch and made Caroline moody and short-tempered. I tried to get her to seek help, but she refused. Finally, the children helped me stage an intervention.

"She'd been clean for nearly two years when Funt gave her those pills. I could have strangled him. But I didn't. She swore to me she only took one, but you can understand why I may not have believed her. And now you say her name is on some list of people who Funt sold drugs to. Do those drugs include painkillers?"

Guin nodded and looked down at Mr. Simms. He no longer looked like the confident man who had barked at her only a few minutes before. Instead, he looked broken.

"I'm sorry," said Guin. And she was. Addiction was a horrible disease. But she couldn't let her emotions get in the way of finding out the truth. "So if you had nothing to do with Funt's death," she asked him, "tell me, where you were the evening of Sunday, September 23?"

"Let me check my calendar," said Mr. Simms, composing himself.

He rooted around in his desk and pulled out a little black book.

"Ah yes, I was out of town that weekend, and Mrs. Simms was with me."

"Can you prove it?" asked Guin.

"Really, Ms. Jones," he replied, giving her a stern look and putting away his little black book. "My word should be good enough."

"I'm afraid the police will require more than that," said Guin.

"Should they come calling, I'd be more than happy to tell them I could not have possibly killed Frank Funt, nor could Caroline have," said Mr. Simms.

Just then his telephone rang. He went to pick it up, but there was a knock at the door.

"Mr. Simms," came a familiar voice.

Guin turned to see the detective standing in the doorway.

"I'd like a word with you," said the detective, looking at Mr. Simms. "In private," he added, turning to look at Guin.

"Of course, Detective O'Loughlin," said Mr. Simms. "Ms. Jones was just leaving."

Guin looked from Mr. Simms to the detective.

"Detective," she said.

"Ms. Jones," replied the detective.

He held the door open for her.

As she left, Guin took a final look at Mr. Simms, then the door closed behind her.

Guin stood in the parking lot, imagining what the detective and Mr. Simms were discussing. Was Mr. Simms telling the detective the same story he had just told her?

She reached into her bag and pulled out her phone to check her messages. There was a text from Craig, asking her to call him. She immediately dialed his number.

"It's Guin," she said, as soon as he picked up. "What's up?"

"I thought you'd want to know, they released Jimbo."

"That's great," she said. "What about Sally?"

"She's still being held, but probably not for much longer. Jimbo got her a lawyer."

"Who?"

"Tricia Parker."

"Well, if anyone can help her, Tricia Parker can," said Guin.

Tricia Parker was well known on Sanibel and Captiva as a tough defense attorney, handling everything from speeding tickets to murder. She wasn't cheap, but her clients swore she was worth every penny.

"That's what I told Jimbo," said Craig. "So, anything new on your end?"

"As a matter of fact, I just met with William Simms."

"Oh?" said Craig.

"His name was on that list, so I thought I'd stop by and ask him about it."

"And what did he have to say for himself?"

"He at first claimed to have no idea why his name might be on Funt's list. But when I pressed him, he gave me a sob story about his wife being addicted to painkillers in the past. Though he swore she was clean now."

"Interesting," said Craig. "Do you believe him?"

"Actually, I do," said Guin. "But it's possible he could have been lying. I don't know who to trust anymore."

"Understandable," said Craig.

"I was going to ask him more, but then Detective O'Loughlin showed up."

"He did, did he?"

"Yeah, and I was asked to leave."

"No doubt the police are vetting everyone whose name appeared on that list."

"Speaking of the list," said Guin, "did Jimbo happen to know who else might have been on it?"

"I asked him," said Craig. "But he said he had no idea. The detective wouldn't show it to him."

"Figures," said Guin. "Did the detective ask Jimbo if he knew where the pills might have come from?"

"He did, but Jimbo had no idea about that either."

"Do you think it's possible that someone planted that container at my house?"

"It's possible, but I have to believe it belonged to Funt," said Craig. "He probably hid it there as a kind of insurance policy, figuring no one would look there."

"So what happened? Did someone find out about the list and kill Frank to make sure it never saw the light of day?"

"Good question," said Craig.

"And what about those pills we found? Did they belong to Big Lou or did Frank get them from someone else? You want to give Mr. Antinori a call, see if he's missing any pills?"

"I can call him, but don't expect an answer," said Craig.

"Understood," said Guin. "Anything else?"

"No, that's it for now."

"Well, thanks for the update."

They ended the call and Guin drove over to Jean-Luc's. He was about to close, so Guin took her sandwich to go.

She devoured it as soon as she got home, then did some work. When she was done for the day, she took her phone out of her drawer and saw that she had a voicemail from Glen.

"You rang?" she said, after he had picked up.

"I did."

"Don't tell me your guys found another mystery box."

Glen laughed.

"No. But I did hear back from Felix."

"And?" said Guin.

"And I was right. They're opioids."

"All of them?"

"The different colors were different dosages," Glen explained.

"Ah."

So Frank *had* been dealing drugs. Guin again wondered if his killer had been one of his customers.

"Any news on your end?" he asked.

Where to begin? thought Guin.

"One of my neighbors said he saw a vehicle pull into my driveway around ten-thirty the night Funt was killed."

"Oh yeah?" said Glen.

"Yeah," said Guin. "So I checked with another neighbor, who has a couple of those surveillance cameras, to see if they caught anything."

"And?"

"And I'm waiting to hear back from them."

"So are the police any closer to finding Funt's killer?"

"Your guess is as good as mine," said Guin. "I just saw the detective over at the Island Trust Company. He was questioning William Simms."

"You think he did it?"

"No, but I'm not positive."

She thought about telling Glen what Mr. Simms had told her, but it didn't feel right somehow.

"Hey, I've gotta run," said Glen. "Just wanted to give you the news. See you Saturday?"

"See you Saturday," said Guin.

CHAPTER 37

Guin had a restless night and woke up feeling tired Thursday morning. She looked at her clock and saw it was just past six. She thought about trying to go back to sleep, but Fauna, sensing that Guin was awake, had positioned herself in front of Guin's face and began tapping it with her paw and meowing.

Guin rolled over, covering her head with the sheet, but Fauna just walked over her shoulders and resumed pawing her head.

"Fine, you win," said Guin, throwing back the sheet and causing Fauna to yowl. "Just give me a minute."

She got out of bed and went to the bathroom, then headed down the hall to the kitchen. Fauna followed her.

Guin gave her a can of wet food, then poured herself a glass of water. The sun would be coming up soon, and even though she had work to do, Guin needed a beach walk.

There were already several vehicles parked at Bowman's Beach when Guin got there. No doubt some of them belonged to fishermen, though she guessed most of them belonged to beachcombers, like herself. She got out of the Mini and sprayed herself with insect repellent, though the noseeums seemed immune to the stuff.

It was a humid morning, and Guin could already sense her hair frizzing, even though she had tied it back in a ponytail. She headed across the bridge down to the beach. She looked left, then right, then decided to head west.

She kept her head down, focused on the wrack line. There looked to be a decent amount of shells, and she quickly found a nice fat lettered olive, a big apple murex, and a deep-brown nutmeg.

"Don't move," said a voice.

Guin froze.

"You were about to step on that banded tulip."

Guin turned to see a woman, probably in her seventies, wearing a Shell Ambassador t-shirt.

"Oh, I've got plenty of those," said Guin, smiling. "You can have it."

The woman picked it up.

"I've got plenty of them, too. But I'm collecting shells to give to the Shell Museum."

"I should give some of my shells to the Shell Museum, too," said Guin.

"I'm Marcy, by the way," said the woman.

"Guin," said Guin. "I don't think I've seen you around here before."

"We just got down," said Marcy. "It's my first morning out."

"And I see you're a Shell Ambassador."

Marcy smiled.

"Yup. Got certified this year."

"Congratulations!" said Guin.

Marcy beamed.

"You find anything good?"

Guin showed her what she had found.

"Very nice," said Marcy. "You ever find a junonia?"

"Not yet," said Guin.

"Me neither," said Marcy. "One day. Though people keep telling me I should head down to the Ten Thousand Islands. I hear you can find lots there."

Guin nodded.

"I've heard that, too. Well, good luck."

She didn't want to be rude, but she wasn't in the mood to chat.

"You too!" said Marcy.

Guin smiled, then continued to make her way down the beach.

Guin made herself coffee and breakfast as soon as she got back to the condo. As she was eating, she checked her messages. But there was no word from Mrs. Bregman or Tony Del Sole or the detective.

She took a last sip of her coffee, then washed out her mug. She glanced up at the clock on the microwave. It was a little after nine. She picked up her phone and called Mrs. Bregman.

"Hello?" said a female voice.

"Mrs. Bregman?" said Guin.

"Speaking. Who's this?"

"Mrs. Bregman, it's your neighbor, Guin Jones."

"Oh, Ms. Jones! I was just going to call you."

"You were?" said Guin.

"I told Mr. Bregman about the footage, and he said he sent it over to the Sanibel police."

Guin was crestfallen.

"But he said he thought it would be okay if you wanted to come over here and take a look."

Guin immediately perked up.

"You still have the footage? That would be great! When can I come over?"

"Yes, we kept the original footage," said Mrs. Bregman. "Mr. Bregman just sent the police a copy. I have a luncheon at noon, but you could stop by before then. I'm afraid there isn't much to see, though. At least, that's what Sam said."

"I could be there at ten," said Guin. "Would that be okay?"

"That's fine," said Mrs. Bregman. "See you then."

"See you then," said Guin.

Guin parked in her driveway, then walked next door and rang the Bregmans' doorbell. Mrs. Bregman opened the door a minute later.

"Ms. Jones, so nice to see you again," said Mrs. Bregman.

"Please, call me Guin," said Guin. "Thank you for allowing me to come over."

"Think nothing of it," said Mrs. Bregman. "And you must call me Sadie. Now, come in, come in."

Guin glanced around the house as Sadie led her to a room towards the back.

"This is Sam's study," said Sadie, opening a door to a small office.

There was a desk against a wall with a computer on it and another wall was lined with bookshelves.

"Sam's out playing golf, but he said he cued up the footage before he left. Just give me a minute."

Guin watched as Sadie sat down in Sam's chair and woke up the computer. She typed in what Guin assumed was her husband's password, then got up.

"There you go," said Sadie. On the screen was a video, which had been paused. "Just click 'play.'"

Guin hesitated.

"Go on, have a seat," said Sadie. "It's okay."

Guin went over and sat in the office chair.

"I'll be down the hall if you need anything," said Sadie.

"You can stay, if you like," said Guin.

"That's okay," said Sadie. "You seem pretty trustworthy."

She smiled at Guin, then left.

Guin doubted she would be so trusting of a stranger.

She hit the arrow for 'play,' then watched the video.

As Sadie had said, there wasn't much to see. It had been dark out, and all you could really see were headlights going towards her house around ten-thirty. She replayed the video several more times, trying to make it as bright as possible. But all she could tell was that the vehicle was a pickup truck.

She glanced around, to make sure Sadie wasn't around, then pulled out the thumb drive she kept in her bag and slotted it into Sam's computer. A minute later, she had transferred the video onto her memory stick. Then she got up.

"I'm all done," she said to Sadie, who she found in the kitchen.

"I'm sorry it wasn't more helpful," said Sadie.

"That's okay," said Guin, clutching her bag. "I appreciate you even sharing the footage with me."

"Sam enjoyed it," said Sadie, smiling. "Made him feel like he was playing detective!"

Guin smiled back at her.

"Well, tell Sam thank you from me."

"I will," said Sadie. "Can I get you something to drink or eat before you go? I should have asked you before, it's just that Sam doesn't like anyone eating in his office. Except for him, of course."

"That's all right," said Guin. "But thank you."

Sadie walked Guin to the door.

"Let me know when you're all moved in."

"I will," said Guin. "And thanks again for your help."

They said their goodbyes, then Guin walked back to the Mini.

As soon as she got back to the condo, Guin went to her computer and uploaded the video. She watched it again, but again found it difficult to make out anything, other than that the vehicle was a pickup. She picked up her phone and called Glen.

"Hey, can you edit videos?" she asked him.

"Of course, why?"

"Even if they're really dark?"

"It depends," said Glen. "Why?"

"I got the video clip from my neighbors, the Bregmans, the ones who have the surveillance cameras. But you can't see much, just that a pickup truck drove by not long before Funt was killed. Could you take a look and see if you can clean it up? Maybe if it's lighter we'll be able to see the license plate or if something's written on the side."

"I can give it a try," said Glen. "Can you give me till later? I'm a little busy right now."

"Sure," said Guin.

"Tell you what, let me send you a link and some instructions for a site I use to transfer big files."

"Sounds good," said Guin. "As soon as I get it, I'll upload the file."

They ended the call and Guin browsed social media while she waited for Glen's email. A few minutes later, she heard a ping and sure enough, there was an email from Glen in her inbox. She opened it and read the instructions. Then she clicked on the link and uploaded the video.

"There!" she said, when she was done. Now it was up to Glen.

CHAPTER 38

It was after three and Guin was finding it hard to concentrate. It was too quiet, and she was anxious for news.

She had begun to pace when her phone rang. She lunged for it and was somewhat disappointed to see it was just Ginny.

"Hey," she said.

"Hey yourself," said Ginny. "So, you ready to tackle another book?"

Guin groaned. It wasn't that she didn't like books. She just didn't like reviewing them.

"Do I have a choice?" she asked.

"This author specifically asked for you."

"She did?" said Guin. She didn't think she knew any authors, at least not personally.

"It's a he, Wren Finchley."

"Wren Finchley?" said Guin. "I'm pretty sure I don't know any Wren Finchleys. What's the book? Please tell me it's not another romance."

"It's a mystery," said Ginny. "His first one was a big success. I'm surprised you haven't heard of him."

"Wren Finchley," said Guin. "Nope, haven't heard of him. And you say he asked for me specifically?"

"Yup, that's what his agent said."

"Huh," said Guin. "Is he local?"

"No, but his agent said he comes to Sanibel quite often."

"Have you ever met him?"

"Not that I'm aware of," said Ginny. "I understand he's a bit of a recluse. But he's agreed to give a book talk at the Captiva Yacht Club just before Thanksgiving. It's to benefit the Ding Darling Wildlife Society. And he specifically requested you be the one to interview him."

"Why me?" said Guin. "I've never met the man. How does he even know about me?"

"Maybe he reads the paper."

Guin looked dubious.

"Is he on Sanibel now?"

"No," said Ginny. "He's not coming down until just before the talk."

"So it'll be a phone interview?"

"No, he'll contact you when he arrives. You can meet with him then."

"Will I have enough time?"

"You'll figure it out."

"So how do I reach this mystery man? Does he have an email address?"

"He does," said Ginny. She then gave it to Guin.

"And what's the title of his new book?"

"*Shot Through the Heart.*"

Oh God, thought Guin. It was another romance novel!

"He wouldn't secretly be Jon Bon Jovi, would he?"

"No idea," said Ginny. "You can ask him."

"So, you have a copy of the book?"

"I do," said Ginny. "You can pick it up anytime."

"I'll stop by tomorrow. Anything else?"

"Nope," said Ginny. "See you tomorrow."

They ended the call and Guin immediately did a search for "Wren Finchley." But there was little online, not even a photo.

"That's odd," she said.

She looked up his first book, *Death in the Jungle*, which had received rave reviews. It was about a spy posing as an ornithologist who seeks out and catches a group of Asian rare bird poachers. She read the author bio, but it didn't reveal much. And there was no author photo.

It seemed Wren Finchley was an even bigger mystery than his books.

She reread the description of *Death in the Jungle*. Something about it struck Guin as familiar, but she couldn't put her finger on it.

She sat back in her chair and stared at her monitor. She had never had this much trouble digging up information about someone. Maybe "Wren Finchley" was a pen name. Who knows, maybe he really was Jon Bon Jovi.

The thought made Guin smile.

She was about to lean forward and begin typing when Fauna jumped into her lap and dug her claws into Guin's thighs.

"Ouch!" said Guin, throwing Fauna to the ground.

Then her phone began to ring. It was Glen.

"Hey," she said. "You get the video?"

"I did," he replied.

"And?"

"And a pickup truck definitely drove by your neighbor's house and into your driveway around ten-thirty."

"Were you able to see a license plate or any identifying marks?"

"I was able to clean it up, but I still couldn't see much. Though you can make out some kind of logo on the side of the truck. I think it was the sun."

"The sun?" said Guin.

"Or it could have been a circular saw. Hard to tell."

"A sun…" said Guin, mostly to herself. "A sun…"

She suddenly sat bolt upright in her chair.

"A sun! Of course!"

She quickly typed on her computer and found what she was looking for.

"I'm going to send you a photo. Can you tell me if it looks like the image you saw on the truck?"

"Sure," said Glen. "But like I said, the image in the video was pretty grainy."

Guin copied the photo she had found and sent it to Glen.

"I just sent it," she informed him.

"Got it," he replied.

Guin waited.

"I can't say for sure, but they do look similar."

"I had a feeling," said Guin.

"You think they had something to do with it?" asked Glen. "Maybe they were working in the neighborhood."

"At ten-thirty on a Sunday night?"

"I often work at night. As you recall, I was at your place just last weekend."

"True…" said Guin. But she was sure she was correct. "Can you send me the edited version of the video?"

"Sure," Glen replied. "Look for a link in your inbox in a few."

Guin thanked him, and they ended the call. She turned back to her monitor, where the image she had sent Glen was still displayed.

"I think it's time I pay another call on Sunshine Builders," she announced.

Guin arrived at Sunshine Builders a little before four-thirty. There were lights on, which meant someone was probably inside. She tried the door and found it unlocked. She opened it and went inside.

"Hello? Anyone here?" she called, looking around. The place seemed empty.

A minute later, Phoebe appeared, seemingly out of nowhere.

"You," she said, glaring at Guin. "What do you want?"

"Is Tony here?" asked Guin, looking around.

"No," said Phoebe. "Why?"

"I need to speak with him."

Phoebe was eyeing her suspiciously.

"It's important," said Guin.

"Tony's at a meeting."

"Do you know when he'll be back?"

"No," said Phoebe. "It's off-island."

"Will he be in tomorrow?" Guin asked.

"Maybe. He's very busy."

"Well, can you ask him to get in touch with me? I've left messages for him, but he hasn't returned my calls."

"I'll let him know you stopped by."

"Thanks," said Guin. Though she had a feeling Phoebe would do no such thing. "How's Nick?"

"Not so good."

Guin noticed that Phoebe's expression always softened when she talked about Nick.

"I'm sorry to hear that. Any idea when they'll release him?"

Phoebe shook her head.

Guin hadn't been back to the hospital or called to check on Nick since her last visit, partly because she was worried about running into Phoebe or the detective. But in light of what she had just discovered, she felt she needed to speak with him again.

"You speak with his doctor?"

"They say he's making progress, but they're still not sure he'll walk right," said Phoebe.

"Well, I hope he heals and gets out of there soon," said Guin.

"Me, too," said Phoebe. "It's driving him nuts being stuck in that bed."

"You visit him often?"

"As often as I can. Like I said, we've been real busy. Everyone wants their place fixed up before Christmas."

Guin understood.

"Well, goodbye," she said.

Guin got in the Mini but didn't start it. Instead, she sat behind the steering wheel, staring at Sunshine Builders. She got out of the car and walked down the driveway, to the back of the building. There was a white Honda Civic parked there, along with a white pickup truck with the words *Sunshine Builders* and their logo, a circular saw that looked like a sun, emblazoned on the side.

She wondered who the pickup belonged to and if Sunshine had more than one. Probably. Though could Phoebe have been lying and could Tony have been inside? It was possible. More likely, though, the pickup belonged to Nick.

Guin stood there, staring at the truck, wondering if she should go back in. Instead, she walked back to the Mini.

Guin hadn't planned on driving to the Health Park. But she found herself in the parking lot 20 minutes later. She turned off the engine and wondered if they would let her go upstairs again.

"Well, nothing ventured, nothing gained."

She got out of the car and made her way to the front desk.

"I'm here to see Nick DiDio," Guin told the woman seated there.

Guin had thought about just going upstairs, to his room, but there was a chance Nick had been moved to a different room.

"And you are?" she asked Guin.

"Guinivere Jones."

She took out her driver's license and slid it across to the woman.

"Guinivere," she said, looking down at Guin's driver's license. "That's an unusual name."

"My mother was into Arthurian legends," Guin explained. "She thought Guinivere sounded romantic."

The woman at the front desk typed something into her computer, then handed Guin back her license.

"Room 432," she said, handing Guin a visitor badge.

Guin thanked the woman and headed to the elevators.

That was easy, she thought. She had expected to be grilled.

She got off on the fourth floor and followed the signs for Room 432. She knocked on the door and a male voice told her to come in. She cautiously opened the door.

"Okay to come in?" she said, spotting Nick in bed with his eyes closed.

"I said come in," he replied, not opening his eyes.

Guin went inside and shut the door behind her.

"How are you?" she asked, moving closer to the bed.

"How do you think I am?" he said, his eyes still closed. "Go ahead and take my blood or whatever it is you're here to do."

"Actually, I just wanted to ask you a few questions," said Guin.

Nick turned his head and opened his eyes.

"You're not the nurse."

"No, I'm not," said Guin, smiling at him.

"But I've seen you before."

"You have," said Guin. "I was here the other day. I asked you about Funt and the Son."

"That's right," said Nick, closing his eyes again. "They catch the guy who killed Frank?"

"Not yet," said Guin. "But they're getting close. That's actually why I'm here."

Nick opened one eye, then closed it again.

"I was hoping you could answer a few more questions."

She waited for Nick to say something. When he didn't, she pressed on.

"The night Funt was killed, a truck bearing the Sunshine Builders logo was seen by my house. You know anything about that?"

Nick's eyes remained closed. Guin wondered if he had fallen asleep.

"Did that truck belong to you, Mr. DiDio?"

"No," said Nick, opening his eyes and looking at Guin. "I don't even know where you live."

Guin told him the address.

"Oh, so you're the one."

"Excuse me?" said Guin. "I'm the one what?"

"The one who was giving Frank a hard time."

"I was only giving him a hard time because he was dragging his feet about getting the permit."

"Yeah, well Frank doesn't like being told what to do."

"So I gather. So where were you the night he was murdered?"

"When did you say that was again?"

Guin told him the date.

"I don't recall. But I guarantee I wasn't at your place."

"Can you prove it?"

"Not from this hospital bed."

He had a point.

"What about your new boss, Tony Del Sole?"

"What about him?"

"Could he have been meeting Frank at my place that Sunday?"

"It's possible. Now if you'll excuse me, I need to get some rest."

Guin had wanted to ask him some more questions, but he had already closed his eyes.

"Thank you, Mr. DiDio," she said. "I hope you feel better soon."

Nick didn't answer. Had he fallen asleep?

Guin quietly saw herself out.

On her way down in the elevator, she replayed their conversation in her head. Was he telling her the truth, or was it his truck that had been at her house the night Frank was killed?

CHAPTER 39

Guin was driving home when her stomach started to rumble. She glanced at the clock on the dashboard and saw that it was after six. When had she last eaten? She couldn't remember. (*I really should keep a bag of nuts or a protein bar in my bag*, she thought, not for the first time.) She saw the Bimini Bait Shack up ahead and pulled into the parking lot.

She took a seat at the bar. They were showing the MLB pregame show. (She had almost forgotten about the baseball playoffs.)

"What'll you have?" asked the bartender.

"Just a glass of water for right now. Could I see a menu?"

He placed a menu in front of her, then said he'd be back with her water.

"You a regular now?" said a familiar voice.

Guin turned to see the detective standing next to her.

"What are you doing here?" she asked him.

"Getting a beer. You?"

"Here you go," said the bartender, placing a glass of water in front of Guin.

"Get me a beer, will ya, Charlie?" the detective asked the bartender.

"Coming right up," said Charlie.

Guin stared at her menu, trying to ignore the detective.

"You planning on getting some food?"

Guin nodded.

Charlie placed a beer in front of the detective and turned to Guin.

"You decide?"

"I'll have the jumbo lump crab cakes, please."

"And I'll have a Cuban," said the detective.

"You two together?" asked Charlie.

"No," said Guin, as the detective said "yes."

Charlie smiled and shook his head.

"Let me know what you two decide."

"So how come you're not having dinner with Maggie?" Guin asked the detective.

"She's not around."

"Where'd she go?"

"Back up north, to Boston."

"Oh?" said Guin. "Why? When did she go?"

"Said she'd had enough of Florida and left last week."

"Is she coming back?"

"I doubt it."

He drank his beer and watched the pregame.

Guin continued to look at him.

"You going to go up there and talk to her?"

"Why bother?" he said, continuing to watch the TV.

"So, did you two break up?"

"You could say that. She said she never wanted to see me again."

Guin signaled to the bartender.

"Your food'll be out in a minute," Charlie told her.

"Actually, can I have a beer?"

He reeled off her choices and Guin ordered a High 5.

Charlie looked over at the detective.

"You want another one?"

"Sure," said the detective.

"So, what happened?" Guin asked him.

The detective continued to look at the television.

"We had a difference of opinion."

Guin waited for him to go on.

"What about?" she finally asked him.

"She wanted to get married. I didn't."

"Here you go," said Charlie, depositing their food in front of them. "Be right back with your beers."

They ate in silence for several minutes, the detective's eyes on the television.

"So, you figure out who killed Funt yet?" Guin asked him when they were nearly done.

"Working on it," said the detective.

"You have a good chat with William Simms?"

"Good enough," he replied.

Guin was getting frustrated. Would he just look at her already?

"What about Sally Bates? You don't really think she killed Funt, do you?"

"You'll be happy to know Ms. Bates is no longer a guest of the Sanibel police department," replied the detective, finally turning to look at her.

"So Tricia Parker got her released?"

The detective didn't reply. He was once again looking at the television.

"I spoke with Nick DiDio again," Guin said, hoping to catch his attention.

The detective turned to look at her again.

"I heard one of Sunshine's trucks was spotted over by my place the night Funt died."

"And where'd you hear that?" asked the detective.

Guin ignored the question.

"You speak with Tony Del Sole and ask him where his trucks were that evening?"

The detective signaled to Charlie for the bill.

Guin reached for her wallet, but the detective stopped her.

"I've got this."

"Thanks," she replied.

The detective left some cash on the bar, then got up. Guin thought about staying, then decided to follow him.

They made their way silently down the stairs.

"You want to come back to my place, watch the game?" asked the detective, when they had reached the parking lot.

Guin stared at him.

"I'm sorry. Did you just invite me back to your place?"

"I know how you love baseball."

"I love *Mets* baseball, not all baseball," Guin clarified.

The detective shrugged.

"Suit yourself."

Guin stood there, trying to decide what to do.

"So you and Maggie are quits? You're not going to jump if she calls?"

"Nope," said the detective.

"How do I know that?" said Guin.

"Because," said the detective, taking a couple of steps and placing a hand under Guin's chin. "Maggie wasn't the one I wanted to be with."

Guin froze.

"She wasn't?"

The detective shook his head, then pulled Guin into a kiss.

Guin was so startled, she didn't know how to react at first. Then she closed her eyes and kissed him back.

"You wanna come back to my place and watch the game?" he asked her again, after they had stopped kissing.

Guin was seriously tempted, but she didn't want to give in that easily. The detective had put her through hell the last six months.

"Thanks," she said. "But I should get going. Another time."

"Suit yourself," said the detective.

He turned and headed to his car.

Should she run after him? No, not this time, she said to herself.

Guin replayed the kiss several times on her way home. She had so many thoughts running through her head. It took all of her energy to concentrate on the road.

Had the detective broken up with Maggie for good this time? And did that mean the two of them would now start dating? Though hadn't he said he wasn't big on relationships?

She reached over and turned on the radio, cranking the volume.

Fauna was waiting for Guin when she got home.

"Hey, there, kitty cat," Guin said, looking down at her.

Fauna meowed and batted Guin's leg with her paw.

"Let me guess, you're hungry."

Fauna meowed again, then turned and trotted into the kitchen.

Guin followed her and shook some dry food into her bowl. Then she made her way to her bedroom/office. She booted up her computer and waited for it to start. Again, she thought about the detective.

"Focus, Guin!" she admonished herself. "Figure out who killed Frank Funt, then worry about the detective."

She closed her eyes and took a deep breath, then slowly exhaled and opened them.

"Okay," she said, looking at her monitor. "Let's see what

we can find about Mr. Tony Del Sole."

She typed his name into her search engine and hit enter. The screen immediately began to fill.

She quickly scanned the first page, but it was mostly mentions of Sunshine Builders. She clicked on the Images tab. She began scrolling when a photo of Tony with another, older man caught her eye. She clicked on the image. The caption read "Tony Del Sole and Lou Antinori."

Guin clicked on the link. It took her to an article for a fundraiser for Drug-Free Lee County, a local nonprofit dedicated to fighting drug abuse. Lou Antinori was a sponsor of the event, as was Sunshine Builders. Guin raised an eyebrow. A man linked to selling drugs a sponsor of an event raising money for reducing substance abuse? It was actually perfect.

She read the article, then did a new search for "Lou Antinori and Tony Del Sole."

The search engine returned two pages of hits. Guin scanned the first page. She stopped at a headline that read "Keeping it all in the family: How one immigrant family built a real estate empire from the ground up." Then she clicked on the link and began reading.

Guin had known Big Lou owned real estate. But she hadn't realized he also owned or co-owned a roofing company, a plumbing business, an electrical company, and... Sunshine Builders, which was run by his nephew, Tony Del Sole. Guin sat back in her chair.

"Well, I'll be," she said, staring at her monitor.

She continued to read the article, which was from a year ago. According to the author, Mr. Antinori had arrived in Florida nearly penniless as a young man and worked his way up in the construction business, eventually buying out the owner of the company he worked for. He then proceeded to purchase other contracting businesses, hiring members of his extended family to run them.

There was also a paragraph about Tony. He had received a degree in Management from Florida State University in Tallahassee and then gone to work for his Uncle Lou, before starting his own business, Sunshine Builders, on Sanibel. The article also mentioned that Lou and Tony were looking to expand the family business, buying up other contracting firms.

"So that's why Tony was interested in Funt and the Son Construction," Guin said.

She picked up the phone and called Craig. He picked up after a few rings.

"So did you know Big Lou was Tony Del Sole's uncle and that he and Tony were in the process of buying up contracting businesses around Southwest Florida?"

"No, I did not," said Craig. "How'd you find that out?"

"I stumbled across the information when I was doing a search online for Tony Del Sole. One of his trucks was spotted driving by my house the night Frank Funt was killed."

"You think he was involved?"

"That's what I'm trying to find out. But he seems to be avoiding me."

"Avoiding you?"

"Every time I stop by his office, he isn't there, and he hasn't returned any of my calls. I spoke with Phoebe, who, by the way, is his new office manager, and she told me he's just been busy. But I'm not buying it."

"She could be telling you the truth," said Craig. "It is the busy season for contractors, or starting to be."

"Yeah, but I've got a feeling it's something else," said Guin.

"If Tony is Big Lou's nephew, you need to watch your step, Guin. These people are dangerous, and they don't like folks sticking their noses in their business."

"What if Tony killed Frank?"

"Then the police will arrest him."

Guin made a face.

"I need to know, Craig."

"Please, Guin, let the police handle it. You don't want to mess with Big Lou or his family."

"Speaking of Big Lou, you talk to him again?"

"Not yet," said Craig. "I left a message with his assistant."

"Okay," said Guin. "Well, let me know if you find out anything."

"You know I will."

They said goodnight, then ended the call.

CHAPTER 40

Guin had yet another restless night and woke up determined to get some answers. She called over to Sunshine Builders a little before nine and was immediately dumped into voicemail. She then called Tony Del Sole's cell phone, which also went to voicemail, telling him she needed to speak with him.

She paced around her little kitchen, wondering who else she could reach out to when it hit her: Frank Funt, Sr. She immediately dialed his number.

"Hello?" said a male voice.

"Mr. Funt?"

"Who wants to know?"

"This is Guin Jones, Mr. Funt. We met a couple of weeks ago, at your apartment. We talked about your son, Frank, Jr."

"Guin Jones..." said Mr. Funt. "The name sounds vaguely familiar. You that redhead?"

"That's me," said Guin, though she wanted to correct him and point out that her hair was strawberry blonde. "Would it be okay if I stopped by later this morning? I have a few more questions."

"About Frank?"

"Actually, about Funt and the Son Construction."

"If you're interested in buying it, I'm afraid you're too late," said Mr. Funt.

"I'm not interested in buying it," said Guin. "Though who are you selling it to?"

"Sunshine Builders. They made me an offer I couldn't refuse."

He chuckled as he said it.

"I see," said Guin.

"Tony's coming over here later this morning, so we can sign the papers."

"At what time?"

"He said he'd be here around eleven."

Guin looked up at the clock. It was just past nine.

"Would it be okay if I stopped by beforehand? I won't stay long."

"Suit yourself," said Mr. Funt.

"Thank you," said Guin. "Would you let them know at the front gate?"

"How do you spell your name?"

"G-U-I-N."

"Never met a Guin before. Knew one or two Gwens, back in the day. But no Guins."

"Yes, I've been told it's an unusual name. Anyway, I'll see you around ten-thirty."

Guin ended the call, then went to her bedroom to change.

She called Craig before she left, to let him know she was going to meet with Frank Funt, Sr., and hopefully Tony Del Sole, but her call went into voicemail. So she left him a message instead. No doubt he was out fishing, as he often was on Friday mornings. She grabbed her things and headed out.

This time Guin had no trouble getting through the front gate at Frank Funt, Sr.'s retirement community. The guard at the gate had her name on his list, and he gave her a tag for her car.

She drove over to Frank Funt, Sr.'s building and found a place to park. Then she checked her phone. There was no word from Craig. On impulse, she sent a text to the detective, telling him she had gone to speak with Frank Funt, Sr. Then she stashed her phone in her bag.

She rang the doorbell and waited. A minute later, it was opened by Mr. Funt. He looked the same as he did the last time.

"Hi, Mr. Funt. Thank you for letting me come over."

He stood in the doorway.

"May I come in?" she asked.

He continued to look at her for several more seconds, then gestured for her to come in.

"Thank you," said Guin.

"So what did you want to ask me?"

"Shall we sit?" Guin suggested, gesturing towards the sofa and chairs.

Mr. Funt took a seat in one of the chairs and Guin sat opposite him on the couch.

"As I was saying over the phone, I wanted to ask you about your business, Funt and the Son Construction. You said you were selling it to Sunshine Builders?"

"That's right," said Mr. Funt.

"Did you know that Mr. Del Sole had been in talks to buy the business from your son?"

"He mentioned it."

"Did he happen to mention why the deal fell apart?"

"I assume because Frank screwed it up somehow," said Mr. Funt.

"Did you know that Frank owed a lot of money to Tony's uncle, Big Lou Antinori?"

"Big Lou is Tony's uncle?"

Guin nodded.

"Frank was working off his loan by selling drugs for Big Lou."

"How do you know that?" asked Mr. Funt.

Guin couldn't tell if he was shocked or angry or sad or some combination of the three.

"An old cookie tin filled with pills was found hidden in one of the houses Frank was working on."

"What did the tin look like?"

"There was a snowman on it," said Guin. She remembered because she thought it was odd to see a tin with a snowman on it here in Florida.

Mr. Funt hung his head.

"Frank loved that tin. His mother gave it to him."

So the tin definitely belonged to Frank.

"There was also an envelope inside the tin, with a list. The police believe the list contained the names of people Frank had sold drugs to."

Mr. Funt shook his head.

"He told me he was done with that," he said softly. He looked up at the ceiling. "Why Frank, why?"

"Are you okay, Mr. Funt?" Guin asked him.

"I told him drugs were the devil's work," Mr. Funt replied, angrily. But did he listen? He never listened," he said a few seconds later, more softly, shaking his head again.

Guin was about to say something when the doorbell rang.

"That must be Tony," said Mr. Funt.

Guin stood up. Here was her chance to confront him.

"Hey, Frank. Hope it's okay I'm a bit early," said Tony, entering the apartment.

He spied Guin and smiled.

"Oh, I didn't know you had company," he said, winking at Frank, Sr.

He went over to Guin, extending a hand.

"Tony Del Sole," he said. "And you are?"

Guin knew it was pointless to lie.

"Guinivere Jones."

Tony frowned.

"You! What are you doing here?"

"I had a few questions for Mr. Funt, about the business and Frank, Jr."

"You don't have to tell her anything, Frank," said Tony, looking over at Frank, Sr.

"Why? I've got nothing to hide, Tony," said Mr. Funt.

"If you'll excuse us, Miss Jones," said Tony, turning his attention back to her. "This is a private business matter."

Guin didn't move.

"Speaking of business," said Guin. "Does Mr. Funt here know that your uncle, Big Lou Antinori, is the real owner of Sunshine Builders?"

"Is that true, Tony?" asked Frank, Sr.

"Is what true?" he said.

"That Big Lou is your uncle and owns Sunshine?"

"Yeah, he's my uncle. So what?"

Frank, Sr., continued to look at him.

"And was Frank working for him?"

Guin could see how hard this was for the elder Funt.

"My Uncle Lou is a very respectable businessman and one of the biggest developers in Southwest Florida," stated Tony. "Many people would kill to work for him."

An interesting choice of words, Guin thought.

"And was Frank selling drugs for your uncle?" she asked.

"If Frank was caught with drugs, it's because he was a junkie. Sorry, Frank," he said, turning to Frank, Sr.

"Frank told me he was clean," mumbled Mr. Funt.

"Clean?" said Tony, shaking his head and letting out a laugh. "Frank couldn't go a day without swallowing a handful of blues. Why do you think I nixed the deal with him? I don't do business with junkies."

Frank, Sr., was looking down at the floor.

"Did you also nix Frank?" Guin asked him.

"I have no idea what you are talking about," said Tony.

"I think you do," said Guin. Suddenly she saw it all. "My guess? Frank was pushing pills for your uncle and went rogue. Big Lou got wind of it and asked you to have a little talk with Frank, contractor to contractor."

Tony had his arms crossed over his chest.

"Frank probably denied it—or maybe he offered you a cut? That's when you decided he was more trouble than he was worth. So you lured him over to one of the sites he was working on, one that he had shown you, that you knew was vacant. Maybe you got some help from your girlfriend, Phoebe."

Tony continued to glower.

"Frank shows up, and you two get into it. Maybe he says something that pisses you off and you lose it. You rough him up to teach him a lesson. Then, as he's lying there unconscious, you get a better idea. You knew Frank had a drug problem. So you drag him into the bathroom and put him in the tub. Then you shoot him up with fentanyl, so it looks like he's OD'd and passed out, not knowing or caring what opioid Frank actually took."

"Everyone knew Frank was addicted to painkillers," Tony said icily.

"He took oxycodone, not fentanyl," said Guin. "And the autopsy report said the track mark on his arm was recent."

"So, maybe he needed something stronger and injected himself."

Guin shook her head.

"If he injected the drug himself, what happened to the syringe?"

Tony was glaring at her.

"You killed my son?" Frank said, looking at Tony, his face full of pain.

"It was an accident," Tony said coolly. "Frank took his own life. He OD'd. Don't listen to her."

Frank, Sr., shook his head.

"Frank hated needles. He would never stick himself."

Guin decided now would be a good time to leave and began to move toward the door. But Tony grabbed her before she could get far.

"And where do you think you're going?" he said, holding her arm tightly.

"Let go of my arm," Guin commanded, trying to sound much braver than she felt.

"You going to make me?" said Tony, grinning now.

Guin glared at him.

"Let her go, Tony," said Mr. Funt.

"Are you kidding me, and have her run to the cops?"

"Let her go, Tony," Frank, Sr., repeated. "We'll tell the cops the truth, that it was an accident, that Frank OD'd."

Tony made another face, and Mr. Funt took a couple of steps toward him.

"Don't come any closer, Frank," Tony warned.

"Let her go, Tony," Frank, Sr., said, softer this time.

"Stay right where you are, Frank," said Tony, removing a small handgun from the back of his waistband.

Frank, Sr., stopped moving and held up his hands.

"Now back away," Tony commanded.

Frank, Sr., took a step back.

"What are you going to do, shoot us both?" said Guin.

"You, shut up," said Tony, pointing the gun at her. "Phoebe said you were trouble."

"Does Phoebe know you killed Frank?" Guin asked him.

"Phoebe knows what's good for her," Tony replied.

"So how are you planning on getting rid of us, Tony? You shoot us and the neighbors will hear and come running."

Tony laughed.

"Have you seen the people who live here? Half of them are deaf and the other half are blind or crippled. I doubt any of them will come running."

"Still, my colleagues at the paper will suspect something is up if I don't report in," said Guin. "I told them and the police I was on my way over here."

"Nice try," said Tony. "You're bluffing."

"They're probably on their way here now," said Guin, trying to stall for time.

"I said, shut up!" said Tony, holding Guin more tightly and poking the gun into her back.

Just then there was a loud pounding on the door.

"Police! Open up!"

Tony looked over at Frank, Sr.

"Go, answer the door."

Frank, Sr., hesitated.

"Go on, get the door!" Tony ordered him.

"Police! Open up!" said the voice a second time.

Tony pointed the gun at Frank, Sr., and he reluctantly went to open the door.

"Not one word out of you," Tony hissed to Guin.

Frank, Sr., opened the door. There were several officers from the Fort Myers Police standing there, along with Detective O'Loughlin. Guin wanted to run over and hug him, but she didn't dare make a move.

They stepped inside and the detective spotted Guin.

"You okay, Ms. Jones?" he asked.

Guin nodded. She could feel Tony's gun against her back.

"Mr. Jeffers got worried when you didn't answer his calls or texts."

"As you can see, detective," said Tony, smoothly, "Ms. Jones here is perfectly fine."

The detective continued to look at Guin, who could feel herself perspiring.

"I'd like Ms. Jones to tell me that herself," said the detective.

"Go ahead, Ms. Jones, tell him," said Tony, nuzzling her back with the gun.

The three police officers and the detective were all looking at Guin.

"I'm fine, detective, really," she said, while telepathically telling the detective she was not fine.

"Mr. Funt and I were just having a little business meeting," explained Tony. "Ms. Jones here was a witness."

"Oh?" said the detective.

"I'm buying Funt and the Son Construction," said Tony. "And I had some papers I needed Mr. Funt here to sign."

"And does Mr. Funt know you killed his son?" asked the detective.

Tony froze for a second, then smiled.

"Now how could you go accuse me of doing something horrible like that, detective?"

"We just spoke with your girlfriend and Nick DiDio," he replied. "They're both willing to swear that you were responsible for the death of Frank, Jr., and for Mr. DiDio being thrown off that roof."

"That bitch!" said Tony. "I knew I shouldn't trust her."

The detective began to read Tony his rights.

"You've got nothing on me," Tony spat.

"Gentlemen, would you please escort Mr. Del Sole out of here?" said the detective.

"I don't think so, detective," Tony replied. "Unless you want Ms. Jones here to have a hole in her back."

The detective signaled for the officers to stop.

"That's right," said Tony, grinning.

The next few seconds were a total blur. Frank, Sr., who no one had been paying attention to, had somehow managed to sneak up behind Tony and grab the hand holding the gun while shoving Guin aside, narrowly avoiding her getting shot.

When Guin came to (she must have fainted), she was lying on Frank, Sr.'s couch with a cool washcloth on her forehead, the detective seated next to her. There was no sign of Tony Del Sole, or Frank Funt, Sr., or the police officers.

"What happened?" said Guin, glancing around. "Where's Mr. Funt? Is he okay?"

"He's fine," said the detective. "He's at the Fort Myers P.D., giving a statement."

Guin breathed a sigh of relief.

"He saved my life."

The detective was looking at her.

"What?" she said.

"You could've been killed."

"But I wasn't," she said, feeling some of her strength coming back.

"That's not the point. You took a foolish risk."

"I needed to find out the truth," Guin retorted. "I had no idea Del Sole would have a gun."

The detective was still looking at her.

Guin sat up, removing the washcloth from her forehead.

"Really, detective, I'm fine." Though she felt a bit woozy.

"You don't look fine," said the detective.

"So, did you arrest him?"

"We did," he replied.

"So how did you know it was Del Sole?"

"We had a strong hunch he was involved. Word on the street is he was in line to take over the business from his uncle, Lou Antinori, and was his enforcer."

"So Big Lou told Tony to kill Frank?"

"Mr. Antinori denies any such thing, but we know that Mr. Del Sole met with Frank at your place that evening."

"I still don't understand why my place."

The detective's mouth curled up.

"That was Ms. Costanza's idea. I don't think she's very fond of you."

"Ya think? So was Phoebe in on it?"

"She claims she had no idea what Tony was really up to."

"Yeah, right," said Guin

Guin stood up. She suddenly felt woozy again and had to place her hand on top of the couch to steady herself.

"You okay?" said the detective. "You bumped your head pretty good when Funt pushed you away from Del Sole."

"I'm fine," said Guin, straightening up. "Really."

"You're coming with me," he announced, placing a hand on her arm.

"You taking me in for questioning?" Guin asked him.

The detective's lips quirked into a partial smile.

"In a manner of speaking," he replied.

He led her out of the apartment to his car.

"What about the Mini?"

"You're not driving anywhere in your condition," said the detective. "Now get in."

Guin silently obeyed.

"Where are we going?" Guin asked him as they drove out of the retirement community.

"Back to my place."

"What about Tony Del Sole? Don't you need to question him?"

"The Fort Myers Police have him well in hand."

"But," Guin said.

The detective shot her a look.

"You can ask questions later. For now, we're going to my place. Any objections?"

Guin looked out the window. She knew resistance was futile.

"No, detective," she replied.

The next morning Guin woke up and was amazed to see the detective still asleep next to her. She smiled. She knew he was normally an early riser, but they had been up late, talking and doing… other things. She lay there glancing over at him, feeling happy. Just then the detective let out a loud snort and rolled over. Guin wanted to laugh. It felt so normal and so right somehow.

She got out of bed, dressed in the detective's Boston Bruins jersey, and made her way to the bathroom. When she was done, she tiptoed down to the kitchen, to make some coffee. She had just poured herself a mug when the detective came in.

"Smells good," he said.

"You want some?" she asked.

"That's one of those rhetorical questions, right?" he said.

Guin smiled.

"Coming right up."

She poured him some coffee and handed him the mug.

"Thanks," he said.

Guin watched him as he drank.

"Not bad," he said.

Guin smiled.

"I've been told I make a mean mug of joe."

They stood in the kitchen, sipping their coffee, neither saying anything for several minutes. Finally, the detective spoke.

"Ms. Jones, Guin, I…"

Guin held up a hand to stop him.

"There's time for that later. For now, let's just enjoy our coffee, okay?"

"Okay," said the detective.

EPILOGUE

Guin looked around her new home. True to his word, Glen and his buddies had managed to get the place mostly done by the time she had to be out of the condo.

Guin had hired local movers to help her move, the Mini being too small to fit all the stuff she had acquired over the last couple of years. It had been bittersweet. She had loved living in the condo, but she was excited to start the next chapter of her life in her very own home.

There was still some work to be done on the house, but Glen had promised her the place would be completely done by Christmas.

As for Tony Del Sole, his trial was scheduled for January, though Guin had a feeling that his uncle would find a way to get him off.

As for Frank Funt, Sr., he did wind up selling Funt & the Son Construction after all, to Nick DiDio, who had recovered the use of his legs. Though it would be a while until he could walk without the aid of crutches. Nick had always wanted to run his own business, and he had offered Frank, Sr., a fair price. And, of course, he had made Phoebe his office manager.

How she got off, Guin didn't know.

Now Guin was about to head over to the San Ybel Resort & Spa to meet with the mysterious Wren Finchley.

She had prepared for the interview as best she could, reading his first book as well as the new one. But that was really all she could do. There was so little she could find about him. She would just have to wing it. (She had emailed him some questions in advance, but he had replied that he would prefer to answer them in person.)

She checked one last time to make sure she had her notes, her microcassette recorder, her notebook, and a pen. Then she left.

It was a short drive from her new place to the San Ybel, and Guin arrived a few minutes early. Ginny had texted her Wren Finchley's room number, so she wouldn't need to stop by the front desk. Apparently, Finchley didn't want anyone knowing he was there. Though obviously the hotel knew.

"Are you sure this is safe?" Guin had texted her back. "This whole thing sounds like a setup. Just promise me that you'll call the police if you don't hear from me."

"You'll be fine," Ginny had replied. "He's just very private."

Guin took the elevator to the top floor and paused outside Wren Finchley's door.

"I'm going in!" she texted Ginny. "Remember to call the police if you don't hear back from me in a couple of hours."

Guin put away her phone and knocked on the door.

"Mr. Finchley," she said, trying not to be too loud. "It's Guinivere Jones, from the *Sanibel-Captiva Sun-Times*."

"Come in," replied a male voice. "The door's open."

Guin turned the knob and entered.

The man standing a few feet away was smiling.

Guin couldn't believe it.

"Birdy!" she said, staring at him. "What on earth?! Don't tell me *you're* Wren Finchley!"

"Please come in and close the door, Guinivere," said Bertram "Birdy" McMurtry, the noted wildlife photographer and ornithological Indiana Jones, whose life Guin had saved not that long ago.

"I thought something about those books sounded familiar!" said Guin. "Like I had heard those stories before. But I don't understand. Why the pseudonym and all the secrecy? And what are you doing here?"

"I will explain everything to you momentarily," Birdy calmly replied. "But right now, I need your help. Now please, take a seat."

To be continued...

Look for Book Seven in the Sanibel Island Mystery series, *A Perilous Proposal*, available in 2021.

Acknowledgments

First, I'd like to thank *you* for reading this book. If you enjoyed it, please consider reviewing or rating it on Amazon and/or Goodreads.

Next, I'd like to thank my first readers, Amanda Walter and Robin Muth, who have provided invaluable advice and suggestions over the course of the series and have caught many embarrassing typos. And speaking of typos, any you may have found are solely my responsibility and not the fault of my wonderful proofreaders, Kirsti Scott, who is the editor and publisher of *Beachcombing Magazine*, and Sue Lonoff de Cuevas (aka Mom), who is, fortunately, nothing like Guin's mother.

I would also like to thank Kristin Bryant, my talented and funny designer, for creating yet another great cover, and Polgarus Studio, for making this and all my books look as good on the inside as they do on the outside.

Lastly, thank you, Kenny, for listening to me grouse and making me dinner every night. Guin should be so lucky.

Oh, and one final thing: having now personally gone through a nightmarish home renovation on Sanibel, I highly recommend you visit www.sanibel-renovation.com before you buy or remodel a home here. It's an invaluable resource with many good tips.

About the Sanibel Island Mystery series

To learn more about the Sanibel Island Mystery series, visit the website at http://www.SanibelIslandMysteries.com and "like" the Sanibel Island Mysteries Facebook page at https://www.facebook.com/SanibelIslandMysteries/.

CPSIA information can be obtained
at www.ICGtesting.com
Printed in the USA
BVHW030236080421
604472BV00015B/59